THE MORETTI MEN

HUNTER'S KEEP

JILL RAMSOWER

HUNTER'S KEEP

JILL RAMSOWER

SERIES RECAP

Jill's books are interconnected standalones. While readers do not need to read earlier books in a series to follow along in later books, there are some themes that carry over from one book to the next.

Hunter's Keep is book 3 in *The Moretti Men* series. If you have not read book 2, *Death's Favor*, and prefer not to hear any spoilers, please skip ahead to the next track. For those of you who would like a very brief refresher of where *The Moretti Men* series left off, keep listening.

In *Death's Favor*, Danika runs from her Russian mob boss father, Biba Mikhailov, to escape an arranged marriage. She finds refuge in the hands of Italian hitman Tommy Donati, who pretends to work with Biba in the assassination of the Reaper. However, Tommy double-crosses Biba and kills him, instead. With Danika safe and no reason to start trouble with the Reaper's organization, Tommy abandons the original assassination plan and spares the lives of the Reaper and his men.

We begin *Hunter's Keep* with unrest in the Russian underworld as powerful individuals vie to take over leadership in Biba's absence.

CONTENT WARNING

Before you begin reading, please be aware that this book touches on matters of self-harm and the loss of loved ones. If you are particularly sensitive to these topics, this might not be the book for you.

*For those of us who understand that
only a morally gray hero has what it takes
to burn down a world wrought with corruption.
We need that man now more than ever.*

CHAPTER 1
Terina

PRESENT

"Why does it feel like you're kidnapping me?" I tug away from my brother's hold, only to receive a withering glare.

"Because I am. Now, get in the damn car." Renzo opens the passenger door to a black Escalade and practically shoves me inside.

"Whose car is this? And what the heck is going on?" I call out as the door shuts.

I have to wait until he's slid into the driver's seat for my answer. He caught me off guard when he ambushed me after yoga class, thus the resistance, but now that it's clear something is wrong, and he wasn't just being a dick older brother, my defiance is fading. That won't stop me from getting answers, though.

Renzo starts the car and merges into traffic. "It's my car—got it for the baby. And Biba Mikhailov's funeral was yesterday. Today, his oldest son, Simeon, seized control of the entire Russian organization and ousted his younger brother, Pasha."

Okay, the car makes sense now. His wife, Shae, is very pregnant. But what about the rest?

"Sounds messy, but what does that have to do with me?" I'm vaguely familiar with the Russians, but Renzo doesn't exactly keep me well-informed with his Mafia world. I don't ask, and he certainly doesn't volunteer.

"There's a solid chance they could blame us for Biba's death."

"Because...?" I prod him.

Renzo's eyes cut meaningfully to mine, but he doesn't say a word. He doesn't have to.

Holy crap!

Did someone in the Moretti Family off the Russian mob boss? I had no idea we'd been responsible. My understanding was that some psycho called the Reaper was the one to blame. But as I already noted, I'm not exactly kept in the loop.

"So ... what does that mean?" I ask quietly, the reality of the situation settling heavily on my shoulders.

"That's exactly what we're going to discuss at Mom's

place. She's making grilled fish and caponata. Shae and DiAngelo are meeting us over there."

My heart stumbles at the mention of my brother's best friend.

I don't run into DiAngelo often, but when I do, I find my brain tends to malfunction. Nerves get the better of me, and I'm not even sure why. It's not like I'm interested in him or care what he thinks of me. Not that he thinks anything of me at all. His blatant indifference toward me makes that fact obvious.

He's simply the man who helps Renzo run the Moretti Family. That's it.

So why's he joining us for dinner?

"What about Tommy and Danika?" Our younger brother and his new wife will surely be there if this is a normal family dinner.

"Busy."

No one's too busy when Mom cooks caponata—she takes the time to use exclusively fresh ingredients and roast the eggplant properly. Tommy's absence is telling. If this isn't a run-of-the-mill family dinner, then what is happening here?

Judging by the tension radiating off Renzo as his steely gaze regularly checks his mirrors and scans nearby cars, I decide it's best not to push for more. That sort of restraint isn't easy for me. I get anxious when I don't know what's happening, but I've been snapped at enough over the years to learn to pace my questions.

Thirty minutes later, we're gathered in Mom's large kitchen, which still bears hints of its 1980s construction in the glass blocks despite modern updates. Steam rises from two tarnished pots on the stove, and the black granite island is dusted with flour. My stomach growls at the rich aroma of freshly baked bread saturating the air. She's an expert at sourdough. I would be absolutely thrilled about the unexpected feast we're about to have if it weren't for the awkward tension pressurizing the room.

"Hey, sweetie. How was yoga?" Mom flashes a grin at me while starting to chop vegetables. Vigorously.

"It was good. How are you?" My eyes cut to Shae, who is engaged in a hushed conversation with my brother, her gaze flitting to me briefly before she gives me a tight smile.

DiAngelo watches me from his seat at the small kitchen table in the corner. He says nothing. No nod. No greeting. Just watching. Assessing.

Why do I feel like I've just walked into an intervention?

Mom waves her knife in the air nonchalantly. "Oh, you know. Life is life. We do what we can."

If that isn't unsettlingly ominous, I don't know what is.

"What's going on here? Why are you all acting so strange?"

"Told you in the car," Renzo answers vaguely.

"You told me the Russians think we killed Biba. That's it." I round the island and take the knife from my mother. "Let me do this before you slice off a finger."

"What do you mean? I'm fine. This is how I always chop peppers." Despite her argument, she acquiesces and shifts to cleaning up the flour dust. "It's not like this is the first time things have been dangerous in this family, but I wish it wasn't happening when the baby is coming."

Shae rubs her rounded belly. Despite being nearly full-term, she's not all that big around. I suppose it's all that jujitsu. She has better abs than any woman I've ever known.

"That just means it's even more fitting for you to stay with us. I know we'll need the help."

My brows furrow. "Mom's staying with you guys?"

"Just for the time being," Shae explains. "Until things calm down."

"I don't want her to be alone right now," Renzo adds.

I still my slicing and look from him to Mom, back to him, then let my eyes travel to DiAngelo, who is still sitting silently in the corner of the room, watching our conversation unfold. If Renzo had wanted me to stay with them as well, wouldn't he have already mentioned it? Definitely. He doesn't beat around the bush. So if he thinks it's dangerous, and we need protection, but I'm not staying with them, that means his plan to keep me safe is...

"What is DiAngelo doing here?" I blurt.

Renzo sighs, then closes the distance between us. "It's just temporary, okay? He's going to shadow you, that's all."

"What does that mean?"

"It means," DiAngelo cuts in, his deep voice filling the room with authority. Everyone stills. Even the boiling water on the stove seems to settle to a quiet simmer. "You don't leave your place without me beside you."

His words spark my body to heat in places it shouldn't.

That is, until their full meaning settles in, and deathly chill takes hold.

I've been assigned a bodyguard. Someone to stand in the way of danger to protect me with their life. Maybe another woman might be relieved or even honored, but those are the furthest emotions from my mind. All I feel right now is dread.

My eyes survey the giant man who dwarfs my mother's kitchen chair—from the disheveled brown curls on his head to his chiseled jaw and down the corded muscles of his arms that make the tattoos on his skin dance when he moves. He's too beautiful for his own good. He's also a tank.

I'm tall for a woman. Five-foot-eight.

He's got to be six-five if he's an inch.

But that's somehow only a fraction of the story. DiAngelo's gargantuan presence has everything to do with the air of power he exudes without so much as saying a word. He's the man your eyes are drawn to in a crowded bar not because he's the loudest or the tallest but because a primordial part of your brain tells you he's the most dangerous predator in the room.

Silent.

Calculating.

Ruthless.

All the best qualities for a Made Man, yet none of them mean anything when up against a bullet. He's precisely the type who would sacrifice himself to keep me alive.

I would rather kill myself than let that happen.

And I'm sure the grumpy brute will be a bastion of understanding and patience about my perspective. Of course, that's why the rest of them are walking on eggshells. They think I'll refuse.

I should.

But I doubt any of them will let me. It's a fact I've had to come to terms with since deciding years ago to stay close to my family rather than distance myself, as my older sister, Bria, did. She told us when she and her husband moved away that it was purely about job opportunities, but I know there was more to the decision. They wanted a different life. Something rural and quiet.

Too much of my heart is here in the city. There's no way I could leave, so I have to figure out how to have a bodyguard without putting him at risk.

"Okay," I finally respond after the maelstrom of thoughts settles in my mind. "I can manage that."

Renzo pulls me into a relieved hug. "Thanks for understanding, Rina. None of this is easy, especially in light of the baby coming." He pulls back and pops a chunk of carrot into his mouth.

"I get it. This stuff happens." *When you're like us. When you're part of the Mafia.*

A huff draws our attention back to DiAngelo. "I'll believe it when I see it." He takes a slow draw from his glass of ice water.

"Believe what?" I jab back. "That I'm not upset?"

"That you're going to cooperate."

My hands go to my hips as the insult raises my hackles. "What exactly are you insinuating?"

"I'm just curious if you're actually going to play along or if you're simply telling us what we want to hear."

I open my mouth to snap back at him when Renzo beats me to it.

"D, we talked about this," he warns in a menacing tone.

DiAngelo shrugs one shoulder. "I'm just trying to do my job. She needs to know that I can't keep her safe if she doesn't cooperate."

My jaw drops. "You have got to be kidding me. Just because I don't like that no one deigned to include me in this new security protocol doesn't mean I'm going to be difficult."

"Of course not. You don't sound difficult at all. And you certainly don't have a habit of seeking forgiveness rather than permission."

"Like you would know. You're so impossibly—"

"*Rina*, that's enough," Renzo barks.

I gape at him as though he's sunk a knife in my back. He's my brother. He's supposed to be on my side.

"All I'm saying," he continues, "is you should take this seriously."

Deciding she needs to join in the ambush, Mom adds her two cents. "We just want you to be safe. And hopefully, it won't be for long."

Sufficiently chastened, I slide my carrot slices into a strainer and mumble, "I didn't realize you all thought I was so reckless."

"It's not that, Ree," Renzo tries to reassure me. Or is he placating? Now, I'm not so sure. "We know you prefer to run your own ship, and this isn't a great time for that."

"Don't you think I understand that?" I snap back, years of guilt and shame sharpening my words. "Don't you think I know how easily bad things can happen?"

My unexpected outburst renders the room silent as we all acknowledge the memory of my dead husband. Yes, I'm painfully aware of the dangers in this world. They left me a widow after only a year of marriage.

Craig died a violent, tragic death because of my Mafia family. Did they think that after only five years, I'd somehow forgotten what can happen just because I don't openly mourn him anymore? That my pursuit of happiness somehow banishes my fears?

I am the way I am *because* of those constant dangers, not in spite of them. Spontaneity and optimism are the only things that keep me sane because they give me hope and a surprising sense of control in a world where I am effectively powerless.

I live life on my terms. And when I can't, darkness descends. I hate the dark times and do everything I can to avoid them, so yes, I know what's at stake.

Four pairs of pitying stares are a thousand tiny needles pricking at my skin.

I can't do this. I need a breather.

"I need to wash up before we eat." I rinse my hands and quickly dry them. "And no need to worry. You guys have made your point crystal clear."

"We'll let you know when the food's ready," Mom calls to my back. "Take your time."

Instead of responding, I take one last parting glance at DiAngelo on my way out of the room. I don't know why. I'm certain it'll only irritate me to see his smug face, but the satisfaction I expect to see after winning our little tête-à-tête is decidedly absent. Instead, his hazel eyes flash with determination.

I don't understand that man, and I suppose I never will. All I can do is hope Mom is right and the danger doesn't last long because if she's wrong, DiAngelo and I might end up a greater threat to one another than the Russians ever could.

The loud scrape of chair legs cut through the quiet air before I hear my brother's frustrated plea echo down the hallway.

"Just leave it, D."

Heavy footsteps pound behind me.

DiAngelo is on the move, and he sounds pissed.

CHAPTER 2

DiAngelo

PRESENT

I'M ON MY FEET BEFORE I KNOW WHAT I PLAN TO DO. Renzo's going to kick my ass for ignoring him, but that doesn't matter. All that matters is getting his little sister to understand the danger surrounding her. Even if that means she sees me as part of the threat. Otherwise, she'll make this impossible. I've seen how she plows through life like a bull in a China shop.

In some ways, I respect the hell out of how she's handled the loss of her husband. That shit couldn't have been easy. But her reckless disregard will get her killed, and I refuse to let that happen.

Not on my watch.

I made a promise to Renzo—the man I consider my closest friend. His father was the boss of the Moretti Family when I first became a Made Man many years ago. Renzo and I worked our way up in the organization together, though he advanced faster than I did because of his father. When Renzo's Uncle Gino declined to be next in line for succession, the title went to Renzo. He took over as underboss at only twenty-eight. It wasn't easy. He needed loyal men around him that he could trust to keep the Family in line. I helped during the transition, and we've been close ever since.

I won't fail him.

I wouldn't want to fall short of his expectations on any front because I respect him, and this task is more important than anything else. He's relying on me to keep his sister alive. Not even *he* will get in the way of my fulfilling that duty.

I made a promise, and I'll keep it, no matter the cost.

And the tab will be steep because I've already started to pay the price. I've spent years steering clear of Rina Donati to make sure she doesn't so much as cross my mind. She's a beautiful woman and totally off-limits—two things that don't pair well.

I don't do relationships, and I refuse to disrespect my best friend by screwing around with his little sister. No reason to tempt myself with something I can't have. Therefore, I've always kept my distance.

Until now.

Terina has become my responsibility, and after only a handful of minutes into this new dynamic between us, she's already clawing her way under my skin. Drawing emotions from me that are normally well-controlled. I don't like it. Not one bit.

She's just started up the winding staircase at the front of the house when I reach her. She doesn't look back, even though she has to know I've come after her. I wasn't exactly quiet about it.

Her stubbornness reinforces my determination.

I ignore the way her perfectly sculpted ass looks in her gray yoga pants and grab her wrist to stop her progress on the second step. "You acting like a child does jack shit to reassure me you're going to follow instructions," I chide her.

She yanks herself free of my hold and crosses her arms over her chest. "Being upset doesn't mean I'm acting like a child. I have a right to be frustrated when you all dictate how I'm to live my life."

She looks just as furious as I do, which is the whole problem. She shouldn't be angry. She should be grateful someone is looking out for her during such a dangerous time. That anger is how I know she needs a new perspective.

It's time to prove a point.

In two seconds flat, I have my hand clamped tightly over her mouth and her entire body held against me, her back to my front. With one arm around her middle, I'm able to completely incapacitate her and sweep her down the stairs and out the front door with hardly a sound.

She puts up a hell of a fight. I'll give her that. But she's simply too small and ill-equipped to fight off a man like me.

That's the reality I want her to experience.

A possibility I need her to understand.

To fear.

Once we're outside and around the front of the house, I still don't release her. Not fully. I keep her body pressed against mine and try to ignore how well she fits against me. She's on the taller side, which I like more than I should. She's a decade younger than me, but she's still a full-grown woman. A woman with curves in all the right places.

Am I seriously thinking about this right now? Jesus Christ.

I give myself a mental kick in the nuts.

"No one is dictating how you should live your life," I growl close to her ear. "They just don't want awful fucking shit to happen to you. If you're not careful, you could get yourself killed, and I've made a promise that I won't let that happen."

I'll be goddamned if the little hellcat doesn't get her teeth around my fingers just enough to bite me. Hard.

"*Fuck*, woman." The hissed words are a mix of fury and wonder.

I let her go and shake the smarting hand. She didn't break the skin, but she was close. My bad for letting my guard down.

Message received.

"You're assuming an awful lot. You don't know anything about me," Terina shoots back at me, her chest heaving with angry breaths.

"I know you well enough to know you always assume everything will work out for the best, and that could get you killed. Do you see how easy it would be for someone to take you? I didn't even work up a sweat."

I inch closer until her back is against the stucco exterior of the house, and her eyes have to lift to hold my stare. I place my palms on the wall on either side of her and lean that little bit closer so that my body is inches from hers. "The Russians could pluck you off the street just as easily as I took you from the house. If I were some other man, I might already have my cock buried deep inside you, and there wouldn't be a damn thing you could do about it."

The ragged scrape of my lust-filled words paints a graphic image. I see it perfectly, and I know she does too, when she draws a shaky wisp of air through her parted lips.

"You're a real dick, you know that?" she breathes softly. Only problem is, her statement doesn't carry the insult she intended because the heat in her eyes is no longer fueled by anger. Those mossy irises spark with a totally different kind of heat that stuns me.

Little Terina Donati is turned on by the thought of me fucking her.

Jesus Christ.

That is not information I should possess, and now the notion is seared into my brain. I'll never be free of the visual.

Doesn't matter. She's off-limits, and you'd do best to remember that.

"I know exactly what I am, and if being a dick keeps you alive, I'll wear the title proudly. Now, get back inside. I think I've made my point."

I slowly draw away from her and wonder if it's moisture in her eyes or a trick of the setting sun. Surely, it's the sun. I can't imagine a woman as headstrong as her would let an ass like me get to her so easily.

"Anyone ever tell you that you catch more flies with honey than vinegar?" She charges past me toward the front door.

I let her go because I don't need to catch a fly. She's already in my grasp.

All I need to do is keep her there. Alive and untouched.

Renzo is trusting me to protect Terina, and that should be my sole objective. I will not let him down.

CHAPTER 3
Terina

PRESENT

Infuriated doesn't begin to describe how I feel. Frustrated, insulted, homicidal—God, so many emotions—but more than anything, it's internal conflict that eats away at my insides as I stomp up the stairs to my childhood bedroom.

I want to scream at DiAngelo that I know exactly how serious the danger is. That's why I don't want him or anyone else risking themselves on my behalf. I'm not being difficult for the pure joy of it.

I'm terrified.

And for that man to judge me when I haven't even had a

chance to wrap my head around it all ... let's just say, it's mystifying how someone with so much strength and beauty could be so dense.

Then, on top of it all, I'm so frustrated with myself for letting him get to me. Who cares what he thinks of me? I shouldn't care one bit, but I clearly do because his rush to condemn me was a white-hot poker in my gut.

Is it because he's so close to my brother? Maybe I'm worried he'll tarnish the way my big brother sees me. I'm not sure why else his opinion of me would matter. I don't know him all that well. He wasn't around my family much until Renzo took over the Moretti Family after our father died. The two work closely together, but I'm rarely around DiAngelo. When we are together, we rarely interact. That's why I was so confused to see him at the house for dinner.

Ugh, dinner.

I still have to go downstairs and pretend I don't want to plant my fork in his chest. That broad, muscled chest that pressed against mine only minutes ago, igniting a yearning in me that I haven't felt in years.

How *dare* he!

Of all the pigheaded, self-righteous meatheads out there, why does he have to be the one to send tingles down my spine and into my fingertips like I've touched a live wire? Sure, I've always felt a little unsteady around him, but nothing like this. When he suggested how easily I could be fucked by a man like him while the heat from his body feathered across my skin, and the spiced scent of his masculine cologne filled my lungs, I could feel the phantom penetration of him thrusting inside me, and dear *God*, did it feel incredible.

I wanted to kill him and kiss him in the same breath.

See? Conflicted.

I'm a certified hot mess, and I need to get a grip on myself. Fast.

Lucky for me, I have a fully stocked room at Mom's place. We grew closer after I lost my husband, Craig. And everything I went through gave me the perspective to help her through Dad's passing. Even though we've both moved past the losses we suffered, I don't always feel like going home to an empty apartment. Staying here is a nice reprieve.

After five long years, I don't miss Craig so much as I miss companionship. While I miss the excitement of new love, I've let go of the man who swept in and out of my world within two years. But there's one thing I can't seem to escape.

Guilt has been my constant companion since Craig was murdered.

My shame haunts me.

He wasn't a bad man and didn't deserve how drastically his life deteriorated after meeting me. I wanted to believe him when he assured me he didn't feel pressure to live up to some artificial standard set by my family's money. None of that was ever important to me. I only ever wanted us to be together. Maybe if I'd told him just a little more often...

I shake away the morose thoughts.

The mental quicksand of self-doubt is a trap I've already wrestled with and refuse to get stuck in again. Nothing can be done about the past. I've learned my lessons and won't forget them anytime soon.

For now, the best thing I can do is take a quick shower and try to calm down.

The hot water helps to soothe my turbulent emotions, but it does nothing for the incessant pull still pulsing between my thighs. If anything, the sting of the water makes it worse. And the towel brushing across my sensitized skin while I dry off...

My entire body shivers, though I'm not remotely cold.

It has to be one of those strange reactions people have, like laughing at a funeral, because I am not into DiAngelo Farina.

So you're not into him. Doesn't mean you can't enjoy the unexpected perk of your argument.

Are you suggesting...?

My eyes drift from the bathroom mirror over my shoulder to the nightstand in my bedroom. The closet isn't the only thing I keep stocked at Mom's house. Not that I take advantage of it all that often, but I do have a shiny bullet vibrator waiting for me in that top drawer.

You were just thinking how you miss that excitement of attraction...

Yeah, but I don't actually want DiAngelo.

Does that matter? Enjoy the feeling and don't worry about where it came from.

I could.

It's not like anyone would have to know. And good Lord knows when I'd feel that itch again.

Oh, hell. Why not? It might be the best way to calm my nerves and help me get through dinner.

I make sure both bedroom doors are locked—my room is half of a Jack-and-Jill suite with a shared bathroom between the two. I hang up my wet towel, then open the nightstand drawer. Bingo.

I twist the small device to turn it on.

Nothing.

Yeah, it's been a while.

The batteries are dead, but it's no problem. I have spares. Once I reload two fresh triple As, I try again, and my girl bits electrify with anticipation at the happy buzzing sound.

This shouldn't take but a minute.

CHAPTER 4

DiAngelo

PRESENT

Renzo hasn't stopped staring daggers at me since I came back from my talk with Terina. He put in his two cents that my tactics weren't helping, though he didn't actually ask what happened. I reminded him that when I agreed to protect his sister, I insisted it had to be done my way or not at all. There wasn't much he could say after that, though his glare is plenty loud.

Fortunately, I have no problem ignoring him.

I work on emails and security plans, instead. The next

thing I know, Renzo's mother, Azzurra, announces that dinner is ready.

"Someone needs to get Rina," she adds.

"Don't look at me, Zuzu," Shae says with her hands raised helplessly. "I'm way too pregnant."

Renzo scoffs at his wife. "You still go to the gym daily, but you can't walk up a few stairs?"

"I didn't say that. What I said is I'm too pregnant for you guys to make me do it without looking like total jerks, and I'm using my free pass while I still can."

Renzo smirks, likely thinking the same as me—we wouldn't have asked her to go anyway, so she can have her win.

My friend leans back in his chair and brings his icy stare back to me. "Might be a good chance for you to go apologize. I suspect you might owe her that much."

I grimace as I stand, only because Renzo doesn't get it. I may have been harsh, but it was necessary. If I apologize, I'll undo any ground I might have gained.

I need Terina to be upset.

I need her unsettled.

Judging by the look in her eyes before she tore back inside, I hit my mark. With that satisfaction in mind, I head upstairs in search of my charge. I've never been on the second level of the house, so I'm not sure what room she's in. Two of the doors are closed, which makes them a safe bet.

I listen at the first door but don't hear anything. When I go to the next one, I can detect a faint buzzing sound coming from within. I'm not certain what to make of it. I could just knock, but that's not how I operate. I prefer to learn what I can when my presence is unknown. This is an excellent opportunity. But what am I hearing?

It's not loud enough to be a hair dryer. I heard the water running earlier, so I assume she showered. Maybe it's a small fan. There's no telling.

I'm about to give in and knock when I hear something else.

A soft moan.

The unmistakable moan of a woman's pleasure.

Suddenly, the buzzing makes perfect sense.

Fuck.

Me.

CHAPTER 5
Terina

PRESENT

MY ORGASM IS AN ATOMIC BLAST IGNITING ME FROM THE inside out. I can't fathom how such a storm could have built so quickly. A handful of minutes, and my entire body is glowing with radioactive pleasure.

I usually take longer to reach the finish line. My body was primed for release, and I choose to believe that is entirely due to the lengthy lull since the last time I touched myself. It has nothing to do with the scene that played out in my head while I fingered myself with that devious little bullet teasing my swollen clit. Nothing about DiAngelo screwing me against the outside of my parents' house, pounding into me from behind, was hotter than any other fantasy I've ever had.

Not remotely.

Whatever the reason, the orgasm was exactly what I needed. Now I—

DiAngelo's masculine rumble follows two sharp knocks at the door. "Time to come down."

My thighs snap together so fast my skin claps.

Sweet mother of God, I hope he didn't hear that.

"What?" I'm so damn disoriented that I can't scrape together a thought.

"Dinner. It's time to come down for dinner."

"Okay, I'll be right there," I holler a bit too loudly.

Dinner. That's right. I need to get dressed for dinner.

I bolt into action, throwing myself together faster than a pop singer manages a mid-concert costume change. The whole time, I reassure myself that even if DiAngelo heard my thighs slap together, he wouldn't have a clue what I'd been doing. It could have been my hands clapping for all he knows. Maybe I was scrolling, saw a hilarious video, and slapped my thigh with hysterical silent laughter.

It could happen.

Dinner is a master class in artful avoidance. I engage with my family as though all is forgotten while successfully pretending DiAngelo doesn't exist. My gaze never strays in his direction. His stare, on the other hand, borders on obsessive. It heats my skin like shards of sunlight on a crisp winter morning.

I bask in my refusal to acknowledge him, despite the

temptation. And that temptation is incessant. I want to see the turbulence in his multicolored irises. I want to confirm he's as unsettled by me as I am by him. But I hold strong throughout dinner, not caving once.

"You square things away with D?" Renzo asks me after we eat while the others are relaxing in the living room. I slipped away to go to the restroom and find my brother waiting for me in the hallway when I return.

"What do you mean?"

"Did he smooth things over?" Creases settle into my brother's forehead.

"No, why?"

Renzo frowns. "When he came down after getting you for dinner, I caught him smiling. I was hoping he'd apologize and that maybe you two had come to an agreement."

Tremors of unease tickle the skin on the back of my neck.

"That would have been nice, but no. He's not exactly the apologetic type."

"It's not that," Renzo starts with a sigh. "He takes protection duty very seriously. It's nothing personal."

I clear my throat to hide my scoff because everything about our encounter outside felt very, *very* personal, but I'm not about to tell my brother that.

"I get it, and I'm not planning to give him any trouble, so you can stop worrying." My smile is genuine because I truly don't want to make this situation any harder for Renzo than it already is. He must sense my sincerity because his features soften before he pulls me into a warm hug.

"Thanks, Rina. I really appreciate that."

"You're not leaving, are you?" DiAngelo's baritone voice is rugged in a way that only maturity can accomplish. He's a few years older than Renzo, which puts him close to ten years older than me. The innate authority in his words refuses to allow me to ignore him any longer.

I finally bring my gaze to his.

"We need to talk first." He spears me to the spot.

My brother jumps into motion. "Yeah, of course you do. I was just going to check on Shae." He scurries away to *check on* the woman who might just be a bigger badass than he is, leaving me alone with DiAngelo.

Traitor.

I cross my arms and lift my chin. "You need something?"

Did I just see the corners of his lips twitch? The motion was so fleeting, I question whether I saw it at all.

"I need your number, and we need to talk about schedules. I don't want you taking a step outside without me."

"I hope you realize that if someone wants me dead badly enough, there's nothing any of us can do about it." I'm not sure where the sentiment comes from. It's morbid and reeks of defeat—two descriptors I wouldn't normally use to label myself. Even when I think I'm over the past, it haunts me in new ways I'm not expecting.

This seems to be one of those times.

DiAngelo's eyes flash with conviction as though I've laid down a personal challenge.

I don't understand it.

I don't understand *him*.

"What's that supposed to mean? Are we not even

supposed to try to prevent it? You have a death wish I need to know about?"

"No, I'm just saying that crazy people do crazy things. I'd prefer not to have your death on my conscience because some Russian lunatic decides he wants me dead."

"That's not your choice to make," he counters firmly.

"Isn't it?"

His hulking form inches closer. My breath catches.

"Someone kills me because I'm protecting you, only two people are responsible—me and the twisted fuck who manages to catch me by surprise."

"But if I'm the target—"

He stops me with a raised hand. "That. Isn't. Your. Fault."

A wave of emotions crashes over me. Suffocating me.

But I can't let him see my struggle.

DiAngelo has no way of knowing that he's touched on the most sensitive, exposed nerve that I possess. And he's the last person I'd be willing to open up to about something so deeply painful.

My only defense is anger.

So I do what I have to and cling to my outrage. I encircle myself in its decadent velvet embrace and wear my fury like a crown.

"The outcome's still the same, so you'll excuse me if I'm not in favor of your sacrifice, no matter how voluntary or honorable." I poke his chest with my finger as the anger surges.

DiAngelo wraps his huge hand around mine and tugs me so close our noses nearly touch.

"Good thing for both of us, I'm a hard sonofabitch to kill."

He suddenly looks down at our hands as if to examine them.

His shift in focus derails me, leaving me flailing, unsure what to feel. I can't imagine what's going through his head until he slowly lifts my hand toward his face and takes a long, heady sniff of my fingers.

His multihued eyes dilate.

And somehow, I know that he knows what I was doing before dinner.

I locked the doors.

I scrubbed my hands.

I was nearly silent.

But like a wild animal scenting prey in the wind, DiAngelo knows. And he likes it.

My lips part, and blood floods my cheeks.

"Like it or not, Rina, I'm your new shadow." His gravelly voice rakes across my skin. "You won't take a single breath without my knowledge. Not a whimper ... or a moan."

Dear God.

This is so much worse than I ever imagined. DiAngelo is so much *more* than I realized—more intense, more aware, more *raw*.

If masculinity were a drug, most men would be mild recreational users, whereas DiAngelo is freebasing enough to stop an elephant's heart. And it's natural to him, not some manufactured facade to compensate for insecurities. He's the real deal, and it's intoxicating.

I've never known a man like him.

I can remember thinking Craig was a man's man—watching action movies and getting excited about spotting rare sports cars. Looking back, I realize he was rather average in that department, and not in a bad way. He was exactly what I was looking for at the time.

I was different back then.

Life was different.

Had I met DiAngelo back then, he probably would have terrified me. I wish that were the case now. And while he causes adrenaline to course through my veins, fear has nothing to do with the electric energy heating my bloodstream. His mere presence causes a chemical reaction inside me that's impossible to ignore.

If Craig was a twinkling sparkler on the Fourth of July, DiAngelo is an all-consuming atomic blast.

Both serve their purpose. And while sparklers don't excite me like they might have before, there was a time when that was exactly what I needed.

CHAPTER 6
Terina

PAST

"Three weeks from now? But you've only known each other for a few months!" My mom's eyes are bulging so big I can see the whites all the way around her irises. I knew my parents would freak out when I told them Craig and I were engaged and planned to get married in less than a month. That's why I insisted on telling them without him here. I didn't want their objections to hurt his feelings.

"We'll have been together for six months at that point," I clarify.

Mom tosses her hands in the air. "Oh, six whole months.

That changes everything. Terina, you're only twenty-two. What's the rush?" She freezes, her head whipping back around to spear me with her penetrating stare. "Are you pregnant?"

"No, Mama. I swear. There's no rush, but we just don't want to wait." I try to explain my perspective. "If we love each other, and we want to be together, why delay?"

"Why rush?" she counters.

"You and Daddy okay if I move in with him, then?" My retort is dangerously sassy but only because I know the answer. Dad wasn't thrilled when I told him I was dating someone outside the Moretti Family, and while he wasn't going to force an archaic arranged marriage on me, I know that shacking up with a boyfriend would be absolutely forbidden.

"Terina," Dad warns in a low rumble.

"I'm sorry, Daddy. I don't mean to be disrespectful." I speak with deference, trying to get this discussion back on track. "You know how I feel about Craig, and you gave me your blessing to date him. Why is it a problem now that he's proposed?"

Mom's shoulders sag. She peers searchingly at my father, who has been unusually quiet since my announcement, then back at me. "Because, Rina. You're still children—you hardly know yourselves, let alone one another." Her words are spoken gently, and while I know they come from a place of love, I don't want to hear them.

"You were married just as young," I remind her.

Sensing the conversation is going nowhere, my father

finally speaks up. "Rina, explain to me why Craig isn't here having this conversation with us?"

"I knew you guys might have concerns, so I told him not to come."

Dad nods, his lips pulled into a thoughtful frown. "And he was okay with that choice?"

My eyes dart from him to my mother as uncertainty fills me, though I'm not sure why. "Yeah? He respects my opinion."

Again, my father nods. "He knew this might be hard for you."

"Yeah?" Why do I feel like I've walked into a trap?

"Yet he didn't insist on being here to support you and come to us as a unified team?"

There it is.

I might as well have given him the gun and the ammunition for him to fill me full of holes. That's Dad, though. He's reserved and calculating, only making his move when the killing blow is in sight. It's what makes him such a powerful Mafia boss. It also makes it so hard to ever live up to his standards.

My chin quivers, and tears flood my eyes. "I told him not to come." It's the only thing I can think to say in our defense.

Dad stands and closes the distance between us, pulling me into a loving hug. "Sweet Ree Ree. You have the biggest heart of all my children. You love with all your might, and I only want to make sure you don't end up hurt."

"I won't be, Daddy. I love him," I force past the emotions clogging my throat.

He pulls back to meet my gaze, wiping the moisture from my cheeks as he studies me. "If you're sure, then of course, we support you." Dad presses a kiss to my forehead, and it fills my chest with warmth.

"Thank you, Daddy." I give him a watery smile, then steal a glance at my mom. Her hand is covering her mouth while tears stream down her face. I start to doubt she's going to be so easily swayed when she spreads her arms wide, calling me in for a hug.

I rush over and cling to her.

"My baby girl," she says, her voice swimming in tears. "We're going to have to do some fast planning. Three weeks isn't much time to plan a wedding."

A hiccup hitches my laughter as I pull back and grin at her. "It doesn't have to be fancy."

"We'll do our best to make it a perfect little ceremony." She takes my hand and tugs me toward the kitchen bar. "Come tell me what you're envisioning, and we'll take notes. Tomorrow, we can hunt for a dress and make some calls."

We spend the next hour strategizing. Churches. Guest list. Simple reception or none at all. There are so many decisions to be made that I'm giddy to finally talk to Craig when he calls that evening.

"How did it go?" he asks right away.

"Better than I expected, I think."

"You think?" He chuckles.

"It was a bit rough at first, but they're on board now. Mom and I talked a bunch about plans."

Craig is quiet for a moment. "Your dad, too? I should have

asked his permission," he says almost to himself. "I bet that upset him."

"No, they were just concerned a little about how quickly it's all happened, but after I assured them how much we both want this, they were supportive."

"I guess that's good."

I grin, though he can't see it. I can't help myself, I'm just so blissfully happy. "Everything is amazing. You have an incredible new job, and in three weeks, we'll be married. Life is going to be wonderful for us."

"Because of you," he says warmly. "You're the best thing to ever happen to me, you know that?"

If my heart weren't confined to my chest, it'd expand to fill the entire room.

My cheeks ache from the intensity of my smile. "I love you, too, baby."

"Three more weeks, and you're all mine."

"Yours forever."

CHAPTER 7

DiAngelo

PRESENT

"I know I'm partly to blame," Renzo admits with a weariness I can hear across the phone line. "I sheltered my sisters for a long time without meaning to. They weren't a part of the business and didn't need to be caged in the middle of things for no reason. Then, Dad got sick, and Tommy was ... Tommy. I just did my best to protect all of them."

I feel for him. I do.

He was still relatively young when he was thrust into a shit ton of responsibility, even before his father got sick. And I know what it's like to want to protect your family.

"I get it," I say with a sigh. "But she has to be exposed to this world to some extent just so she appreciates the dangers. She needs more perspective."

I'm certain she understands loss and that she wants to avoid it. I think that's why she has such a strong need to be independent. It gives her a sense of control. She needs to learn that sometimes the safest plan is to defer to others—whether that means asking experts for help or simply letting someone with experience take the reins.

"Agreed," Renzo responds. "I'll do my part on that front. And for what it's worth, I'm confident she'll fall in line. She's not naive per se. She's just been through a lot."

My lips press thin as I stare at the woman in question.

Her long auburn hair is wound into a soft knot on her head as she smiles. She's wearing a baggy yellow sweatshirt over leggings, with an olive-green sports bra strap visible where the collar of her shirt has drifted down over her shoulder. She exudes a carefree elegance that mystifies me.

"That why she's out having coffee with a friend even though she never mentioned she had plans?"

"You're shitting me."

"Wish I was, man. I came by this morning to do some recon of the building and spotted her in the lobby. You called before I could confront her." I refrain from going into detail about her breezy laughter to save him the same infuriated frustration I've been battling for the past fifteen minutes. It's barely been twelve hours since our confrontation outside her mom's house, and she's already defying me.

"I don't know what to say except thank you for doing this.

I have a real bad feeling Biba's sons are going to want revenge, and if it's blood-for-blood they want, they'll come after a family member. Rina and Mom are by far the easiest targets."

"I've got your back—as my boss and my friend. I promise I'll keep her safe."

Those six words cycle through my head on repeat after the call disconnects.

I promise I'll keep her safe.

The only way I can be certain to keep my promise is if I have her complete cooperation. I can't guard against the Russians and corral her at the same time. That sort of chaos creates too many variables. Too many uncertainties.

Variables are like leaks in a ship. Once the water starts flooding in, there's nothing any one man can do to keep that boat from going down.

No matter how tempting the lust in her eyes, no matter how sweet the musky scent on her fingers, no matter how tragic her past, I *must* make her safety my only priority. Empathy and desire will only muddy the waters.

I *have* to remember that.

Because I know what it's like when emotion compromises judgment.

Lives are lost, and the guilt never fades.

CHAPTER 8
DiAngelo

"You told them it was your yacht, and they believed you?" The skepticism in my brother's voice adds to my irritation. My hangover isn't helping, either.

"No, dumbass. I showed them pictures of me on the yacht and told them Dad was connected, which he is. If they falsely assumed I was a guest on the boat rather than cleaning it, that's not my fault."

Elio chuckles. "If by connected you mean a childhood friend who grew up to join the Mafia, then fair enough. Bet the girls were all over you after that."

I finally crack a smile. "You should have seen it, man. Like I was a god or something. Best damn summer job ever—way better than your busboy gig." Sure, I have to do some shitty jobs like carting around heavy restocking supplies and scrubbing the outboard, but it's worth it to get access to the incredible boats. What I wouldn't give to own one someday.

"Yeah, sorry I couldn't make it. It took hours for that damn headache to fade." Elio's had a lot of headaches and other excuses lately for missing all kinds of activities. I don't know what's up, but something's definitely not right. He claims I'm reading too much into things every time I bring up my concerns.

"You sure you don't need to see a doctor?"

"Definitely. In fact, I feel a hell of a lot better than you look."

I rub my eyes with a wry huff of laughter. "That's because I'm hungover as shit. Work is going to suck ass today." We're only seventeen, but one of the benefits of being huge for our age is that no one ever questions our fake IDs. It's too damn expensive to go out often, but when I do, I make sure to enjoy myself. I'm pretty sure my parents know what we get up to, but they're pretty chill so long as we don't get into any real trouble.

"I tell you what, to make up for skipping out on you last night, I'll work for you today. It's my day off, anyway."

"No way, man. You serious?" I stare at my twin brother as if he had offered me his kidney. As bad as I feel, he might have to do that, too.

"Sure, gives me a chance to finally see these boats you've

been obsessing over the past month, assuming you can walk me through everything."

Elio and I are identical in every way. Most people can't tell us apart, and we don't exactly try to differentiate ourselves. It's easy for us to switch places—we have seventeen years of practice.

But a niggling doubt pricks at my conscience.

Am I taking advantage of my brother? He shouldn't have to do hard labor just because I threw a tantrum about him not going out. And what if my boss realizes something's up? I don't want to lose my job.

Mom's voice plays in my head.

One of these days, you're going to be sorry you tricked people like that.

She gets so irritated when we switch places, and she might be right, but surely, there's no real harm in Elio working for me today. It's not like we're sleeping with each other's girl-friends, or something twisted like that.

I know we probably shouldn't, but damn, it would be nice to sleep off this headache. And if he's willing...

"I can absolutely walk you through what to do. I can even text one of the guys I work with—he's trustworthy. I'll let him know what's up."

Elio extends his hand, initiating our snap handshake that we've done since we were six. We grin mischievously at one another, both relieved to be back on the same team. We're so close that even the slightest rift between us makes the world feel off-kilter. I don't know how other people exist without a twin. We're too much a part of one another to ever let anything serious come between us, and a life without him wouldn't even be worth living.

CHAPTER 9
Terina

PRESENT

"My dad has started escorting me everywhere, though he said the threat is likely greater for your family. I can't imagine how terrified you must be." My good friend Isa chews on her lip, her brows drawn together.

I filled her in about my new bodyguard as soon as we sat down for coffee. Her father is Cosimo Costa, Renzo's consigliere, so she understands my life better than most. I'm so grateful to have someone I can share with, even if I choose to keep some things private.

"It's definitely unsettling, but we don't have any concrete information from what I'm hearing. Though there's always a chance Renzo's keeping things from me—it wouldn't be the first time," I add under my breath.

"At least he's got you well protected. DiAngelo takes his job very seriously."

I scoff after sipping from my coffee. "So I've noticed. The man is a little deranged."

She shrugs. "He wasn't always that intense. Not sure if I ever told you, but our dads are friends. We sort of grew up together."

"Really?" I'm stunned. "How have I never heard about that?" I'm reminded that Isa is several years older than I am, so she's closer in age to DiAngelo than I am.

She tucks a strand of her golden hair behind her ear, eyes downcast. "Guess I've never had much reason to mention it. My brother was closer to him and his twin than I was."

"*Twin?* DiAngelo has a brother?" I gape at her, wondering if I've had my head in the sand or if there's a reason all this is only coming out now.

"*Had* a twin," she corrects me in a somber tone. "He was killed. DiAngelo was never the same after Elio died."

"What happened?" My question is no more than a hushed whisper.

Isa fidgets in her seat. "He was kidnapped, though it's hard to recall the details. That whole time period is fuzzy in my memory. It wasn't long after that when Ario and I were in the car crash." Her voice wavers at the mention of her brother and his tragic death. "Mostly, I just know what I was told after the fact."

I don't push her. How could I when she's so clearly still bothered by the mere mention of the event? Neither of us tends to talk about our pasts, but I know she ended up in the hospital. That entire year was a traumatic series of losses for her.

Pain scars a person in places the eye can't see, but like recognizes like.

While my struggles came seasoned with an extra dash of guilt, we were served the same bitter dish. I instantly sensed a kindred spirit in her when we reunited at a Moretti Family event about a year after Craig's death. Isa and I are generous when it comes to grace and understanding, and in a way, we find solace in one another's darkness. I'm grateful to have her as my friend.

"I had no idea he'd been through something so awful. Renzo never said anything."

"The twins were seventeen. Ario was nineteen, but they were close despite the age difference. After I lost Ario, I kept my distance from DiAngelo because seeing him reminded me of my brother." Isa looks down at her coffee, and I'm reminded of the tragic series of events. An aneurysm took her mother, then came her brother's accident less than a year later.

Back-to-back losses are extra devastating—a fact I know well since my father died not long after my husband. Sometimes I have to remind myself I'm doing surprisingly well, all things considered.

Not wanting to force those memories upon her, I decide

it's time for a change of subjects. Our meetup has already been heavier than I'd intended, though I'm glad to gain some insight into the man who has barreled his way into my world.

The image of DiAngelo's smoldering stare as he sniffed my fingers floats in my mind's eye for the thousandth time since last night. I'd say I was reading into things, but I could see in his eyes that he knew. I could never mistake the smug satisfaction glinting in his eyes.

I have no idea how I'm going to face him.

I tap my knuckles on the table and smile. "Tell me what your plans are for the day."

Grateful for the shift in focus, she grins back at me. "Well..." Isa starts into a breakdown of her plans, but I only half hear her because a text notification lights up my phone and snags my attention.

It's from my mother-in-law. Ex mother-in-law? I'm not sure what to call her now.

I shouldn't read the message for multiple reasons, including not wanting to be rude to my friend, but I can't help myself. I have to see what it says.

I discreetly swipe the screen to open and take a glance at the message.

Kristi: his tombstone was covered in bird shit, but I don't suppose you knew that since you never visit

My stomach twists into knots, and I have to set down my coffee.

I knew I shouldn't have looked, but I feel so bad for her. I can't imagine what it would be like to lose a child, no matter how grown they are. She's not always the nicest, but it's the pain talking. Craig was her only child. The least I can do is not shut her out.

"You okay?" Isa asks gently.

A wave of embarrassment crashes over me. "Yeah, just a stupid spam text. Sorry about that."

I'm way too embarrassed to tell her about Kristi. I know she'd tell me I shouldn't tolerate the woman, but my life is more complicated than simple black and white. Our choices have consequences, which we have to live with, no matter how painful. The best we can do is learn from our mistakes and keep from repeating them, which is why I've refused to even consider a new relationship—romantic or otherwise. I won't put another life in danger the way I did with Craig.

Fortunately, Isa skirted my rule. Already a part of my Mafia world, our friendship doesn't put her in any additional danger than she would be in already.

I suddenly realize my hand is inadvertently scraping my nails across my belly in search of soothing. Not hard, but it's enough to engulf me in shame. I hate that sometimes my life overwhelms me to the point where I feel out of control. I have no idea how some people shrug off the past. If I could, I'd pack it away into a box and bury it deep inside my subconscious so that it could never find its way out.

Isa doesn't question my excuse. "I hate that stuff—texts about toll fees and calls for business loans—the scams are constant."

"No kidding." I smile, but I'm in desperate need of a

moment alone to collect myself. "I'm going to pop into the bathroom real quick."

I flash a reassuring smile and head to the single-unit restroom. When I open the heavy door, an automatic light flicks on just as a large body collides with mine. Huge arms encircle me, a hand clamping over my mouth. I'm forced forward into the bathroom as the door clicks shut behind me.

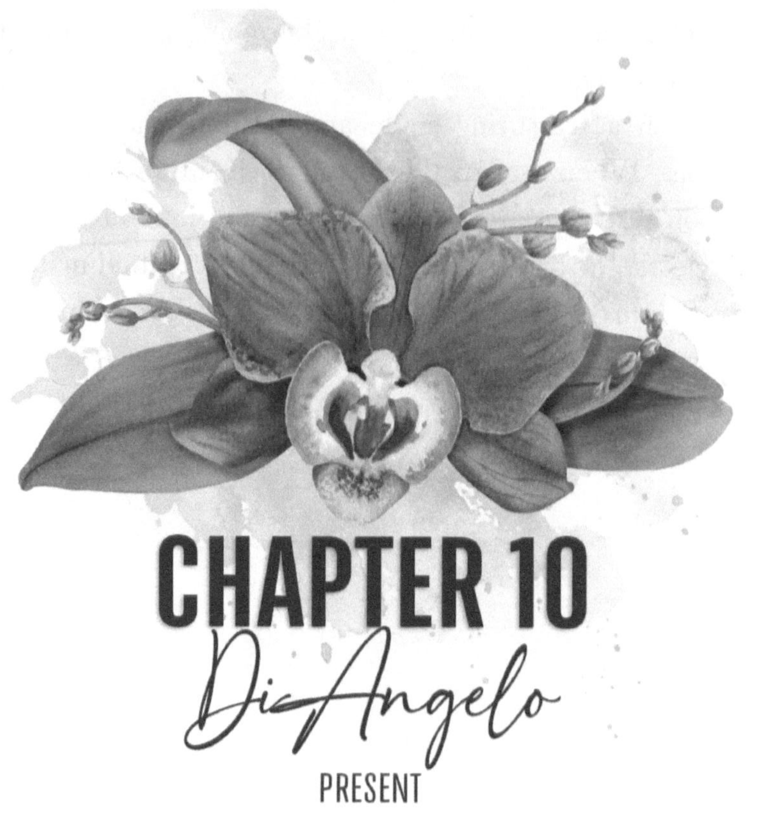

CHAPTER 10

DiAngelo

"What did I say about not taking a step outside without me?" I demand, holding Terina much like I had the night before—one hand over her mouth, and the other holding her tight against my body.

She's totally helpless, not that her vulnerability seems to bother her. It hasn't been twenty-four goddamn hours, and she's already undermining me. I had a feeling something like this would happen. It was the reason I was over at her place, preparing to have cameras installed. Not even I had expected her to be so reckless so soon, but I won't make that mistake again.

When she realizes who has her, she calms, her body relaxing against mine. Our eyes meet in the small mirror, and I remove my hand from her mouth.

"I didn't step foot outside," she says as though genuinely shocked.

"What do you think this is?" I raise my arms to my sides with exasperation.

Terina turns to face me, her eyes still wide. "We're still in the building."

"Semantics, Rina. You left the safety of your apartment, and you see how easy it was to get to you? Don't pretend you didn't know this was dangerous."

Her expressive lips dip with a frown as her eyes soften. "You're right. I think I'm a little in denial, but I never meant to intentionally defy you. I just don't want anyone to be in danger."

Her forested stare peers up at me earnestly, and fuck if it doesn't tame my anger.

I reach for her, cupping the back of her neck and coaxing her closer. Her lips part at my touch, and she breathes me deep into her lungs. For a fraction of a second, I envision the feel of my lips colliding with hers, my tongue tasting hers...

It's the most idiotic thing I've thought in years. I don't know what the hell's come over me.

I shake off the ridiculous fantasy and sentence myself to an extra thirty minutes on the treadmill in the morning.

I must remember my purpose.

Yet ... there's value in knowledge. Fucking her is off the table, but understanding Terina might help me keep her safe. If I can anticipate her thoughts, it's one less variable to worry about.

My thumb absently strokes her throat from top to bottom and back.

"You feel responsible for your husband's death." She didn't say it in so many words, but I can put two and two together. She feels helpless against threats and worries that if something happens, it'll be her fault. I'd be willing to bet those beliefs are an offshoot of the past.

"Let's just say that I know if someone is determined to hurt another person, there's no stopping that."

"You think it's fate when someone dies?" I ask, an unintended chill frosting my words.

"I think life and death decisions aren't always up to us."

I lean in closer, my hand tightening around her throat, and whisper, "If I kill you now, would that be fate?"

Her eyes light with a mix of fear and something else.

Something wistful and chaotic.

Something I never imagined I'd see.

Excitement.

I only meant to make a point, but it seems I've uncovered something else entirely. Something that speaks to a darkness inside her and has woken a feral beast inside me. He claws his way from the radioactive sewage deep in my mind and blindly sniffs the air for prey.

The last thing I need is for the animalistic side of me to take interest in my best friend's little sister, yet the temptation of corrupting Terina has me teetering on the verge of losing control.

I wrench my hand away so fast my momentum pulls me backward a step, though my eyes never leave hers.

It's the one point of contact I can't seem to sever.

"*Fuck* fate," I bark viciously. "Fate is for cowards, so you need to decide real quick—are you a coward, or are you a fighter?" My outburst gives me whiplash; I can only guess at what she must be thinking. Something along the lines of her brother having saddled her with a lunatic.

Let her believe what she will. I need to know her answer. It's imperative.

My lips part to push for a response when a knock sounds at the door.

"Terina? You okay in there?" Isa has come to check on her with the absolute worst timing.

I hold Rina's gaze captive, my stare commanding an answer.

For a second, I think she's going to comply before a shutter falls across her eyes, effectively severing our connection. She swings open the bathroom door and transitions seamlessly into a lighthearted explanation to her friend as though our entire conversation never happened.

CHAPTER 11
Terina

PAST

I've been asking myself that for weeks, and I know it can't be good. Not already.

As I swipe through wedding photos, it's hard to believe only six months have passed. It seems like a lifetime.

I've been struggling with doubts about my marriage. It's been so much harder than I imagined. I understand now what my parents had been trying to tell me, but it's not the sort of information you can impart. This sort of life experience has to be earned.

My gaze drifts out the window from the gorgeous high-rise apartment my family bought us toward the financial district in the distance. My husband is somewhere over there, working himself into the ground to build a life for us. I've told him I don't need to have the sort of money my parents have, but I don't think he believes me. Whatever the motivation, he's been working sixteen hours a day, seven days a week, for months. I hardly see him, and when I do, I don't recognize him.

I massage my aching chest with my palm.

As much as the loneliness hurts, I prefer the pain to the constant doubts that plague me. Did I rush into marriage? Getting married at twenty-two after only knowing one another for less than a year seems fast, but it felt so right. Why have things changed so drastically? Will it get better? If so, how and when?

I keep myself as busy as I can to avoid answering the questions. I even accepted a role as a board member at a local soup kitchen where I volunteer. The extra responsibilities are a good distraction, and I get to indulge my love of exploring new recipes while keeping hungry people fed. I like what I do, but I'd prefer it if it were a choice rather than an escape from the loneliness.

Every day I pray that someone will tell me what I can do to fix this, and every night my tears are my only answer.

As if on cue, my phone buzzes with a call, sending my heart into orbit.

Craig's beautiful smiling face appears on the screen. His contact photo was from a day we spent at the Bronx Zoo back when we were dating. We got to feed huge pieces of lettuce to a giraffe, and he was endlessly tickled by the experience. It was such a blissfully happy moment—one I love to relive every time my phone lights up with his calls—and a perfect reminder of what I'm fighting for.

Because I *am* a fighter.

I love Craig, and I want our marriage to work. I'm not ready to give up.

"Hey, baby," I say with a smile that I hope he can hear.

"How's my beautiful girl?" His words are sweet, and his tone is warm, but I can't ignore the hint of distraction that's ever-present these days.

"I'm good. Looking forward to dinner out with you tonight."

"About that..." he draws slowly. "I can meet for dinner, but I'll need to head back to the office after."

"Back to the office so late?"

"Yes, Ree." Exasperation sharpens his words. "We've talked about this. It won't be forever."

I can hear a pen rapidly tapping on his desk. I know it's a pen because I've seen him do it at home, too, when he's agitated.

"Is everything okay?" I ask warily. It's the same question I've asked dozens of times before. I don't know why I keep asking. He gives me the same response every time.

"Everything is fine. You worry too much." His brush-off feels dismissive, but I don't have a chance to comment when he continues. "Hey, did my passport arrive yet?"

It's the second time he's asked in a week. And is that strain in his voice?

Why would it matter if his passport arrived?

We don't have any trips planned. He hardly has time for dinner, let alone a trip. Unless... Could he be planning a surprise getaway for us? A six-month anniversary excursion? God, that would be amazing. We desperately need some time together—away from the city.

"I haven't checked the mail, but I'll make sure to do that on my way to dinner, okay?" I ask brightly, buoyed by the hope of a fresh start.

"Yeah, that works. I'll see you in an hour."

"Sounds good. Love you."

"Love you, Ree Ree."

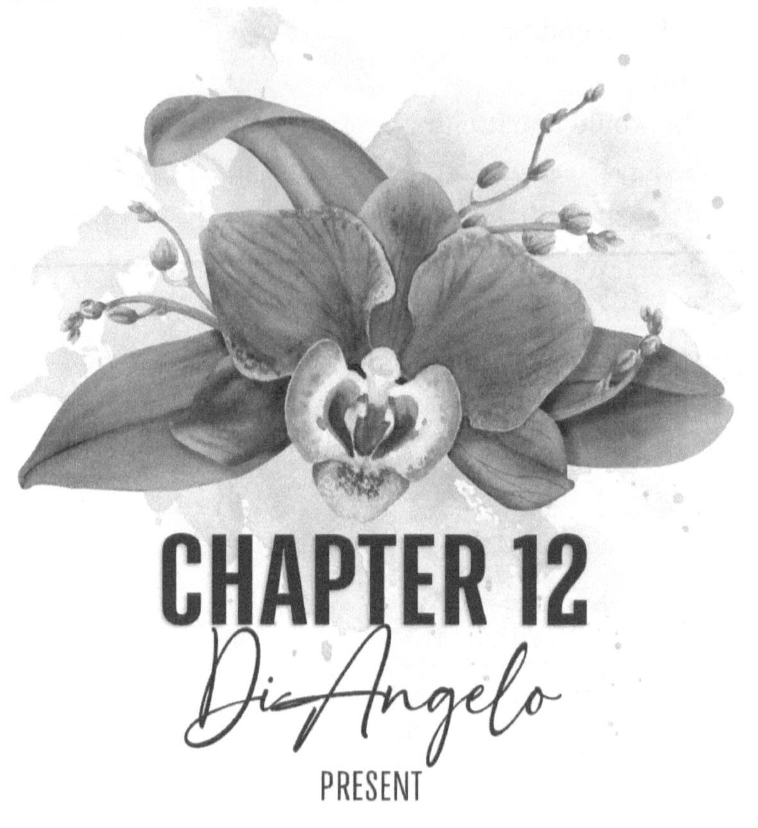

CHAPTER 12
DiAngelo

PRESENT

A COWARD OR A FIGHTER? TERINA NEVER GAVE ME AN answer, and I haven't pushed for one. I doubt she could forget the question if she tried. I can see it dancing behind her eyes when I catch her watching me.

We've spent the better part of a week settling into our new normal. She's been cooperative, which I appreciate, but I don't like how strictly she keeps to routine. Yoga at the same studio, the same time, nearly every damn day. Walks in the park using only one designated route. Dinner with her mom and coffee with Isa, both twice a week—Wednesdays and Sundays with her mom, and Tuesdays and Fridays with Isa.

I discovered their usual coffee shop is several blocks away from her apartment. Rina had moved their meetings to the shop in her building to minimize her outings. I hadn't realized she'd done that and appreciated her efforts, but a set coffee date, no matter where it is, is still too dangerous.

Routine might as well be an engraved invitation to the Russians.

Before dropping her off last night, I asked her to come up with a randomized schedule for next week. She wasn't thrilled, but she said she'd work on it. I wonder how much she'll be able to deviate from her established norm.

Terina is surprisingly structured for someone I thought tended toward impulsivity. She's an unusual mix of the two. While she can afford a cleaning service, she cleans the apartment herself but has no set cleaning schedule. She prefers to cook her own food rather than eat out, but doesn't plan her meals. Instead, she buys whatever ingredients look good when she's out shopping and concocts a recipe later.

I get the sense her need for control is more of a coping mechanism than an innate part of her personality. I'd be curious to ask Renzo if she was like that before her husband died. I wasn't close to the family at that point, so I wasn't privy to the details of his death. It was a mugging gone wrong, which I only learned about after dinner at her mother's house.

It's an unfortunate way to go. Loss is bad enough on its own. Overcoming a violent, unexpected death can shatter a person.

I should know.

My brother's death happened twenty years ago, and I still struggle to think about it. Her husband's only been gone for five years. That's not long in the grand scheme of things.

My phone rings, drawing my attention away from the computer screens where I've been scanning through the video footage of her building to see if anything suspicious jumps out at me.

"Yeah," I answer.

"How's everything going over there?" Renzo wants to know how things are going with his sister. His timing is perfect.

"Nothing to report at the moment, though I did have a question."

"What's up?"

"I was wondering what you could tell me about Terina's husband's death." I toss it out there and hope I'm not over-stepping.

"Why you wanna know?" Renzo asks with a hint of wariness.

"Just thought it might help me understand her better."

He sighs, spiking my curiosity. His reaction isn't quite what I anticipated.

"The guy wasn't terrible, but he got into some shit—drugs and gambling. Terina never knew about it, and we decided not to tell her. Hell, I didn't realize until the guy was dead. No reason to hurt her further by dragging him through the mud. It was over. End of story."

Interesting.

"How much does she know?" I ask to make sure I don't share anything I'm not supposed to.

"Just that he was stabbed in an attempted mugging. Wrong place, wrong time."

"I'm surprised you didn't get a read on him earlier."

"Me, too. The guy was a finance bro. Worked on Wall Street and had never been in any trouble before. Took his first big corporate job right before they got married, and someone there must have got him coked up is all I could figure."

I huff, knowing how ruthless it is in the financial district. Cops love to peg us for all the crime in the city, but that white-collar shit is nuts. Those guys would piss down their own mother's throats to get a leg up.

"Sounds like she's better off, no matter how shitty that is."

"Hope so, since there's nothing we can do about it now. Listen, I called to let you know we've got word on the Russians."

"I'm listening." A mild understatement. My heart suddenly slows to a quiet thrum as if to help me hear every possible detail.

"We got confirmation that Pasha isn't rolling over easily and has stayed in the city despite Simeon's warning to leave. He's pissed about the ouster, though there's not much he can do about it. Only a handful of guys went with him. I'm hoping the two brothers focus their grievances on one another and forget their beef with us."

"Any idea where he's holing up?"

"Nope."

"Then we still don't know much," I grumble.

"I know, but we've got our ears to the ground."

"You still okay with Terina on the street?" At some point, if things get too dangerous, I'll make the call myself to keep her sequestered somewhere safe. Renzo doesn't want to resort to that if possible, nor do I. Rina herself offered to stop going to yoga. I insisted classes were fine so long as we varied the schedule.

"Yeah. I know you've got her covered. Besides, the whole thing may blow over. It's hard to say."

It's wishful thinking, if you ask me, but he didn't, so I keep my thoughts to myself.

"Sounds like a plan."

"Later."

As soon as the call ends, another rings through. This time, it's Rina. She usually texts, so I'm immediately on guard.

"Yeah?"

The terror in her voice plunges me into an icy river.

"*D, you need to come over here fast! Please, hurry.*"

CHAPTER 13
Terina

EXERCISE CLASSES HAVE A CULTURE. ANYONE WHO HAS regularly attended a step class, Zumba, or any group fitness class knows they function like mini families. Sure, there are always a few stragglers who come and go, but the regulars get to know one another. It's understood that Shannon from Vermont always works out in the front corner, and Jessi with the red hair keeps to the back because she has two small kids and is *always* late. If you go to the morning class, the instructor is super chill and always has chakra candles burning, while the lunch-hour instructor's energy levels rival that of a toddler on a sugar binge.

Every class is different in its own unique way, so switching classes is more than just a schedule change. It's with that in mind that I assess my yoga class options for next week. Do I like the instructor for the 3 p.m. class? Does Tammy with the horrible body odor go to the 11 a.m. session? And if I go to class in the morning, do I shower right after or wait until my usual evening shower?

So many considerations, and I'd bet good money DiAngelo has zero clue.

I understand his reasoning, though, behind asking me to randomize my schedule. And as much as changing my routine normally bugs me, I'm happy to do it if it means less chance of putting him in harm's way. And despite what he may think, I'm not about to roll over and let the Russians get either one of us.

Are you a coward or a fighter?

His challenge took me back to a place I didn't want to be, a time when I had to face a very similar question, so I avoided answering him. I've been avoiding him altogether, if I'm honest. My reactions to DiAngelo are too unpredictable. Too raw. I don't trust myself around him. It's best to keep things professional and respectful. After all, this situation won't last forever. Once the danger dissipates, life can go back to normal.

I wish that sounded more appealing than it does.

Don't be silly, Rina. You'll be much happier that way.

I hope so. It's worked for me these past five years. Why change?

The buzz of my phone relieves me from having to answer the question. Thank goodness.

"Hello," I answer politely after seeing it's the front desk calling.

"Miss Donati?" asks a man's voice, rugged with age.

"Yes."

"You have a delivery. We were going to send it up, but wanted to make sure you were home to receive it."

"Yes, that works. Thank you."

"Our pleasure. Have a lovely day."

"You, too."

It takes a good ten minutes before there's a knock on my door. I spend the entire time racking my brain over what the delivery might be. A look through the peephole confirms that building staff have arrived with a white box in hand. I give the young runner a tip and take my elegant Neiman Marcus box inside. It's wrapped in a beautiful black satin ribbon, and the notecard on top simply reads *R.*

Did Renzo send me a gift?

That's not exactly his norm, but he's been extra accommodating since sticking me with a bodyguard. Plus, I think Shae's pregnancy has softened him, though I'd never tell him that.

Maybe this is a thank-you gift for dealing with his brute friend for the past week. It makes sense.

I untie the bow, a smile blooming on my face as I remove the lid. I start to pull apart the white tissue paper inside when I catch a glimpse of black-and-yellow stripes ... and scales.

I shoot backward so quickly that the chair I had rested my knee on crashes to the floor.

A black glistening snout peeks from the box, its forked tongue flicking the air.

I scream and scramble for my phone while keeping a frantic eye on the creature at the same time. My hands are so damn shaky that I struggle to hit a few simple buttons. Eventually, the line rings.

"Yeah?" The strong tenor of DiAngelo's voice envelops me with relief.

"D, you need to come over here fast! Please, hurry," I say in a rush.

"What's going on?"

I can hear the strain in his voice. He's already in motion, confirmed by the sound of a door slamming in the background.

"I think it's a snake in a box. I thought it was from Renzo. I'm sorry, I shouldn't have opened it. I didn't think. I—" My flood of frenzied words is cut short.

"Slow down, Rina," he says calmly. "I need to know if you're hurt. Did it bite you?"

"N-n-no." I shudder at the thought.

"Where is the snake now?"

"It's still in the box on my kitchen counter. Its head is poking out, but it hasn't tried to go anywhere."

"Good, you stay the fuck away from it. I'll be there in five."

It doesn't even take him that long. The man must have flown to get here so quickly. When he arrives, he lets himself in with a key I didn't know he had and finds me clutching my phone in the living room—the farthest I can be from the snake while still keeping sight of the midnight scales on its head.

"It's still in the box. I've been watching. I made sure." The staccato words sound distant to my own ears, and my eyes refuse to disengage from their focus.

DiAngelo crosses my line of sight and forces my wide gaze to his. The instant our eyes meet, my lungs empty with a relieved breath, and my entire body begins to shake like a Chihuahua left out in the cold.

It's the strangest thing.

The snake is still alive and well. I could have been killed. Neither of those things has changed, but something about having DiAngelo nearby gives my body permission to come apart.

He places his hands on either side of my face. "Breathe, Rina. I'll handle the snake. You just breathe, okay?"

I nod shakily.

"Good girl."

Then he does something that I never expected. Something that pulls the rug right out from under me. DiAngelo Farina places a tender kiss on the top of my head, infusing my body with a steadying warmth.

"Scared the shit outta me," he murmurs with his lips still pressed to my hair before pulling back.

"Me, too," I whisper.

The tiniest of smirks teases the corners of his lips. "Go pack a bag while I deal with this." He gives me an authoritative lift of his brows, then turns toward the kitchen.

"A bag?"

He peers back at me. "You're not safe here. I'm moving you in with me, where I can protect you better. If you want to take anything with you, I suggest you get moving." His brows rise again as his gaze shifts toward the bedroom, an unmistakable order for me to make myself scarce, but I can't.

"What if you get bitten? I'll be in there sorting cosmetics while you're out here dying. I don't think so."

D sighs. "Fine, but don't come a *single* inch closer."

"I won't. Promise." I raise my hands in surrender.

"You have a broom?"

My brain glitches for a second with the subject change before I nod, then hurry to the coat closet where I keep my vacuum and broom. I grab it and take it to him, then swiftly retreat to a safe distance.

DiAngelo prowls toward the snake. He positions himself to the side of it, the peninsula portion of the counter giving him a range of approach options.

Once in place, he pokes the snake.

I shit you not. The man pokes the snake until it slithers farther outside the box and rears up protectively.

My heart is lodged in my throat, terrified the snake will dart off the counter and disappear into my apartment. But before that can happen, DiAngelo presses the wooden broom handle down over the snake right behind his head. The second the snake is secure, he picks it up with one hand.

PICKS. IT. UP.

With ONE hand.

He dangles the snake in front of him, exposing the full

length of the black-and-yellow-striped creature—about four feet in total. The tongue flicks faster, and the body writhes and sways agitatedly, but without the leverage to accomplish anything.

In my head, I'm yelling at DiAngelo, demanding to know what the hell he's doing. All my body manages to do is gape at the scene with my jaw hinged wide open.

"Now what?" I finally squeak.

D brings his eyes to mine, hazel bleeding into a stone-cold gray that sends a chill down my spine. His free hand clamps around the snake next to his other hand before he swiftly snaps its spine. Bent at an unnatural angle, the snake goes limp. Not skipping a beat, DiAngelo carefully coils the dead creature back into the box. When he puts the lid on top, he notices the card and picks it up to examine it.

"I thought it was from Renzo," I try to explain.

"Looks kind of like an 'R,' but I'd be willing to bet it's a 'P.'"

"Why's that?"

"Pasha Mikhailov. He's chosen to target you." His gaze returns to mine, the stony stare now razor sharp. "Pack that bag. It's time to get out of here."

CHAPTER 14

DiAngelo

PRESENT

"You don't think it was venomous?" Rina listened intently to my conversation with Renzo on the ride to my place and is now peppering me with questions. I'm glad. It shows she's worried.

She should be.

"That's not what I said. I said that I didn't think it was meant to kill you. I think it was a message more than anything."

The snake was too fucking exotic not to be deadly. It looked like something Nat Geo films in the middle of a South

American rainforest. The sleek scales glistened in the light, the stripes so stark they appeared painted on.

"And what message is that?" she asks quietly.

My eyes study her as the elevator doors close us in. "You've been marked. Things just got a lot more dangerous."

The color drains from her face.

It's the appropriate response, and in a way, I'm glad, but at the same time, it pisses me the fuck off. Terina is an innocent victim in all this. We may have been responsible for Biba's death, but that bastard was far from innocent. Painting a target on Renzo's sister is a whole other level of evil.

I won't let them lay a finger on her.

When I open the door to my apartment, Bonny is waiting in the entry.

"Oh! Who's this?" Terina asks with renewed life, not at all intimidated by the 100-pound Rottweiler across from her. She extends her hand for Bonny to sniff, then scratches behind her ear. My guard dog grins like a buffoon.

"That's Bonny," I tell her with a note of disapproval.

"Bonny? You named your big, scary dog *Bonny*?"

"You don't seem so scared." I drop the duffel bag she packed next to her suitcase.

She continues to make friends with Bonny, smiling and cooing at her. "I would have expected a name like Onyx or Xena."

"As in ... the warrior princess?" I give her an incredulous look.

"Yeah, exactly. Not something soft and sweet."

"It's not soft and sweet. She's a pirate." Fuck, that sounds dumb. I shouldn't have said anything, but she was dissing my dog.

Terina finally turns her focus back to me. "A pirate?"

I run my hand through my hair and sigh. "Dog was as clumsy as a drunken sailor when I first got her. Anne Bonny was a famous pirate in the 1700s. Thought it was fitting. We done with twenty-one questions now?"

The smile that splits her face could power the city for a week. "A pirate. I love it."

I grunt, ignoring the small swell of pride that warms my chest. "Come on, I'll show you around."

My apartment is a good size—a four-bedroom with two of those used as an office and a workout room. I appreciate how spacious each room is. At six feet, five inches, a lot of places can feel claustrophobic to me. The high ceilings and big rooms here allow me to breathe.

"You can take my bedroom," I tell her as we enter the main suite.

She looks at me with wide eyes, making me realize the implication of my words.

"Relax, I won't be in here with you. I'm staying on the couch."

Her brows crease. "But you have a guest room. One of us could easily stay there."

"I want to be close to the door, and you're safest back in the primary."

"You're going to sleep on the couch? What if this goes on for weeks?"

"Then I sleep on the couch for weeks. My comfort is insignificant when your life is at risk."

Her teeth graze across her lip. "I'm not sure what to say, except thank you."

Fuck, the sweet side of Rina Donati does things to me. Things best ignored.

"I made a promise to your brother, and I intend to keep it," I speak the words out loud more as a reminder for me than a response to her, which is probably why they come out gruffer than I intend.

I don't throw around promises I don't intend to keep because I know what it's like to break a promise. That sort of failure can haunt a person for the rest of their life.

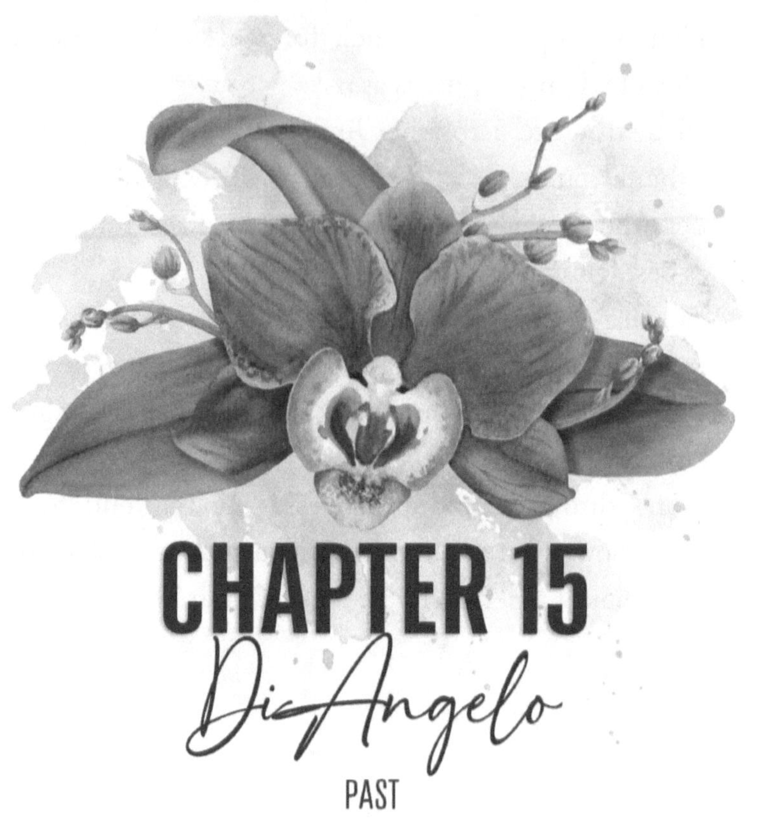

CHAPTER 15
DiAngelo

"What do you mean he hasn't come home yet?" I stare at my mom, confused. It's nine in the evening. I've just returned from the movie theater after catching an early evening show to find out my brother still hasn't come back from working my job at the pier.

She stares back, equally confused. "He was working, right? He hasn't come home. Maybe he decided to eat with a friend after work."

That might have been the case had Elio been at his own job busing tables in the air-conditioning, but it was ninety degrees today, and he was scrubbing boats at the pier. I know from experience that the only thing you want to do at that point is get home to shower.

I check my phone and show no missed calls, so I try his number.

No answer.

What the hell is he up to?

Maybe he stayed at work late and has been too busy to help, or his phone could have died. We're both usually good about remembering to keep the phones charged since we've only had them for a year. It took ages to convince our parents to let us have cell phones and was the main reason we both got jobs.

With nothing better to do, I decide to head to the pier to look for him. I bound down the stairs, let my parents know I'll be right back, then go in search of my brother. As I get closer to the pier, I dial his number again, and a phone begins to ring nearby.

I stop and search for the ringing. Confusion has me doubting myself because I could swear it's coming from a sidewalk trashcan.

I end the call and wait. The ringing stops.

I dial his number again.

The ringing resumes.

My stomach fills with an inky black dread.

Yanking off the metal top, I pull out the bag and dump it onto the ground. My gaze quickly snags on the silver Nokia phone. I got a black phone, and he got the silver so it would be easier to tell them apart. The screen shows a missed call from D.

It's Elio's phone.

Something is horribly wrong.

Using my own phone, I call my friend from work.

"Dude, your bro was a no-show." His words ice over the blood in my veins until the chill causes my entire body to shiver.

"Thanks, man," I murmur distractedly before hanging up on him, my hand shaking as I put my phone back in my pocket.

Elio would never intentionally not show up. Something bad has happened, and I have no idea what it is or what to do about it, except go home and tell my parents that Elio is missing.

❦

I could hear my mom crying in the night. None of us slept. We called the police. They told us we have to wait until Elio has been missing for twenty-four hours before we can file a missing person's report, which is absolute bullshit. My twin didn't run away without me.

We checked hospitals. No one with his name or description has been admitted. Plus, that wouldn't explain his phone getting trashed. I've gone round and round all night thinking about it, and I can only guess that he's been kidnapped, but why? Dad's an engineer and Mom teaches school. They don't have enemies. We have decent money but aren't rich. Elio isn't exactly ideal for trafficking since he's six feet and nearly

200 pounds. What reason does that leave? Why the fuck would someone take him?

The questions haunt me relentlessly.

We sit silently in the kitchen the following morning while torturous seconds tick by. I decide to go back to the street to keep looking for clues when Dad's phone rings. The chime slices through the thick air with cheery violence.

His large hands fumble with the device. "Hello?"

I watch and listen breathlessly. Could it be Elio? Is he okay?

"Who are you?" Dad demands. "Why are you doing this?"

The pit in my stomach expands, its thorny spines digging into my insides. It's not Elio, and judging by Dad's tone, we've been right to worry.

Dad's face drains of blood. "I don't have that kind of money," he stutters quietly. "No, no. Don't hurt him. We'll find a way. Please, just don't hurt him." After a minute, he pulls the phone from his ear and stares at it in disbelief.

Mom's trembling hand covers her mouth in horror as we stare at my dad, waiting for the worst to unfold.

"Someone has Elio—I have no idea who. He wants five hundred thousand dollars ransom in forty-eight hours or ... or..." He swallows, unable to finish.

"Why would someone do this? Why?" My mother's broken words claw at my heart.

Dad shakes his head. "I don't know. I don't understand at all. He said he'd know if we contacted the police and told me to use my connections to get the money, but I don't know what that means. And ... I think he thinks he has you, D." He peers up at me from where he sits at the kitchen table. "He started by telling me he has DiAngelo."

Use his connections.

Jesus, no.

Tell me this isn't all my fault. Tell me someone didn't take my brother because I made a bunch of strangers at a shitty bar think we were loaded.

My lungs refuse to function.

I stumble against the wall as the room closes in around me.

"D, sweetie. Are you okay?" Mom places her hands on my face, searching my eyes with a worried gaze. She's terrified for Elio, yet still so damn strong that she's checking on me. I should be the one protecting her. I should be the one preventing this sort of pain from ever touching her.

Get your fucking head out of your ass, you worthless piece of shit, and do something.

I regain control of my lungs, regulate my breathing, and shake off my shock. I don't have the luxury of panic. I have to save my brother.

"I'm okay." I nod and gently squeeze her arms to reassure her. "We're going to get him back, Mom. I'll get him back. I promise."

Tears flood her eyes as she chokes on a sob, and I swear to myself I won't let her down. I will find Elio and bring him back one way or another.

CHAPTER 16

Terina

PRESENT

Ouch.

I made a promise to your brother.

DiAngelo's statement made it clear that everything he's doing is out of duty rather than any true affection for me. I've known that from the beginning, so why does it sting so bad?

I'm a job to him. An obligation. And that's how it should be.

I shouldn't want to be anything more.

Heartache is the direct result of attachment, which is why I avoid relationships. No matter how tempting that sense of comfort I experience in his presence, DiAngelo is not for me. I force myself to remember that as I settle into my new temporary home.

His apartment is lovely and surprisingly cozy. I chalked him up to the industrial loft type, but there are no concrete floors or exposed ductwork in his place. In fact, the walls are painted a muted forest green, and the oversized sofa in a soft velour fabric could comfortably seat a small family for movie night. Sheer drapes frame the large windows, softening the harsh city lights and summer sun. Sandy colored wood on the floor gives the place an almost forested feel.

It's surprisingly ... peaceful.

Being forced from home is nerve-racking, but staying here isn't a hardship, aside from near constant proximity to the home's owner. Living with DiAngelo is going to be an adventure.

I survey the bedroom while I unpack. He has a ginormous California king bed. I've never seen such a huge bed, though it suits his size.

I'll be sleeping in DiAngelo's bed. My head isn't sure what to do with that information. I keep trying to tell myself it's just a bed, but the butterflies in my stomach disagree.

Before long, I have all but a few items unpacked. I had no idea how long I'd be here, so I brought more than I probably should have. Specifically, the two items I left in my suitcase. A candle and a lighter. It was weak of me to bring them. I swore to myself I wouldn't use them, but I felt compelled to bring them anyway. That doesn't bode well for my resolve.

Not wanting to think about it, I zip up the suitcase and

stash it in the closet. My clothes are hanging next to his. My toiletries are on his bathroom vanity.

I snicker at the absurdity because my life feels like an AI deepfake. I am Alice in Wonderland without a clue how I got here.

"Cleaners were just here two days ago," DiAngelo says when he joins me, "but you won't hurt my feelings if you want clean sheets."

The bed isn't made, but it's not a mess either. A soft burgundy duvet is neatly folded back, revealing crisp cream-colored sheets. As clean as it seems, my natural tendency would still be to ask for fresh sheets, but that's not what pops out of my mouth.

"It's fine as it is," I say, somewhat dumbfounded by my own words because I know the motive behind them. I'm embarrassed to put words to the feelings, and I'd never admit the thoughts out loud, but I want to know what it's like to wrap myself in his scent. To lay my head where his has rested and feel the comfort of his presence while I sleep.

See, I sound like a freak.

Fortunately, he doesn't press the issue or pass judgment. He wordlessly leads us back out to the living room, where I continue making friends with Bonny. She's cute as a button with her floppy ears and perky tail that curves up in the air like an extension of her smile.

We have a quiet day at home. No yoga. Just television and scrolling, which is a nice change of pace. I even manage to coerce Bonny onto the sofa to watch movies with me.

"Bonny, you know you're not supposed to be on the sofa," DiAngelo says in a low warning tone.

The dog looks from him to me, then rests her large, round head on my lap as though begging for me to champion her cause.

I've always been a proponent of animal rights.

"Don't be like that. She's doing such a great job making me feel at home. So attentive and protective. She wasn't about to let someone bust through that door and hurt me."

He shoots me a look. "Bonny, *down*." His command brooks no argument.

The poor dog lurches off the sofa and skulks toward him.

"That was mean," I mutter.

"She's a guard dog, not a companion. You defeat the purpose of her if you soften her edge."

I disagree, but it's my first day here, so I don't argue with him.

By day's end, I've consumed four movies—two rom-coms, a mystery, and one mindless action flick. DiAngelo makes an appearance every now and then but primarily keeps to his office. After her scolding, Bonny stays with him.

I feel compelled to win her over for some unknown reason. I want to prove to D that his sweet Rottie can be a protector *and* a companion, so she gets the love she deserves. Maybe I'm just selfish, and it serves as a good distraction. Whatever the motive, I commit to my mission.

I offer to make dinner, but DiAngelo already has a meal planned. We eat in companionable silence, and I return to the TV until finally getting the courage to go to bed. DiAngelo makes sure I have everything I need, and while I close the door to get ready for bed, he insists the door remain open at night. I have no problem with that.

After a long, hot shower, I put on a baggy T-shirt and crawl beneath the covers of his bed.

I was right.

It smells like him. Like leather and oak and warm woolen blankets that lock out the cold.

Between the soft cotton against my skin and the masculine scent warming my insides, I'm achingly aroused in record time. I hadn't considered that possibility. Maybe it was naive. Maybe my subconscious knew what it was doing all along, but either way, the tiniest movement of my shirt is exquisite torture for my sensitive nipples.

This feels wrong on so many levels.

His home is his sanctuary, and he's sharing it with me so that I'll be safe, and I'm over here acting like a pervert. What would I think if I knew he jacked off in my bed because he got off on my scent?

That was a bad choice of imagery. Thanks to a vivid imagination, my center is now throbbing so intensely that my spine is flexing and arching to combat the sensation.

I just need a little *relief.*

My mind takes the inopportune moment to picture DiAngelo's strong hands wrapped around the snake. His bravery. His raw strength.

Yeah, this isn't helping at all.

I don't know why him killing something has me so hot, except it makes me think of his large hand wrapped tight around something else thick and hard. Suddenly, my hand is slipping lower toward the apex of my thighs, stunning me.

Am I actually considering this ... in his bed? On a day when I could have been killed?

What a great reminder to live life to its fullest.

The door is open, I point out to the deranged hussy who's taken over my thoughts. I can't touch myself with the door wide open, and he was adamant about that rule. I don't want to cross him, and besides, he'd probably hear if I closed it. He's likely got preternatural hearing to go with his super sense of smell.

I don't care how good his ears are. There's no way he can hear my fingers sliding against my clit.

True. And I can be very, *very* quiet when needed.

Maybe just a little touch. Something to help soothe the ache...

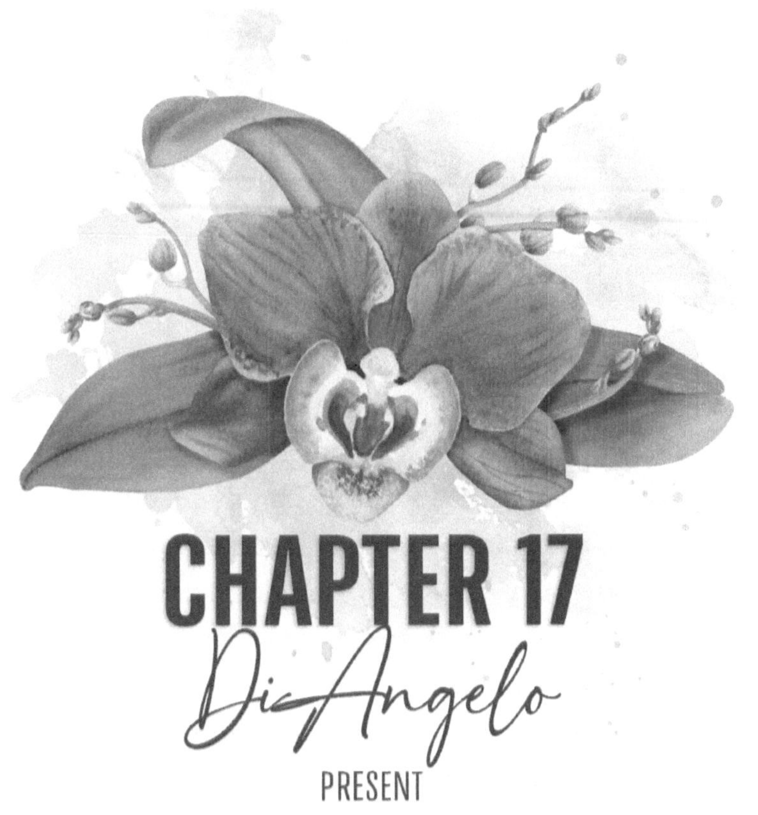

CHAPTER 17

DiAngelo

The lights go out in my bedroom, but I'm still wide awake. It's hard to sleep after what happened today. I didn't want to scare Terina more than necessary, but that snake was a serious message. There's no telling what the Russians will do if they're hell-bent on revenge. Her life is in grave danger.

I'm relieved she came to my place willingly. I feel better with her here. That fact alone should help me sleep, but I can tell that's not happening anytime soon. Especially not when an insidious thought slithers its way into my consciousness and takes root.

I wonder if Terina chose to sleep on my side of the bed.

It's not hard to tell which side I prefer. What would it mean if she chose the same side? That she sleeps on that side in her own bed? That she isn't bothered by sheets slept in by someone else? Or maybe sleeping near my scent makes her feel safe.

Maybe I have my head up my ass and need to stop thinking about things that don't matter.

What is wrong with me? Am I seriously daydreaming about Renzo's little sister? She's ten damn years younger than me ... and she's his *sister*. Have I lost my goddamn mind? Her life is at risk, and I'm overthinking her sleeping preferences. That's exactly why allowing emotions into the mix is a horrible idea. I need to be focused. Practical.

I need to keep Terina safe. Full stop.

If that's the case, it might be a good idea to check on her. She had a traumatic day, after all.

True. I hated to hear how upset she was when she called me. And I wasn't lying when I said she scared the shit out of me. I was so damn worried, I couldn't get there fast enough.

Exactly, and while you check on her, you can settle that little curiosity. Put it to bed, if you will.

Fuck me. I think my inner voice may have it in for me.

He's certainly not helping matters, though he does have a point. If I check on Rina, see that she's sleeping peacefully, and confirm she's not on my side of the bed, then maybe I can get some damn sleep.

I silently rise from the sofa, wearing only the boxer briefs I went to bed in, and quietly pad toward my bedroom. The blackout shades are drawn beneath the shears, but there's still enough ambient light to see. From my stance in the doorway, I can make out her form in the darkness.

Jesus, she's on my side.

Why does that realization send a jolt of lust straight to my dick?

I don't get a chance to adequately chasten myself because Terina's breathing catches in a way that has me worried she's crying. I don't want her in here, upset, all by herself.

I take two steps forward, bringing me close enough to see a tiny bit better, and I realize she's on her back with her legs butterflied open at the knees. I watch more carefully and see the sheet flutter near her center.

My entire body turns to rock-hard stone.

Jesus fucking Christ, she's getting herself off in my bed.

I should walk away. I should go back to bed and cauterize this from my memories. The only problem is, my marbleized legs refuse to budge.

For the second time in a week, I perve on Terina while she touches herself. It's so fucking messed up, yet I can't stop myself. The sounds she's making—tiny panting breaths—and the subtle writhing of her body—it's too much. Too intoxicating.

I think I might come in my fucking boxers. I can't tear myself away from her.

Even worse?

My hand has found its way to my aching cock, squeezing the damn thing through my boxer briefs as though my life depends upon it.

I begin to stroke myself.

Her eyes flit open and lock with mine.

I still, fully expecting her to freak the fuck out. Except that's not what happens. Instead, her parted lips widen a fraction more, and her movement beneath the sheet intensifies.

My heart thuds all the way to the bottom of my balls.

Terina sucks in a lungful of air before her entire body contracts.

I squeeze my dick so hard that I spontaneously combust like a goddamn teenager.

Her eyes never ... leave ... mine.

It's the hottest fucking thing I've ever seen.

You need to get your ass out of here, now.

I don't even recognize myself. I've never been so damn undisciplined in my life.

I take one step, then a second, but not toward the open door.

I inch closer to Rina.

I'm desperate to smell her again. The scent was too faint last time—there but not entirely. I want the unfiltered, unadulterated version.

I don't just want it.

I *need* it.

CHAPTER 18

Terina

PRESENT

I didn't stop.

I didn't stop even though DiAngelo was watching.

Even though he knew I was masturbating in his bed.

And the craziest part is how unbothered I am. The tranquilizing effects of my cataclysmic orgasm have infused me with calm when I should be freaking out. I should be embarrassed, outraged, apologetic, or maybe even all three.

I'm none of those despite being trapped in his feral stare as he stalks closer.

The same enchantment keeps me silent. Transfixed. In part because he seems to be locked in this same magical web.

Golden eyes glint despite the darkness, as though the fire in him burns too bright to be contained. Embers sparking in the ash.

My lungs hitch on a breath when he reaches the bed, towering over me.

"Give me your hand." A murmur has never managed such authority.

Questions fill my mind, but my body obeys blindly. I watch breathlessly as my brother's best friend—the man who has been forced to babysit me—carefully sucks two of my fingers deep into his mouth. When his tongue laves against my skin, my core shivers with renewed hunger because he isn't simply tasting; he's devouring.

Savoring.

DiAngelo Farina is ravenous for me, and I am stunned speechless. This man's irritation, where I'm concerned, knows no bounds. I was certain of that. But now?

I have no idea what's happening.

I'm not about to delude myself into thinking there's anything more to it than a moment of lust, but it still shocks me. What was he even doing in here in the first place? Why keep watching when he realized what I was doing?

Regardless of the answer, his participation wipes away any embarrassment I might have felt and replaces it with stunned curiosity.

I watch raptly as he retracts my fingers from between his full lips.

What will he do next? Will I allow him to take it further?

"Touch yourself again in my bed, and I'll take it as an invitation." He releases my hand, then walks out of the room as though nothing ever happened, while I shiver from the arctic chill that descends in his absence.

It's the perfect reminder of what can happen if I lose my head and let someone in because I know that empty sense of loss all too well. While this instance is only momentary, I know how much worse it can get. I've lived in the unending arctic tundra of grief, and I never want to go back there again.

CHAPTER 19

Terina

PAST

I PUSH THE FOOD AROUND MY PLATE, MY MIND TOO distracted for an appetite. Last week was my first anniversary with Craig. Not only did he not have a secret getaway planned six months ago but he also forgot the date entirely.

I cried myself to sleep that night. Alone. It wasn't the first time.

Six more months have passed, and things have only gotten worse. I'm heartbroken over the distance that's grown between us, with no idea how to fix it. Craig is different lately. Easy to anger. Distracted and even a touch erratic. I've asked myself whether he could be seeing someone else, and it breaks my heart to admit, but I just don't know.

He swears that after his division completes the acquisition they've been working on for the past six weeks that everything will be better. But there was a campaign for a new corporate account before this and an internal audit before that. There's always something demanding his attention. Something that isn't me.

I've tried to be understanding. I've tried to convince him to quit his job or get counseling to help with the stress. I've tried so damn hard, but it's been a year, and I'm sick of tear-soaked dinners in a silent apartment.

If I had years of good times to look back upon, I could use that as reassurance that we can get back to a better place. As it is, I'm worried that marriage with him doesn't get better than this. I'm terrified that I've made a mistake. And as much as I hate to do it, I have to start considering my options.

Am I truly ready to consider divorce?

The universe must sense my reluctance to answer the question, though, because a knock on the door saves me. Security is good in our building—solicitors aren't allowed up—which means unexpected visitors are few and far between.

I hurry to the door and take a look through the peephole. Two uniformed police officers stand in the hallway. I open the door and smile hesitantly. "Can I help you?"

The older of the two takes off his hat and peers at me through weary brown eyes. "Mrs. Kirkland?"

"Yes."

"May we come in?"

"Why?" I don't budge. While I have nothing to hide, I had it ingrained from a young age to never *ever* let the police inside my home.

His lips thin, and the other officer is avoiding eye contact entirely. "There's been an incident. I'm afraid we have bad news."

Tingles start in my scalp and trickle down my spine until my entire body is engulfed. And it's not the good kind of tingles. My bloodstream is flooded with pure terror.

"What?" I ask on a winded breath.

"Today at approximately 4 p.m., we received a report that a man had been stabbed in East Harlem. When we arrived at the scene, the victim was pronounced dead and taken to the hospital. After a preliminary search, the man has been identified as Craig Kirkland. I'm so very sorry."

His words filter through a funnel before they reach my ears, making them sound distant and surreal.

A man was stabbed and pronounced dead.

Identified as Craig Kirkland.

"Not my Craig," I say almost to myself. "He's at work. He works late."

The two officers exchange a pity-filled glance.

"I'm afraid so. Is there someone we can call to come be with you?"

Someone to call? I need to call Craig. I'll call him, and he'll tell them there's been a misunderstanding. Yes, that's what I need to do.

I walk away, leaving the door wide open, and get my phone. Craig's number rings.

Once.

Twice.

Three times.

Four.

Five times.

Voicemail picks up.

I hang up, but refuse to concede that his not answering means anything. "He works all the time. I'm sure he's just in a meeting," I tell the two men who have migrated into the entry.

"Ma'am, who else can we call to come by and help out?" He walks over and places a kind hand on my shoulder, though I don't feel it. I don't feel anything.

I look at my phone and dial my mom's number because no matter how much we may bicker, she's my greatest source of comfort.

"Momma?" Heartbreak sends me back to childhood, my voice sounding small and broken.

"Rina? What is it, baby?"

"Momma, they're saying Craig's dead, but that can't be right. He went to work this morning. He's wearing the tie I gave him for Christmas." My breathing catches, fear carving a jagged hole in my chest. "He can't be ... he's just at work. Tell them, Momma. Tell them he's at work." My chin quivers, and rivers of tears surge down my cheeks.

"*Jesus, Mary, and Joseph.*" Her whispered prayer shatters my glass heart.

"Momma, tell them..." Sobs claw their way up from the depths of my soul. "Tell them..." The phone slips from my hand as my knees give out. I sink to the floor and lose myself to the pain.

I'm only vaguely aware of the officers picking up my phone and placing a blanket around my shoulders. My entire body shivers as my soul bleeds onto the wood floor.

I spend the rest of the day and night wrapped in my mother's arms.

I'm not aware of the passing of time. There is only pain.

Craig is gone.

My husband.

My love.

He's gone, and I'll never be whole again.

Craig's mother identified the body. I couldn't do it. And my father has fought to keep the police away even though he's been very sick lately. He has joined me at every interview and demanded I not be contacted directly. I'm so grateful for his protection right now because simply getting through the day is hard enough. Participating in an investigation only makes everything worse.

One week ago today, my precious husband was murdered.

It was a mugging gone wrong. His wallet and watch were taken. He was stabbed five times.

Five times.

I can't fathom what would bring a person to do something like that. For what? A few dollars? And now, I'm standing in a cemetery, watching my husband's body get lowered into the ground.

A week ago, I'd contemplated leaving him. I was frustrated and lonely. What I wanted more than anything was a joint effort to fix things between us. Now that he's gone forever, I'm riddled with regret and guilt.

None of it seems real.

Every second since the police came to my door has passed in a suffocating fog. A dense haze cuts out all the light with no end in sight, as though the world will forever be saturated in a viscous heartbreak.

The ground clings to my feet, making every step a challenge.

Sleep both courts and rejects me, keeping me shackled to perpetual exhaustion.

And I can't shake the feeling that a part of me has died with him. As I stare at the box deep in the ground, I know I'll never be myself again. Not the person I was before. That naive little girl is beside him in the box, as lifeless as the man at her side.

"Are you ready, sweetie?" Mom places a gentle arm around my shoulders.

"Almost. I'd like just a minute alone with him."

She nods and signals for the rest of the family to give me space. The funeral ended a while ago. Only close family remains. Mostly mine. Craig didn't have much family. Just his mother and him. She's even more alone than I am, since she doesn't have the same support system I do. Craig was her only child. I can't begin to fathom the pain she must be feeling.

Therefore, when she joins me at the gravesite, I allow her to impose on what I was hoping would be a moment for my husband and me.

"He was terrified he'd lose you," she says, eyes fixed on the distance. Her comment surprises me because I never got the sense he was scared of losing me and because of her almost accusatorial tone.

"He was? He never said anything."

"Of course, he wouldn't. But he told me everything," she says in a tone devoid of emotion. "He told me how he was being blackmailed and had to pay enormous amounts of money to keep you safe."

"*What?*" I gasp, having no clue what she's talking about.

Kristi brings her cold stare to mine, her blue eyes ringed in thick black eyeliner. "He died because of you." Her accusation sinks deep into my gut as intended, a killing blow.

My lungs contract painfully with the need for air.

"What are you saying?" I try not to look alarmed, needing to understand what's happening without my family intervening.

"Why do you think he had to work so hard? He was paying protection money to keep you alive. And when he ran short, they killed him."

My head jerks side to side in small choppy shakes. "No, it was a mugging gone wrong. The police determined it was a mugging."

Her impervious stare penetrates deep into my bones. "That's what your family wants you to think. They haven't told you everything. Ask about the quarters." She lets the words sink in, then walks away, leaving me dumbfounded.

Was my husband murdered because of me? Would my family keep something like that from me? Of course, they would. If they thought I couldn't handle it. And it's not like I've been in a state for hard truths.

I have to get to the bottom of it.

I need to know what happened to my husband, so I can make sure something like this never happens again.

CHAPTER 20
DiAngelo

PRESENT

You managed to drag yourself away last night with her taste on your tongue, but it took every ounce of your control. You will not, under any circumstances, let yourself get carried away again. I don't care what side of the bed she's sleeping on or how unabashed she is about touching herself. I don't care if she offers herself up in a pink satin bow and cuffs; you will not cross that line.

Terina Donati is off-limits.

She is your best friend's little sister—a full ten years younger than you. She needs your undiluted focus to keep *her safe. That cannot happen if you're busy imagining her naked.*

Like you're doing right now.

Jesus Christ.

I've been reading myself the riot act all night and since the moment I woke this morning, yet one look at Rina has my imagination rebelling. She's wearing what must be the tiniest pajama shorts on record with a thin, baggy T-shirt. Together, the two tease a peek at the luscious curve of her ass cheeks practically every time she moves.

And her hair ... *Jesus*, her hair—thick and long, a deep auburn color like a redwood forest cascading down her back. A perfect fistful.

She flits about as if she doesn't have a care in the world, an earbud in one ear, and a rhythm to her steps. She's a brightly colored flag waving in an autumn breeze, drawing the eye of anyone who happens by. I noticed her beauty in the past, but never to this degree. I wouldn't allow myself to. With her living in my home, I can't escape her mystifying effects.

I've had a semi ever since she got a coffee mug down from the cupboard.

My body's response pisses me off. I suppose it makes what I'm about to do a smidgen easier because I have to reset the boundary, and if I'm an asshole in the process, it's for the best.

For her safety, and for my honor.

Hell, for my sanity.

I'll pretend last night never happened and ensure we maintain strict boundaries going forward.

"I need to go by Renzo's place today. If you're going to

yoga, you need to go to a session around one o'clock. We'll go to your brother's after. I'm not doing two outings."

There's a hitch in her movements as she processes, but only for a second.

"One o'clock class works for me." She blows on her coffee, then takes a sip.

I expected more of an argument. More of a reaction stemming from last night. I'm not sure what type of reaction, but this isn't it. This isn't anything. It's like she's oblivious, which was supposed to be my trick, and it's pissing me off.

If she's unaffected by my inflexible demands, I'll have to up the ante. I need to do something to drive a wedge between us and keep my priorities straight. When she intentionally drops a corner of her toast on the floor for Bonny to gobble up, I seize the opportunity.

"Do *not* feed my goddamn dog," I snap at her. "You're already wreaking havoc on my life. You don't need to give my dog the shits on top of everything else."

Bull's-eye.

She gapes at me as though I backhanded her across the face. With my mission accomplished, I head for the guest room shower where I plan to punish myself with ice-cold water because I feel like an absolute bastard. But it had to be done.

I'm not okay with her paying for my mistakes, which will happen if I'm not careful. Her sore feelings will heal, but a failure of protection might bring consequences I could never undo. I've lived that misery, and I never want to experience it again.

CHAPTER 21
DiAngelo

PAST

"What's done is done. We can't change that now," my dad says wearily after I explain the deception that likely led to Elio's abduction.

While he didn't berate or blame me, my shame is still overwhelming. As much as I want to crawl in a hole and never resurface, that would be the coward's choice. It's more important than ever that I do what is right, no matter how excruciating it is to bear.

"Would Cosimo help us?" I ask. Cosimo Costa is Dad's childhood friend—the two were neighbors growing up and kept in touch through the years. Dad is an engineer, while his friend became one of the top members of the Moretti crime family. He was my inspiration for the insinuation that my father had connections, even though I knew very well that Dad has never had anything to do with the Mafia aspects of Cosimo's life. "I'll explain to him myself what I did. I'll make sure he knows I'm the only one to blame."

"It's not an issue of blame, DiAngelo. I'll talk to him if needed, and while I never thought I'd ask my friend for money, I would never be too proud to ask for help when it comes to keeping my family safe."

Dad has always maintained that the key to remaining friends with someone in such a different economic situation is to ensure money is never involved. If they go to dinner together, Dad always insists on paying for himself. He never wanted his friend to question whether Dad was after friend-ship or money. Crossing that line will weigh heavily on my father.

"What else can we do? Get a loan from the bank?"

Dad shakes his head. "That sort of thing takes ages. They have to go to underwriters and get liens on collateral—there's no way we'd get the money in time."

My heart races in my chest. "How do we get the money, then?" Rising panic pulls at my voice like guitar strings strung overly tight.

"We'll have to go to a moneylender."

"I thought you said—"

"Not the bank," he corrects me. "This type of lender isn't

restricted to the governmental oversight that drags out the loan process."

"You mean a loan shark?" I can't keep the shock from my voice. I don't mean to judge his choices. I don't have any better suggestions, but this feels like we're walking straight into a pit of quicksand.

"Keep your voice down," he demands, eyes cutting to the living room where Mom is pacing. "It would only be temporary. I could pay him off after getting a bank loan. There's no other way to get that sort of money so quickly. As it is, I don't know that I could get as much as these monsters are asking, but I need to get as much as I can."

"You know who to talk to?"

"I have an idea."

I nod, choosing not to dig further, though I'm endlessly curious how he knows anyone in that line of work. Of course, he's friends with Cosimo, so maybe there's more to my dad than I realized.

He stands and slides his phone into his pocket. "I'm going to see what I can come up with."

I stand, as well. "I'm going to go to the bar and see about getting security footage from that night. Maybe there's some clue that could help me figure out who's behind this."

Dad claps a hand on my shoulder, his steely eyes boring into mine. "That's a good thought. Every bit of information helps. You let me know what you find, and I'll keep you informed as well."

I'm so damn ashamed at how proud he makes me feel when

none of this would be necessary if it weren't for my stupid ego. I don't deserve such amazing parents. I don't deserve them, yet I'll try for the rest of my damn life to honor them and do right by their names. I fucking owe them that and so much more.

Two hours later, I'm in a grungy back office scanning through grainy security footage of the bar. I force myself to watch as past me boasts about his influential connections and passes around my phone to show off photos of the yacht I supposedly rode on. It makes me sick to relive it. At the same time, I'm glad for the discomfort. I deserve that and worse.

Think of Elio and what he might be going through.

I study each face with renewed determination. When the video reaches the moment I leave the bar to go home, I make a breakthrough. One of the men who'd been crowded around our table follows me out the door. And not in a happenstance sort of way. His body almost appears tethered to mine from the second I separate from the table.

Bingo.

It's a relief to have a lead, but I'm also furious with myself for being so shit-faced that I was oblivious to my surroundings. Had the man followed me all the way home? Why didn't he take me right then? I wish he had so that it was me in danger and not my brother. This man probably has no idea I have a twin.

"Is this guy familiar at all?" I ask the bouncer, pointing at the paused screen.

He squints. "Nah, man. Can't really see enough of his face to make him out." He looks a little closer. "Think I can make out the logo on his ball cap. Not sure if it helps, but I think it says ACME."

Sure enough, I can read it, too. "Any bit helps." I take a photo of the screen and thank the guy for his help.

Once I'm back out in the light of day, I call to check in with my dad. He's finished talking to the loan shark, who said he'd take Cosimo's reference in lieu of collateral and would let us know the answer after they talked. Dad was about to call his friend to let him know the situation, so I don't keep him. I can tell him about the man at the bar once I'm home.

A dozen different businesses across the city use the acronym ACME in their names, not to mention the myriad others around the country. Hell, the hat could be Bugs Bunny merch with absolutely no tie to the city whatsoever. It's hard to say, but I have to keep looking. I can't sit and do nothing.

I study the photo until my vision blurs. I try to reverse image search the logo, but it's too blurry for any matches. I also do a reverse number search for the phone number that the kidnapper used but was unable to get any information. By the time Dad gets home, I've listed every ACME business in all five boroughs and plotted their locations on a map.

"What did Cosimo say?" I ask quietly. Mom is asleep on the sofa. She was out of it when I got home. I'm pretty sure she's taken something to knock herself out, and I don't blame her. I'd do the same if I were in her shoes.

"He's going to see if there's any word on the street about

serial kidnappings—anything that might get us information on who this bastard might be."

"And the money?" I'm scared to ask, and my wavering voice shows it.

"He's got to talk to some people and get back with me." Dad looks twenty years older than he did yesterday. The bags under his eyes are a dark gray, and the sagging of his lips into a frown gives him the appearance of jowls. Dad isn't even forty-five yet.

Needing to get away from myself, I bolt to my feet. "I'll cook some dinner." Anything to distract me from the self-loathing.

A half-hour later, I have a bolognese sauce simmering when Dad's phone rings.

Our eyes lock for an elongated second before we both fly into action. He pulls out his phone while I rush to sit beside him.

"Yes?" He rubs his forehead. "No, I don't have the money yet. I'm having a little trouble coming up with that much ... No, please listen ... I'm not refusing."

I can hear the raised voice on the other end of the call, and something inside me breaks. I need to try to fix this. I have to do something, so I grab the phone and start to pace.

"This is DiAngelo. I'm not sure if you know, but you took my twin brother. I'm the one from the bar—I assume you were there, and that's why you think we have a lot of money. The thing is," I hurry to explain frantically, "I lied about it all. I clean the boats. I wasn't a guest. I was putting on a show to look good, but it was all a lie. Please, don't hurt my brother.

We'll give you what we can, but we don't really have that sort of money."

"You don't have the money?" The man's distant voice sounds incredulous. "This won't be good. He won't like that. Not at all."

"That's not what I said. We just might need a little more time," I try to explain.

"*He won't believe you,*" he says in a harrowing whisper that chills me to the bone.

"I'll get the money," I pronounce in no uncertain terms, terror prodding me to lie my ass off. This man's fear of his boss is palpable, and I can't imagine what that means for my brother. "Please, just give us the full forty-eight hours. That's all we're asking."

I wait for a response. All I hear is a bell in the distance before the line goes dead.

I sink into a kitchen chair and stare at my hands. Worthless, pathetic, helpless hands. "I'm so sorry." The words seem so inadequate for how I feel. I'd carve my heart out and lay it at my father's feet if I could.

He scoots his chair closer and pulls me into his arms, holding me in a merciless hug.

"This isn't your fault. You can't know what a crazy person will do." His voice bleeds into sobs, and I join him. Together, we hold one another and allow our fear to leave our bodies until we are drained and ready to refocus our efforts.

I tell him about the ACME hat and show him my map.

"Before the guy hung up, I heard something in the background. Sounded like a church bell, but I'm not sure what to make of it."

Dad studies the map for a while. "Doesn't look like any churches are located near the ACME businesses." He looks at the security photo of the man from the bar, deep in thought. "Instead of a church bell, could it have been a ferry bell? The kind on a river taxi?"

I think back. "Yeah, I suppose it could have been that." I zoom in on the map and scan each of my pinned locations to see if any are located near piers with ferry access. "The ACME Smoked Salmon plant. It's the only one."

"You think you would recognize the guy if you saw him again?"

I lift my gaze to my father's and feel winded at the hope in his eyes. "There's only one way to find out."

"Wait, no. I shouldn't have even suggested it. We should call the police if we have a lead on this guy."

"Dad, he said he'd know. What if he hurts Elio?"

We stare at one another, equally uncertain and terrified. Dad eventually lowers his gaze defeatedly.

"Maybe you watch from a distance and see if you can spot him. If so, then you can call the cops."

I nod, desperately needing to do *something*.

We learn the shifts start at 5 a.m. Dad only allows me to go if I agree to get some rest in the meantime, since we hardly slept the night before. I can't imagine I'll sleep again tonight, considering the speed of my racing thoughts, but in no time at all, my alarm is going off at 4 a.m.

It's dark, but at least it's not cold, and the processing plant has one main entrance, which also helps. I park the family car where I have the best view of the arriving employees, roll down my window, and wait.

The first shift of workers lopes into the building one after another. At midmorning, another crew begins to filter in. I study one after the other until I see a man who draws my attention. I can't be sure without a closer look, so I exit the car.

Yes, this man is definitely familiar.

I'm considering whether to call the police, as my dad instructed me to do, when the man notices me. He freezes, his face blanching with shock, before he drops his lunch pail and bolts in the opposite direction.

Adrenaline has me flying in an instant. It's a good thing, too, because he's fast. We both careen across the main roadway and away from the isolation of the fish plant. He weaves down sidewalks and across busy streets with me not far behind. I can't make up ground, but I'm not losing him either.

We wind our way back toward the riverfront before he disappears into an old building. It's part of an abandoned industrial complex. I follow him inside but slow to a careful creep, not wanting to end up with a bullet in my face.

The place is filthy. Operations ended here long ago, though the equipment is all still present and accumulating dust. I crouch, slinking from one vantage point to another, keeping myself hidden while continuing farther into the building. The sound of frantic muttering has me pausing. I can't make out what he's saying or whether there are other people present.

Noticing a large wrench, I grab it and inch forward.

The man stands in an open area where several thick, rusted chains hang from the rafters. He's pacing back and forth, cursing and chattering nonsensically while pulling at his short hair.

He appears to be alone. I consider calling the police when my gaze is drawn to the ground beneath his feet, where a massive section of concrete is stained bloodred.

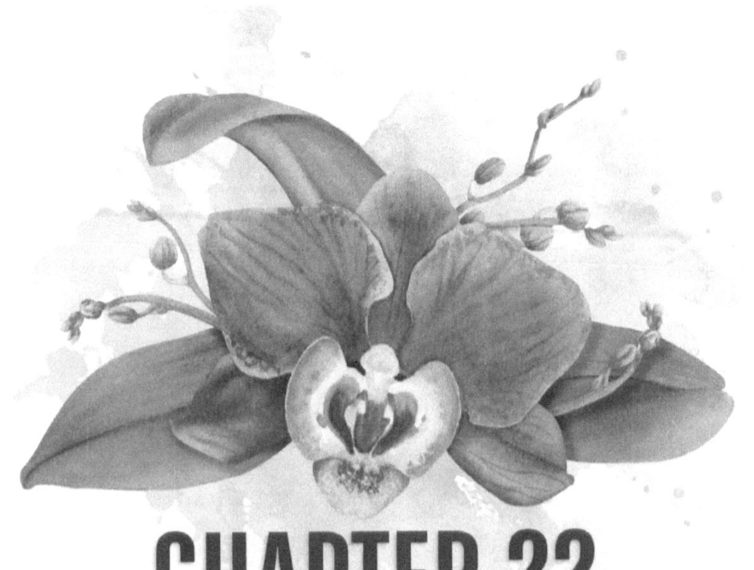

CHAPTER 22
Terina

PRESENT

THE SECOND DiAngelo DISAPPEARS AFTER reprimanding me about feeding Bonny, I give the dog my entire slice of toast, just to spite him. Being angry is easier than being hurt, and damn did his comment sting.

I hate that I'm wreaking havoc on his life. I hate it more than he could ever know. That's why I wasn't over the moon about anyone serving as my bodyguard. I don't want the taint of my life spilling over onto anyone else. Ever.

What I don't get is why he lashed out. It wasn't about the

dog, that's for sure. And tensions between us had settled after the snake incident. We spent most of the day in peaceful coexistence. All I can figure is that the outburst stemmed from his unexpected appearance in the bedroom last night.

He hadn't seemed angry about what I was doing—his thoughts seemed more concerned about his lack of involvement. Why would that upset him? I don't get the sense he feels unjustly entitled. So why was he upset?

I have no freaking clue.

And I'm not feeling particularly forgiving about his behavior. He doesn't get to treat me like crap when I've had no say in any of this. If he has a problem with his bodyguard assignment, he can damn well take it up with my brother.

"Come on, Bonny, let's get cleaned up."

Determined not to let DiAngelo get me down, I take my coffee and my new furry best friend to the bathroom with me. Bonny and I have hit it off exceptionally well, which tickles me to no end. She may be the best part of this whole fiasco.

Bonny lies on the cool stone floor while I do my hair and makeup. We listen to Olivia Dean croon about how easy it is to fall in love with me. I sing along. It's a good reminder that I'm the only person I need.

While finishing up, I realize that my nails are in desperate need of painting. Grabbing one of the cosmetic bags I threw together, I sit on the floor to see what polishes I brought with me. I know there has to be a couple buried in the bag somewhere.

Not wanting to be left out, Bonny gets up and clacks

across the floor to join me. She lies with her front paws extended as if showing off her chunky black nails.

"Oh, Bon Bon. Do you need your nails painted, too? You'd look beautiful in red."

She makes a playful noise and scoots a tiny bit closer. If I didn't know better, I'd say she was goading me.

"I couldn't. He'd go ballistic."

Again, Bonny whines. She even lays her head down as though begging me to dress her up.

"Well, let me see what the internet says. I don't want to hurt you." I'm glad I took the time to check because it turns out human polish is dangerous for dogs.

Duly noted.

"Don't worry, sweetie. There are other options." Who am I to deny a girl some pampering? That would be cruel when nontoxic doggy polishes exist and can be delivered to our door tomorrow.

"If your daddy still has a stick up his butt tomorrow, you get a spa day," I sing to her, scratching her head.

Bonny wags her tail, which shakes her entire back end. I think we're both equally excited.

I'm not super familiar with today's yoga class. I see one girl I know and chat with her briefly before the instructor begins. The lights dim, and I notice DiAngelo bring in a folding chair from the lobby. He plants himself in the seat.

Last week, he waited in the lobby. Is he planning to station himself in the workout room from now on? What on earth will everyone think?

My gaze darts to the class instructor, who has taken notice but appears to be moving on anyway. I dash over to D, trying not to make a scene.

"What are you doing?" I ask in a hushed whisper.

"Same thing I've done for the past week—keeping an eye on you."

"You didn't stand in here last week."

"You hadn't been specifically targeted last week."

"DiAngelo, no one is going to hurt me in here. Look around. They're here for yoga, not murder."

He remains rooted to the spot, ignoring me.

My teeth clench tightly together.

"Fine," I hiss.

It's not like I have a lot of options, so I return to my mat and sync up with the instructor's movements. I can feel DiAngelo's surly presence in the back of the room and wonder if everyone else is as painfully aware of my bodyguard acting like the Secret Service during our hour-long class.

The worst part of all? I sense his eyes on me, and it reminds me of last night. He got off watching me. I saw the enormous bulge in his underwear—the room was dark, but not *that* dark. He was hard as a rock, and knowing how intensely I was affecting him was a dizzying drug injected directly into my bloodstream.

And the way he sucked my fingers?

God, it was like he couldn't get enough.

Touch yourself again in my bed, and I'll take that as an invitation.

His parting statement seemed pretty clear, but the emotions tied up in it still confuse me. He was so damn cold to me this morning. Why?

He's such a mystery. I don't know why I'm trying to understand him. I should be grateful he's erected this wall between us. I don't want to be responsible for another man's death, and it could happen so easily. If the Russians come after me, will DiAngelo give his life to save mine? What if he'd been at my place and inspected that box for me? Would he already be dead?

The thought cinches a vise tight around my ribs until my breath comes in shallow pants.

My vision blurs.

I can't do this here. I have to shut out the thoughts.

I envision myself back in my apartment, alone, with the subtle shift of candlelight warming me from the inside out. After a few minutes, I lose myself in the movements until class is over, escaping the clutches of panic this time around.

"Hey, Rina! You going to keep coming to the class? I'd love for you to come more often." My friend Morgan joins me as I pack up my gear.

"My schedule's a bit wonky lately, so I'll probably be all over the place."

Her eyes cut to DiAngelo. "Yeah, seems like you've got a lot going on. You okay?" she whispers the last part.

I can only imagine what she must think—probably something along the lines of a crazy, possessive boyfriend in my life. Why else would I have a man sit through class with me?

"Yes, I promise! I know it probably looks odd," I try to assure her. "He's my bodyguard and takes his job a little too seriously."

Her eyes bulge. "Whoa! Why do you need security? You some sort of secret princess?"

I have to laugh, which is a nice reprieve. "Nah, just my family being cautious." I lead her toward the lobby and into the gift shop area.

Her gaze continues to drift back to DiAngelo. "Well, sure looks like you hit the bodyguard jackpot. Mr. Muscles and Tats could guard my body any day."

She's joking. I know she's joking.

DiAngelo is undeniably attractive if you like the Hulk sort of look. And I'm irritated with him, so it shouldn't bother me that Morgan is ogling him, but it does. The thorny tendrils of jealousy sprout like vines encircling my arms and legs, squeezing.

"Yeah, he's pretty to look at, but you know the prettiest ones are always gay." Smug satisfaction relaxes my shoulders as the words fly past my lips.

Morgan purses her lips. "Crap, I should've known." She shrugs, then lifts a pair of black leggings from a rack. "These are so crazy cute. I've been eyeing them for ages, but don't have the body for them. You would look amazing in them." She holds the pants still on a hanger up against my lower half. The waist is a V-cut, meant to expose the belly button and below.

That will never happen.

I only wear high-waisted leggings, but I don't feel like explaining myself, so I focus on her instead.

"What? You could totally pull these off. Seriously, you should get them."

"You think?" she asks, bringing the pants to rest against her body.

"I think so, but you're the only one who can decide what you're comfortable wearing. Personally, I say wear what you like and don't worry about what other people think."

Her eyes light up. "You know? You're right. I'm going to do it." She gives me a one-armed hug. "I'm so glad I ran into you. Hopefully, you'll come to more afternoon classes."

"Same! And I'm bound to at some point. You take care."

"You, too!"

Our exchange has an unexpected smile taking up residence on my face until I lock eyes with DiAngelo, who's glowering at me from across the room. It seems I've taken up enough of his precious time.

Not wanting to anger the beast further, I join him at the door. "I'm ready to leave, now," I say haughtily. If I have to look like uptight royalty, I might as well act like it.

His chin lowers, casting his eyes further into shadow before he leans in toward me.

"Act like a brat, and you'll be treated like one," he drawls in a deviously dark tone.

Every molecule of moisture evaporates from my mouth, and something dangerously delicious stirs in my belly.

Here's me thinking I'd test the limits of my authority, only to realize I've brought toy swords to a gun fight.

I swallow. "Lead the way."

God, that impervious smirk. What I wouldn't give to smack it right off his face.

I tally one for DiAngelo, but assure myself I'm nowhere near done with this war.

CHAPTER 23

Terina

PRESENT

Renzo's house is a time machine. The ancient brownstone has been fully updated with modern versions of the materials used in its heyday. The style is an authentic expression of historic charm, but everything is new.

Old homes that preserve original materials rather than remodel with modern replicas seem to cling to the present, haunted by the ghosts of the past. But when I'm at Renzo's, it's different. His house gives the sensation of actually living in a bygone era. It's like walking through a portal to another dimension every time I visit.

Today, it's a little less noticeable since my thoughts are focused elsewhere. And by elsewhere, I mean a lumbering musclehead who finds it amusing to ruffle my feathers at every opportunity. I want to return the favor. It only seems fair.

I'm probably asking for trouble, but holding my own where DiAngelo is concerned is the one bit of control I have left in my world. If I can't stand up to him, what power do I have?

I wouldn't do anything to put either of us in danger. That would be ridiculous. But when my brother asks how things are going, I recognize an opportunity when I see it.

"It's an adjustment. I didn't realize having a bodyguard meant being watched at *all* times," I say the word with just enough innuendo to plant a seed of impropriety.

Renzo's eyes narrow. "What are you trying to say?"

"Nothing," I answer innocently. "I'm sure you and DiAngelo know exactly what you're doing. I just didn't realize I'd have eyes on me day *and* night, but you trust your best friend, so I'm sure his degree of supervision must be necessary."

It occurs to me as I'm talking that if DiAngelo gets reassigned, he won't be in the line of fire any longer. At least, not because of me. I love and hate the idea at the same time, making me realize I have more of a selfish streak than I realized. I want him safe, but I don't like the prospect of losing him either.

When I steal a glance at him, his cutting glare slices into me.

Yikes!

It looks like it's time for a subject change. "Anyway, I

think I'll go wash my hands. I didn't get a chance to wash them after yoga."

Renzo wears a dumbfounded expression as I slip away in search of the nearest bathroom. I take my time, splashing a little water on my face in anticipation that the two men will be in Renzo's office talking for a while. However, upon exiting the bathroom, I discover their meeting has yet to begin because DiAngelo is lying in wait for me instead. It seems ambushing me outside bathrooms is the new favorite pastime for all the men in my life.

Arms crossed, he leans against the wall opposite the bathroom door. "What exactly were you trying to accomplish in there with that little performance?"

"I don't think I said anything that wasn't true." I hold my ground with a small lift of my chin.

"You were trying to get me in trouble." He peels himself off the wall and inches closer.

"If the truth makes you look bad, that's not my fault."

Slowly, he walks me backward into the bathroom. It's a small interior room with no windows, so we're now totally ensconced in shadow. Again, I'm peering up at him in the dark, golden brown irises ringed with green stare back at me. Just like last night.

My thundering pulse pounds in my ears and throat ... and lower.

My body remembers.

It preens and blossoms in his sight.

"As if you didn't get off on me watching you, *literally*," he says in a lazy rumble.

"I ... I was already coming—you had nothing to do with it."

DiAngelo shakes his head slowly. "You and I both know, you didn't come until your eyes met mine." He leans in closer until his lips are inches from my ear. "Seeing me watching you is what pushed you over the edge, and no amount of denial is gonna change that."

I force myself to take a shaky breath and ignore the fact that my center is weeping with need for this man.

"Doesn't mean I wanted you watching me." The fight has left my voice breathy and soft.

"No," he muses softly. "I don't think that's it at all. I think you enjoyed it more than you want to admit, and that's the part you don't like. That's why you want to embarrass me in front of your brother. You want to punish me for exposing your dirty secret, but the problem is, you can't top from the bottom."

I want to lash out at him—to argue and rage at him—but his last words trip me up.

"What do you mean top from the bottom?"

He stands tall, pulling back so that I can see the devilish glint in his eyes. "It means you're pretending to be something you aren't, and I see through the charade. You try to be tough, but you're scared underneath it all. You're frightened, and you're ashamed."

My hand strikes his cheek before my actions register.

I can hardly believe I've slapped him, yet I'm too upset for remorse. "Fuck you, DiAngelo."

His gaze slowly swivels back to mine as smug satisfaction hooks his lips into a smirk before he turns and disappears down the hall. I'm left reeling—my spine rigid with anger while tears pool in my eyes from frustration. I want to rage at him for seeing me more thoroughly than he should.

Who gave him the right to strip me down and expose me like a flower ravaged of all its petals?

I wipe away angry tears and sniffle, making me aware of the pine scent filling the bathroom from a small burning candle. I immediately blow it out, then march to the sitting room at the front of the house. I'm about to sit in one of the two armchairs when I notice yet another candle on a console against the wall.

A new wave of frustration washes over me.

Why are there so many damn candles in this house? It's always like that, no matter the season. We're in the middle of a July heatwave, and my idiotic brother has candles burning all over his house. Who does that?

I round the chair toward the back of the room and suck in a lungful of air, then freeze.

The flickering flame captivates my attention. Mesmerizes.

Its subtle movements reflect off the lake of translucent wax below like a stoic memorial poised in the center of a reflecting pond. It's beauty and danger and comfort and pain all in one. Hope and horror.

I envision myself dipping the pad of my finger into the hot wax and lifting it away to watch the liquid harden as it cools.

A shiver wracks my body. Or is it a shudder?

It's hard to say.

Whatever it is distracts from the ugly thoughts and sings me a sultry lullaby. A siren's song of comfort and peace.

I clamp my eyelids shut.

This is because of the upcoming anniversary—that's why you're feeling weak. Do not let it win.

That's right. The anniversary of Craig's death is only a few weeks away. It always makes July so much harder, and with DiAngelo added to the mix, it's no wonder I'm a mess. But this, too, shall pass.

Feeling a smidgen fortified, I open my eyes and finally blow out the flame. I then press the wooden lid onto the glass container that houses the candle to seal away any further temptation.

Because the candle does tempt me.

DiAngelo may have stumbled upon a nugget of truth, but he wasn't entirely right. A dirty secret does haunt me, but it's so much worse than a sexual kink. Something grotesque and shameful. Something he would likely never understand, and I will never be able to atone for.

CHAPTER 24

Terina

PAST

"I'm surprised to see you here without your father." The detective's gaze sweeps the station as though expecting to find my dad hovering somewhere nearby. He almost looks worried, and I wonder if he's been warned not to talk to me alone.

"He doesn't know I'm here, and he doesn't need to know. I'm a grown adult, Detective Briggs."

"Of course. How about we step into my office, and you can tell me what brings you in." He closes the door behind us, taking one last peek around before doing so.

I sit in the visitor's chair, my hands clutching my purse in my lap, and force all my strength into my voice. "I need to know how my husband died."

His brows cinch together. "He ... was stabbed, Mrs. Kirkland."

"Yes, but I want to know why." I don't waver. I don't allow my grief or nerves beyond the confines of the metal box deep inside me, where I stashed my emotions before arriving at the police station.

Briggs doesn't say a word for long seconds.

"We can't ever truly know what motivates a person—"

"No." I cut him off. "You're not going to feed me a bullshit story concocted by my family to protect me. I want to know about the quarters, Detective Briggs."

"*Fuck*," he hisses, fidgeting in his chair as though suddenly uncomfortable. "You know, none of this changes anything. I hate to say it, but this won't bring him back." He pleads his case gingerly, not wanting to upset me but desperate to end the conversation.

It's my turn to go silent.

I keep my unflinching stare trained on him until he mutters another curse and continues.

"It wasn't a mugging."

"So I've gathered. I want to know what happened, and I promise I won't tell my family I know the truth. I understand why they've kept this from me, but I need to know."

He inhales heavily and relaxes back into his chair. "It was a punitive hit. He must have been doing business with someone he shouldn't have and crossed them in some way that they decided to send a message." He pauses, his jaw flexing. "Your husband had an entire roll worth of quarters shoved down his throat."

Oh, dear God.

I don't want to hear this. I've made a mistake. I don't know what I thought the quarters referenced, but this isn't it. This is so much worse, and I'll never get the image out of my head.

No, Terina. You will not back out of this. That man died for you; the least you can do is learn his truth and honor him.

I unclench my eyes and battle against the emotions threatening to overthrow their confines.

"Show me," I demand quietly.

"No, you don't want—"

"Show. Me." Each word is carved from unbreakable stone.

"*Fucking Christ.*" Despite the vicious hiss of his curse, he starts typing at his computer. Once he pulls up the crime scene photos, he steels himself and swivels the monitor in my direction.

It's a close-up of Craig's bloody lips. The dull shimmer of what I know to be coins rests wedged in the back of his throat.

I swallow and swear I can feel the pain of a phantom coin lodged in my esophagus.

"All of them," I instruct.

Briggs grimaces but clicks through the portfolio of images, one after the other. I don't ask him to slow down. I don't need to. Every photo is instantly seared into my memory. I couldn't forget them if I wanted to.

"Do you know who did it?" I ask once the slideshow is over, guilt and sorrow finally taking its toll on my voice.

"Not yet, but we're working on it. I promise, we'll do our best to track them down."

I nod. "Is there anything else I should know? Anything else my family has instructed you to keep from me?"

"No, ma'am. Not that I'm aware of." The relief in his hurried words leads me to believe he's telling the truth.

"Thank you, Detective Briggs. I think that's all, then." I stand and extend my hand, which he accepts with a remorseful glint in his eyes.

"I am truly sorry, Mrs. Kirkland."

"It's Donati." The correction is unexpected. I hadn't even contemplated changing my name back, but suddenly, I know it needs to happen. I'm not worthy of the Kirkland name. And besides, I can't escape my Donati ties with a simple name change. Not unless I moved away and completely started over. What would be the point in that? The damage is already done.

Briggs nods with a frown. "I'll walk you out."

"No need. I can find my way on my own." I don't wait for him to challenge me because in a small way, I need to prove to myself that it's possible. That I can navigate the world on my own since that is the only acceptable path for me.

A beautiful young man lost his life because of me. A man I loved, despite the flaws in our relationship. He was fun-loving and sweet and had his whole life in front of him—all snuffed out because of the danger surrounding me.

I will never, *ever* allow such a thing to happen again.

When I think of the heartbreak I've caused, I physically stumble from the pain. I don't know how Craig's mother could stomach to look at me. All those people at the funeral—were they all watching me, wondering how I could be so incredibly selfish and heartless?

A barrage of crushing thoughts assails me as I rush home. I need to escape the eyes of the world, but even once I'm alone behind locked doors, there's no hiding from my shame.

I will never stop seeing the blood that stains my hands.

And I don't want to.

I must always remember the damage I'm capable of inflicting on others. And to that end, I allow the images of my dead husband's mutilated body to wash over me, finally giving in to the violence of my grief as I collapse to my knees.

I HAVEN'T LEFT my apartment in a week. I resigned from the soup kitchen. They suggested I might change my mind in a few months. I won't. Everything is different now, and it's never going back to the way it was.

My mom has come by to see me, and though she's worried, she's given me space to grieve. She doesn't realize it's so much more than that.

The guilt is acid eating at my insides.

I hate that I could have been so hopelessly naive, and worry I'll make another similar mistake. What if I see a friend at the market? What if an enemy sees us talking and decides to use my friend as leverage or punishment? Have my eyes been opened wide enough to know when I've put someone at risk?

Without the answers, I can't make myself rejoin the world, which is how I find myself sitting on my bathroom floor at 1 a.m. with a candle in my hand. My sleep patterns are a mess. And television only numbs the pain for so long. I wander my apartment like a ghost stuck in a world where I no longer belong.

Do people use candlesticks anymore?

We were given a pair of Tiffany crystal candlesticks for our wedding. I've never been a crystal sort of girl, so the gift went in a cabinet along with the white candles that go with them.

During my late-night wandering, I didn't want to turn on the harsh lights and remembered the candles. I grabbed one along with a lighter and ended up on the plush rug in front of my bathroom vanity.

Why there? Your guess is as good as mine.

Nothing in my life makes sense anymore. Why should tonight be any different?

I light the wick and am instantly enchanted by the dancing flame. Its soft curves are such a beautiful contrast to its devouring nature. Soothing calm with violent potential.

I wish I were a flame.

The world would be too scared to cross me. But that's not my nature. I can't be anyone other than who I am.

My existential wonderings are interrupted by a sudden searing pain. Hot wax has dripped from the candle onto my inner thigh.

I hiss and jerk my hand away, causing another series of drips to plop across my leg. The pain is intense but brief.

Almost instantly, the wax begins to cool, hardening to an opaque white.

The transformation fascinates me.

As does the newfound absence of my seemingly incessant thoughts.

I slide my fingernail under a dried piece of wax and let it fall to the floor. Despite the dim light, I can see the skin beneath is red and angry, but won't be permanently damaged.

I watch as my hand rises again and tips, drizzling a stream of translucent wax onto the opposite thigh. My teeth grind together as I inhale sharply from the burn. When the sting begins to subside, a blanket of peaceful calm envelops me like I haven't known in weeks. Maybe even months.

The relief is euphoric.

I don't know what's happened in my brain to bring about this change, and I don't care. All that matters is that the torment is gone for however long. And when I peel away the dried wax, I uncover a renewed version of myself.

Stronger.

More resilient.

This Terina is made to survive.

CHAPTER 25
DiAngelo

"Dinner's not going to work this week, and I have no idea when I'll be free. I have someone staying with me to keep them safe for a bit." I could take Terina to my parents' house, in theory. I just don't want to. I'm not up for the questions I'd undoubtedly get from both parties.

Lucky for me, I have a long history of disappointing my parents.

My opinion, not theirs.

They've always been supportive and eager to be as

involved in my life as I'll allow. I'm the one who holds back, and I know that's shitty of me, but being around them reminds me of how different life could have been. I'm reminded of my worst failures and what we all lost because of me.

Is that the coward's cherry on top of the selfish bastard cake? You bet.

A monthly dinner keeps me from hating myself completely where they're concerned. This week was supposed to be our get-together, so I had to call and let them know it isn't happening.

"Oh, that sounds serious," Mom says in a hushed tone over the phone as though someone might try to overhear our conversation. "You should definitely make sure they're safe. We can have dinner with you once things settle down."

Of course, she's genuinely understanding. That's Mom.

"I appreciate that. You guys doing okay?"

"Your dad's just fine, but he keeps trying to give me a heat stroke by turning the AC off. If he doesn't watch it, I'm going to call someone in here to put a lock on the thermostat."

"Why's he doing that? You can afford to be comfortable." They can afford a hell of a lot more than that, thanks to the money I've deposited in their account. It was the first place my money went after I swore my oath to the Moretti Family. One of the things I'm most proud of in my life is knowing my parents retired early because of me.

They know the money isn't exactly clean. Mom wasn't thrilled when I got out of prison and went straight to Dad's good friend Cosimo Costa for work, but she didn't judge me for it, either. Mom and Dad have always maintained that good character isn't always measured in terms of legality. Too many upstanding citizens hide monstrous secrets to pretend a legitimate job makes a person good.

Mom sighs. "I think he's getting old. You know how old people are always cold? That's him. I swear, he has to wear a sweater just to go inside a department store."

A smile tugs at my lips despite the twinge in my heart. Dad is getting older. There are five years between them. I'm glad they can laugh about that stuff, but it's a sobering reminder that they won't be around forever.

"I'll get him some long underwear. I don't want to sweat through our next dinner."

"I'll make sure to have it nice and cold for you," she assures me warmly. "You just let us know when you can make it over here, and I'll put him under a heat lamp like one of those lizards."

"Alright, Ma." I chuckle. "I'll be in touch."

"Better be. Love you, D."

"Love you, too." And I do. I wish I didn't love them so much. It would make stomaching the past that little bit easier.

Yup, I'm definitely a selfish dick.

To my parents and Terina. Her attempt at getting me in trouble with Renzo was probably deserved, but it still pissed me off. That is, until I saw the way she reacted to me. Like aloe on a sunburn, my anger fizzled to a distant hum.

Damn, I wanted to taste her at that moment. Feel her melt beneath me.

Her body is screaming to submit to me, and I don't think she has the slightest clue. Or maybe she knows and simply doesn't want to feel that way. Regardless, her true nature shines through, and the dominant in me hungers for more. That's why I had to say something even though I know better. The last thing I need is to be introducing her to the more basal side of her nature.

Fortunately, that shouldn't be a problem, considering my delivery couldn't have been worse. I'm not even sure where I went wrong. Yeah, I said she was pretending to be someone she's not and ashamed about it, but I didn't expect that to be quite so triggering. I was talking about the way she naturally bends to my will, but she reacted as though I had accused her of stealing money from the elderly.

Something was clearly lost in translation. I let it go, though, because the last thing we need is to discuss our sexual compatibility. Let her be pissed. That's what I'd been after initially, right?

Exactly.

Therefore, I left it alone. A week has now passed since the slap at Renzo's place, and she's been distant ever since. I fucking hate it.

I've asked myself all week if it was the implication of her submissive nature that upset her or the notion of submitting to me specifically that bothered her most?

I'm dying to know what's going on in that head of hers. Patience isn't normally a problem for me, but I seem to be in short supply ever since Terina entered my life. Need claws at me to give her what I know she craves. To force her to surrender.

But once a line like that is crossed, there's no going back.

I know I should fight the desire with everything inside me, yet every time she innately bends to my will, that creature inside me rears its head and howls. Should he demand more, I can't be sure logic would win that battle.

And then there's the bending of her body.

I should tell her no more damn yoga class. It would be safer on multiple fronts. I tell myself I'm letting her continue classes because it's important to her, and that's part of it, but the dirty truth is that I desperately need to watch her. The way she moves, slow and sensuous, like honey begging to be lapped up.

Today's class isn't until midafternoon, so I have a little time to get my head on straight and remember my priorities. Which reminds me that I need to check in with Renzo.

He answers my call almost immediately. "I was just about to call you."

"Hell, that can't be good," I mutter.

"It could be, but it's not," he confirms. "I finally got a call back from Simeon Mikhailov. He says he has no ill will toward us. If his brother's plotting anything, he's not involved."

"And we're supposed to believe him?" I snap back.

"I get it. I was skeptical, too, but his father's death has only benefited him. Why begrudge us what enabled him to seize control? And there's something else. Turns out Biba's old garage hangout burned to the ground last night."

"No shit?"

"Yeah. Word on the street says Reaper's behind it, which got me thinking. We assumed the P on that notecard with the snake was from Pasha. What if Terina was right, and the letter was an R—"

"Fucking Reaper," I breathe, finishing his thought. "I hadn't even considered that." How could I have been so stupid?

"Me either." Renzo's words are heavy with self-disgust. "He's been so quiet, and a Russian attack seemed so likely, it never occurred to me the threat could be coming from another source entirely. It could be a direct attack from him, or he could be trying to stir up trouble between the Russians and us."

"That would be clever—get us fighting, then swoop in and steal our turf in the process."

"Exactly."

"Clever but seriously underhanded considering that asshole owes us—not only did we spare him and his sniper but we also took out Biba for him. Tommy easily could have taken out all of them that day."

"You and I both know others in our world don't operate with the same code we observe. He may see our actions as a weakness to manipulate."

I huff my disgust. "If that's the case, we won't make the same mistake twice."

"Agreed."

I move on. "Well, I wish I had news to report on the snake. The exotic animal dealers our guys have been to all confirm it was a banded krait, whatever the fuck that is, but none claim to have sourced it. They said it's found in Thailand and Asia and is exceptionally hard to import."

"And venomous?"

"One of the deadliest."

A violent curse crosses the phone line.

"Nothing we didn't already know, but confirming it still pisses me the fuck off," he adds.

"I hear you, and I'll have the guys keep working through the list of dealers. There's a fuck-ton of them in the city, especially when you include the black market names. Surely, one of them will give us a lead."

"Let's hope so."

"Next question is, what's our response?"

Renzo lets out a weary sigh. "It's been a week, and no one has taken accountability. I don't think it's right to endanger the entire Moretti organization when there are doubts as to the origin of the threat."

I hate to admit it, but he's right. "What then?"

"We need to see if we can finally make contact with this Reaper lunatic. I'm going to put out some aggressive feelers and see what we can accomplish."

"You need me to put my ear to the ground?" We both know I'm good at protection, but my specialty is intel. I can track down a person better than most bloodhounds.

"Yes, but I want to wait until we see where this inquiry gets us."

"You're the boss," I say grimly, not envying his position.

He gives me a commiserating grunt, then ends the call. I consider stewing in my office, but give in to the grating curiosity and go in search of Terina to see what she's been up to all morning.

The answer is, corrupting my dog.

She has Bonny on the sofa, again, and as I approach, I realize it's so much worse than that.

"You've got to be fucking kidding me." I gape at the two.

A triumphant grin brightens Terina's face. "Doesn't she look pretty!"

Bonny bounds off the couch and prances in circles as if showing off. I know the dog had no say in this, but hell, if she doesn't look proud of herself.

"You painted her goddamn nails?"

"I sure did, and they look so pretty, don't they, girl?" She welcomes Bonny back to her, further exciting the dog. "That's right! The most beautiful girl in the city! Yes, you are."

Un-fucking-believable.

"*Heel*." My clipped command whips through the air.

Bonny races to my side.

"Alert," I add quietly, pleased when my purebred Rottweiler begins to growl, and Terina's eyes go wide as saucers. I'm about to give the *Steady* command to call off the threat when the shock on Terina's face melts to pure joy.

"Oh, you *are* a good girl, aren't you?" She lowers herself to the floor and opens her arms in welcome. My treacherous dog ends her warning without my command and bounds to Rina like a lost puppy. "So scary and strong and the very best protector there is."

Then she's giggling and rolling on the floor as Bonny licks her from head to toe.

I'm speechless.

And not because I'm outraged. It's the damn cutest thing I've ever seen—like the two are long-lost soulmates. My preferences in the matter have zero chance of relevance, and I'm not even mad about it.

Fuck, this is bad.

CHAPTER 26
DiAngelo

PRESENT

Another day, another yoga class. I've been informed that Isa will be at this class. I'm hoping that means a stress-free hour, but my optimism dies a quick death the minute I see the instructor. His name is Chase, which also appears to be his favorite pastime—chasing the women in his class.

The ladies all seem to love him. He's a few years older than me but keeps himself lean and fit. He also wears so much spray tan that his skin has an orange glow and is way too goddamn handsy. I made a comment about him to Rina after a class last week, and she's under the deluded impression he's simply friendly. His touches don't look friendly to me. They look suggestive. The asshole has probably laid half the women in the studio.

That's when it hits me.

He could have already had sex with Terina. She's a grown woman. Nothing says she can't screw anyone she wants, but the thought has my fists balled so tightly that my bones ache.

Now my optimism *and* my mood have left the building.

The lights dim. Sixteen participants, all quiet, focus their attention on Chase. The opening stretch poses begin with Chase leading by example. Once instruction moves to the core of the routine, he makes a demonstrative pass-through before walking among the participants to check their form as they repeat the series of movements.

When he gets to Rina, my shoulders tense.

I watch him like a hawk. His nose doesn't twitch without me noticing. Rina can't see it because he's behind her, but I get a perfect view of the way his tongue swipes over his bottom lip before his hand presses to her lower back.

It's not obscene. Nothing that would earn him a near-death experience, but I hate it, nonetheless.

I have to relax my jaw and move it side to side to prevent me from cracking a tooth.

Not ten minutes later, the little ass-wipe manages to find yet another reason to put his hands on Rina. This time, it's her hamstrings, encouraging her to squeeze her glutes in a bridge pose.

Sounds reasonable, right?

Not to the demon in my head. All he sees is a man trying to touch Rina's ass.

His rage is my rage, turning our vision red.

Chase has moved on by the time I cross the room, but I don't care. We're out of here.

"What's going on?" she asks in a hushed whisper as I help her to her feet.

"Something's come up; we gotta go." Not a lie, but there's no way I'm telling her the full truth. She doesn't need to know the something that came up is a touch of insanity on my part.

Thankfully, she complies, collecting her things and giving Isa a reassuring nod before following me out.

"Is everything okay?" she asks once we're in the car. Her words are hushed with worry, and I feel a tiny tinge of guilt. Not enough to trigger remorse. Just enough to sour my mood further.

"Yeah, it's fine," I answer gruffly, keeping my eyes on traffic.

Neither of us says another word until we're back at the apartment. I thought that meant the subject had been dropped. I was wrong.

I set my wallet and keys on a console in the living room where I always leave them and go to the kitchen for some food.

"DiAngelo, what was that?" Rina asks.

I glance behind me to where she's standing with her hands on her hips, eyes narrowed. Tension coils in my neck at the feeling of a storm brewing.

"We just needed to get out of there, okay?" *Please, leave it at that.*

She's quiet for several seconds. I grab a protein shake and remove the lid.

"Is this ... is this because of *Chase?*" she blurts, her voice rising.

"Who?"

Aren't you too damn old to play dumb?

Apparently not.

"The yoga instructor," she says dryly. "Did you drag me out of there because he was touching me?"

"Don't think anyone dragged you anywhere." I take a gulp of my drink.

Terina marches forward. "You're avoiding the question, which only confirms my suspicion. You made me leave because he was touching me, didn't you? You thought he was some sort of danger?" If she wants to think this was about safety, that works for me.

"I was keeping you safe, like I promised I would."

"Safe from what? A good workout?"

I'll give you a workout, if that's what you need.

Jesus, man. Get that shit outta your head.

I lean in, my eyes narrowing to match hers. "The thing about doing my job is, I don't have to explain it to you."

"*Ugh,* you're impossible," she roars before marching away to the bedroom.

The next six hours are entrenched in silence, at least as far as conversation goes. There's plenty of slammed doors and irritable sighs—on both our parts.

By the time she calls it a night, the tension between us is one spark away from a raging forest fire. And that spark turns out to be the bedroom door. It becomes our line in the sand—the excuse we've both been looking for to air our grievances.

I charge toward the bedroom the second the door slams shut and open it without knocking. "Told you this stays open."

She's sitting on the bed, rubbing lotion into long, sexy legs. "I don't think so. There's absolutely no reason that door needs to be open for my safety. This room doesn't have a secret back entrance. No one is going to get to me in here without going by you first." She proclaims each word with absolute confidence. My guess is she's probably been rehearsing it. It irritates me to think she's been plotting ways to push me away.

I prowl closer. "You thought you were safe in your apartment, but the snake found its way in, didn't it?"

She lifts her chin defiantly. "I won't accept deliveries anymore."

I grab the lotion from beside her and squirt some in my hand. She watches in confusion as I take her foot—the angle forcing her to lie back on the bed. She yips with surprise but doesn't argue as I slowly begin to rub the cool cream into the arch of her foot.

"And what happens if someone slips something in your purse while we're out, or finds a way to mix poison into something seemingly innocuous like ... lotion ... and you have no idea there's a problem until you're all alone in your bed?" I rest her foot on my chest and continue my massage farther up her leg. "With the door closed, I'd never hear you."

I lift her other foot, taking one in each hand before

suddenly using my leverage to flip her onto her stomach. Before she can recover from the surprise, I align my body with hers and take her hands in mine. Nose in her hair, I can't avoid the intoxicating scent of peaches and cream.

"Danger can strike when you least expect it, Terina," I rasp close to her ear. "You don't always see it coming. While your life is in my hands, I make the calls. I decide where you go and when. I decide if the doors stay open and shut, and I sure as fuck decide who gets to touch you."

Rina gasps.

I tense in preparation for a fight, holding her hands that little bit tighter, but am stunned when I feel her press her ass against my swollen cock instead.

"You didn't want him touching me," she breathes softly, as though some mysterious puzzle piece has fallen into place.

"No, I didn't, and if it happens again, I'll break his fucking fingers." I sound like an absolute psychopath and don't care in the slightest. Taking one more sniff of her hair, I drag myself off her. "And the door stays open," I add, noting the petulance in my tone but unable to curb it.

Terina rolls over, and I allow our eyes to meet for a handful of heartbeats. Allow her to see there's not a joking bone in my body. Because I'm the sort of man who will protect her with my life, but I'm equally likely to kill for her, too. She needs to know that. She needs to understand I'm not the sort of man who plays games and haven't been for a very long time.

CHAPTER 27
DiAngelo

PAST

I thought I knew myself. I thought I knew the man I was becoming. I had no idea life could disfigure a person so suddenly into something unrecognizable.

As I step into view of the man who kidnapped my brother and take in the bucket and mop standing in the middle of a large patch of red-stained concrete, a chilling savagery slows my heartbeat and stills my mind. All thoughts of calling the police have evaporated.

"Where's my brother?" My menacing words bring the

man to a stop. Again, he blanches at the sight of me, as if he's seen a ghost.

He shakes his head and returns to pulling at his hair, muttering, "Two of them ... not one ... two ... killed him ... then he was gone ... but not him ... now he's back..." His frantic ramblings grow more panicked with every second.

My brain picks apart every word. Every movement.

Calculating.

Assessing.

"Did you kill my brother?" I stalk closer, the heavy wrench gripped firmly in my hand.

The man's wide eyes cut to a knife on the floor. It's caked in dried blood. My muscles ready to lunge. Should he indicate a move in that direction, we're each a dozen paces from where it lies, but he looks back at me, instead.

"I ... I would never..."

"Then who?" I demand, my booming voice echoing from the rafters.

The pathetic shadow of a man flinches. "I was only following orders. He's the one ... he did it. Not me."

"Tell me his name."

"I can't." He shakes his head in rapid, jerky movements. "I'll never see the light of day again."

Fury pumps liquid violence into my veins. "You don't tell me his name, and you'll never breathe again." I raise my hand with the wrench in emphasis of my snarled threat. "What's his name, and *where the fuck is my brother?*" I roar.

Time stretches thin, then slingshots forward when the

man suddenly dashes for the knife. I launch into motion as well, but I'm not after the knife.

I already have a weapon.

When he tosses himself to the ground to grab the knife, I swing the wrench with all my might.

Not at his hand to disarm him.

Not at his ribs to wind him.

I aim for his head with only death in mind. I'm blind with rage.

This man took my brother. He's just as much a part of this as whoever it is he's working for. Both of them will pay with their lives.

I swear it.

My chest heaves with heavy breaths as I stand and survey the result of my actions. A man not much older than me, his face now smooth and serene, lies unmoving on the floor. Blood pools beneath his head.

Is that how Elio looked on this same floor?

My stomach rebels, spasming violently. I bend and retch. I haven't eaten in over twenty-four hours, so the heaving only results in saliva and bile.

When I'm in control of my faculties again, I check the man for a pulse.

Nothing.

He's dead.

I killed him, and I don't have it in me to panic about the consequences because all that matters is Elio. My brother is gone. The very best part of my world.

My soul has been viciously ripped in two, and nothing will ever be the same again.

It's too much to think about.

Instead, I focus my mind on dealing with the immediate situation. I have a dead body to deal with. I could call the police. And tell them what? That I murdered a man? I could try to say it was self-defense—he was going for a knife, after all. But there's probably surveillance footage of me chasing the asshole down, and the fact that I hit him in the back of the head doesn't look great.

What, then? Think, D. What the fuck do you do now?

Before I do anything, I need to look for Elio. Hell, maybe the guy was delusional and my brother isn't even dead.

I keep the wrench clutched in my fist, deciding I should stay armed if there's a chance his accomplice could be lurking in the building. Over the next hour, I systematically search every inch of what appears to be an old meat processing plant. The place is untouched. I don't see any signs of Elio or any other activity in the rest of the building.

When I return to the body, I go through his pockets. He has a wallet with a state ID and a few bucks, but nothing else of consequence. He also has a small notepad with a majority of the pages ripped out. The remaining pages are blank, though I can just barely make out the imprint of scribbles from what was written on the last page to be removed.

I don't have a pencil to rub across the paper and help me make out the words, but there's plenty of dust. I use my finger to swipe a layer of brown from a nearby machine, then gently rub it back and forth over the page. The added contrast is just enough to make out the message.

They don't have the money.

The iron jaws of an invisible bear trap clamp ruthlessly around my chest.

Is this what sentenced my brother to death? Why didn't they give us more time? What the hell is wrong with them? What kind of evil throws away a human life for no reason?

I stagger to my feet and clutch at the searing pain in my chest. That's when I see the red water in the bucket. Is it truly Elio's blood? Is that all I have left of him?

I lift the mop out of the bucket and notice something glinting at the bottom through the murky, brownish-red liquid. My hand dives into the bloody water without thinking, soaking myself up to my elbow, because I recognize the object.

It's Elio's cross pendant and silver chain, identical to the one I wear. Mom gave them to us for our first communion. We've worn them ever since.

Seeing the necklace drives home the reality of the situation.

Elio is gone. He's never coming back.

His watered-down blood soaking my arm is the closest I'll ever get to having my twin with me again.

"*Elio!*" The lamenting wail claws its way from my ravaged soul and saturates the air with sorrow. Sobs rack my body as I collapse to my knees.

How do I go on living without my other half?

How can I look myself in the mirror knowing it's all my fault?

I wrestle with the hardest truths I've ever known while a granite boulder sits upon my chest. Everything feels impossible, but giving into my self-pity and pain is easy. Their call is seductively sweet. I don't deserve easy.

What would be infinitely harder is forcing myself to live with the knowledge of what I've done. And if I stay alive, I can dedicate my life to honoring his. Doing right by him is all I have left.

A somber sense of clarity and purpose blankets my ailing conscience.

I wipe the snot and tears from my face. I carefully deposit Elio's necklace into my pocket and rise to my feet. There's work to be done. For Elio.

I still have a murderer to catch.

But first, I need to dispose of this body, and I think I know how. While I was searching the building, I saw what looked to be an industrial-sized meat grinder. That should do the trick nicely.

CHAPTER 28
Terina

DiAngelo was jealous of Chase. He could claim all he wanted that he cut yoga class short because of my safety, but I can read between the lines. It came down to jealousy, pure and simple.

What does that mean, though?

I can't deny a chaotic chemistry has been building between us since he first started acting as my bodyguard. Every time he's close, the air seems to thicken a little more. Every touch is a tad more claiming. The mutual attraction between us isn't at question. But getting a hard-on is different from wanting to be with someone.

Jealousy …

That implies a desire to possess exclusively.

It's another story entirely and somehow casts a different light on everything.

The mystery of it all keeps me awake later than usual. I spend ages mulling over the meaning of his actions and how I feel about it all because as confused as I am by him, it's nothing compared to the bafflement I feel at my response.

In the moment, with DiAngelo's body pressed against mine, his cock nestled between my ass cheeks, I wasn't scared or angry or even frustrated. The only thing I felt when I realized he'd been jealous was pure satisfaction. It's the reason my body writhed against his of its own volition. Something deep inside me preened at the idea of belonging to him, and that's the part that has me most unsettled.

I haven't wanted a relationship since Craig died. Not even a little.

When I think about it logically, I still don't want a man. I don't want anyone to get too close to me and endanger themselves. Yet the chemistry simmering between me and DiAngelo overrides logic and scrambles my thoughts like a rake through sand.

I wake in the morning no closer to understanding than when I'd first gone to bed, but leave it to the universe to swoop in and remind me of what's at stake. Kristi messaged me in the night.

Guilt wraps its cold, bony fingers around my shoulders and squeezes.

Kristi: you going to pay your respects tomorrow?

Kristi: it's his birthday, in case you forgot

Kristi: seems like the least you can do

I take a breath before I reply. Craig's mom was never my biggest fan, but she got downright mean after his death. It's the pain that causes her to lash out, and I'm a big reason for that pain. I try to be understanding, but damn does it hurt.

As for the date, I hadn't forgotten, but for once, it hasn't haunted me upon its approach. I've had too much on my mind to remember to feel guilty.

The reprieve was nice while it lasted.

Me: I'm sorry but I can't be there. I'll do what I can to visit on the anniversary.

The anniversary of his murder.

I always go to the cemetery that day. She knows that. It's been five years, though, and she still shames me for not going more often.

But I refuse to let it get to me today. I woke with a buoyancy—an unexpected hopefulness—that I want to take hold of with both hands and never let go. Today feels different. I feel different.

It's dangerous, this new unfurling curiosity, yet I can't quash it.

I don't want to, if I'm honest.

"Do we still have blueberries?" I ask when I join DiAngelo in the kitchen. He's sitting at the bar shirtless and drinking coffee. His hair is still wet from a shower, and his muscles are taut from working out.

My fingers twitch with the need to trace each dip and curve.

"I think so."

"I'm going to make blueberry pancakes. You want some?" I saw syrup hiding in the pantry the other day and decided it would be fun to make a treat. Now that I'm feeling more comfortable here in his home, I'd like to do more cooking. I enjoy the process of making a meal, and I'd love to feel like I'm giving back to DiAngelo in some way since he's done so much to help me. Despite our arguments, I appreciate his sacrifices.

"Yeah, that works."

"Or I can leave off the blueberries, if you prefer," I hurry to add.

"Blueberries are good. I can make eggs, too, if you want."

"I'll do it—you already do plenty for me." I flash him a shy smile. "I can fry some bacon, too. It's a good day for a big breakfast."

"Oh yeah? Why's that?"

"I thought I'd take the day off—no yoga for either of us." I offered to do yoga at home at first, but he insisted I was fine going to classes. While I don't want to become a hermit, I do feel better knowing I'm not leading him into unnecessary danger. Maybe I can alternate between home and class to minimize our outings.

"That is reason to celebrate," he teases wryly as I bustle around the kitchen gathering the items I'll need for the pancakes.

"I don't know how you'd feel about it, but I'd love to see if Isa could come by to hang out later today."

"Fine by me." He's suddenly standing by me with a skillet in hand.

"Thanks." My voice grows unexpectedly husky at his nearness. I hesitantly take the pan then get back to my task, trying to ignore the fact that he's now leaning against the counter behind me. Watching.

"I'm putting in a grocery order today. You have any requests?"

I whirl around, forgetting my nerves. "Yes! I'd love to do some cooking, if you're okay with that."

"You won't hear me complaining. Maybe after you eat, you can put together a list. I'll add it to the order."

"I can do that. Do you have any allergies or preferences?"

His gaze is warm molasses on a crisp October morning. "You make it, Rina, and I'll eat it, yeah?"

DiAngelo's sweet words have stolen all of mine, so I nod and try to keep breathing now that my lungs have forgotten how to work.

Today is definitely different.

This is uncharted territory, and I'm terrified of how good it feels, but I try not to let that fear taint the moment. Breakfast is a success. I'm pleased at how my pancakes come out, and DiAngelo practically licks his plate clean. We clean the kitchen together, then disperse to our separate activities until it's time for Isa to arrive in the late afternoon.

I introduce her to Bonny, and the three of us plant

ourselves in the shade outside on the balcony after we make ourselves some cocktails.

"Mmm, perfect day for a cold drink." Isa sips from her vodka tonic that is mostly tonic.

I raise my glass in agreement. "I should probably drink straight from the bottle after the couple of weeks I've had."

"Yeah, I want to hear all about it. I'm not sure how you breathe with all that tension in the air."

I frown, though I know exactly what she's talking about. "Tension? That's just DiAngelo. You know how intense he is."

Come on, acting skills. Show me what you've got.

Isa chuckles. "My bad—so ... nothing is going on between you guys?"

"No, nothing at all." Not technically.

"Excellent, because I've been thinking, and if you're okay with it ... I'd like to ask him out. Seeing him again reminded me of the old days, and I thought it might be good to reconnect." She peers at me warily as though worried I'll be upset.

My cup clanks onto the glass patio table as the air evaporates from my lungs.

Isa and DiAngelo? I don't even have to say it out loud for the bitterness to coat my tongue, yet the taste is so strong, I have to fight back a grimace.

Maybe I want DiAngelo more than I wanted to admit. More than a simple attraction.

A peal of laughter scatters my chaotic thoughts. Isa grins. "That's what I thought."

"Wait..." I stare at her. "Did you just ... *bait* me?"

She shrugs impishly. "More like nudged you a little."

"It's not what you think, Isa. Things between us are crazy complicated. Sometimes I want to strangle him, and other times I want to..." I can't say what I want. I'm too scared to voice it into being. But I don't have to lay it out for Isa to understand.

She gives me a sad smile. "You do what's best for you, Rina."

"I'm trying to figure out what that is."

"Well, in the process, no one would blame you if you decided to ... test the waters. You know, scratch that itch. No reason not to take advantage of being stuck here together." She sips from her drink, brows rising.

My cheeks flush what has to be bright red, and I can only hope she thinks it's the alcohol. I can't bring myself to tell her what I did in his bed. And besides, she and I don't usually talk about that sort of thing. It may be a little unusual, but it works for us. Neither of us dates. Men and sex simply aren't a part of the equation.

I'm not entirely sure about her reasons. She lost her mother and brother close to one another. I got the sense she never truly processed the loss.

As for me, I haven't wanted to be with anyone—not even just for sex—because sex leads to feelings, and I didn't want that. I don't want that. Right?

My gaze drifts inside the apartment and locks with his. The television is on, but he's not watching it. He's watching me.

Butterfly wings tickle my insides and make it hard to breathe.

"Rina, is Craig the reason you don't move on? Do you still miss him?" Isa's question is so unexpected, and my attention is so fixated on DiAngelo, that I don't filter my answer the way I normally would.

"No, I don't move on because I don't want anyone else to get hurt because of me." I finally force my eyes back to my friend, though I can't hold her gaze long because of the immense sadness I see.

"You weren't to blame, Rina. It was just bad luck."

"Do you actually believe that with our family business, his getting stabbed was a random coincidence?" My words are sober and spoken with a heavy dose of reality.

Isa leans forward. "Do you know something I don't?"

Yes.

But there's no use dredging up the past, so I shake my head. "It's a risky life we lead. You know that better than anyone." Her father is Renzo's consigliere. While there was no proof that her brother's death was a hit, their brakes went out while he was driving. That doesn't usually happen. The only reason she's alive is his decision to steer the car to a stop in a way that saved her but killed him instantly.

She nods, and we both take long swigs from our drinks.

"It's also boring. I don't know about you, but hiding out at my dad's house has me bored to tears. I've been thinking about taking up canning, and I don't even like preserves."

I chuckle. "Then why canning?"

"I like the jars." She shrugs, and we both laugh.

"Seems like a good reason. I should probably take on more than yoga. I used to volunteer at a soup kitchen, which isn't an option while we're in danger, but I could go back to that."

"Yeah? I might would join you."

"Really?" I'm not sure why I'm surprised. She's super sweet like that, and we'd have fun together.

"Of course. Once all of this blows over, we should look at the options."

"That sounds great."

Our conversation continues to wind seamlessly from one topic to another until an hour has passed, and DiAngelo joins us with a plate full of food in one hand and two water bottles in the other.

"This is unexpected," I say with an alcohol-induced grin. We've finished our second round of drinks, and though the vodka ratio wasn't high, I don't drink often, so I'm feeling the effects.

"Figured I'd better bring something so that I'm not stuck holding your hair back all night." His words remind me of the kiwi he's included on the plate—a little rough and prickly on the outside but all sugary sweet on the inside.

The truth is, he's under no obligation to help me if I get sick. He didn't have to bring us anything, let alone spend the time to cut up kiwi and strawberries, slice cheese, and line the plate with rows of crackers and salami.

"You're welcome to join us." My softly spoken offer hangs in the air.

DiAngelo pauses, his eyes lingering on mine before drifting to Isa and Bonny. "I have some things to do, but you make sure to drink some water, yeah?"

Heat radiates from my skin when his gaze finds mine again. I nod, my teeth grazing my bottom lip. Silence envelopes the balcony until he's returned inside and no longer in sight.

"Girl, that tension's so intense, it stole all the air from an open patio. How does that even happen?" Isa fans herself with her hand more for effect than the breeze.

"Oh, God. I don't know. I don't know what to do about any of it." I open my water bottle and take a swig.

Isa does the same, but eyes me the entire time. "You know he'd do it, don't you? He'd hold your hair back all night if that's how long it took."

I chew on my cheek while considering her comment. "I think you might be right," I finally answer in a hushed tone.

Even if I think about all the ways he's been a brute, there are just as many things he's done purely for my benefit. Like the snake—he was under no obligation to be so sweet and reassuring. He's given up his bed, bought a pantry full of food to my specifications, and despite my best efforts, he never even got all that upset when I painted Bonny's nails. He easily could have kept me couped up in his apartment, no yoga or outings whatsoever, if he wanted to make this job as simple as possible.

When I think about it like that, I have to admit, he's been pretty dang sweet.

Oh, crap. Is this a *crush*?

Do I have a crush on my brother's best friend?

"It would be hypocritical of me to push you into a relationship when I'm equally unwilling," Isa says gently, "but I know both of you, and I think you should keep an open mind. I just want you to be happy."

"I'm not sure what happy looks like for me." I whisper my admission, scared to acknowledge the truth to myself.

My friend lays her hand on mine. "I understand probably more than anyone, and I'm here for you. All you have to do is ask."

"Thanks, Isa." I squeeze her hand. "Same goes for you, babe."

Our exchange is sweet, but the ugly truth is, neither of us is willing to take the plunge and actually lay ourselves bare. Maybe one day. But for now, it helps to know I'm not alone.

CHAPTER 29
DiAngelo

"You sure do a fuck-ton of yoga." I shouldn't complain—it could have been worse. Terina could have been into dumpster diving or those creepy porcelain dolls.

"I told you I can practice from home."

I grunt, my gaze scanning the schedule she's put together for the following week. "I'm not complaining."

"Kind of sounds like it," she quips softly. "You could get more done on your phone during class if you went back to waiting in the lobby."

It's been two days since Isa was over, and we've been

balanced on a knife's edge ever since. Thoughtful and civil yet restrained. We're both aware of how precariously we're perched, and neither of us knows if it's better to push or pull.

"Not happening. And if that man is there again and thinks he's going to put his hands on you, you remember what I said."

My bristling words are a figurative push. I didn't anticipate rocking the boat, but the thought of another man touching her riles me beyond rational thought.

Time slows while Rina decides how to respond.

Will she choose to keep the balance of our tenuous status quo? Or will she resist?

She squares her shoulders and crosses her arms over her chest.

Excitement stirs in mine.

She's made her choice.

My fighter is ready to push back and see where we fall.

"Surely, you can hear how ridiculous that sounds. I don't even understand why it matters to you."

Push.

I step closer and glower at the auburn beauty across from me. "Because it's not his job to touch you."

Shove.

"It's not yours either, but that didn't stop you." She takes a measured step of her own while pointing an accusatory finger my direction.

We're now face-to-face, glaring at one another. Teetering on the precipice of unchartered territory. A world of untold treasures that I shouldn't want but can't resist.

"That's different," I ground out through gritted teeth.

"Why is it different?"

"It just is."

"How?" she demands, anger rising in her voice.

The final thread snaps.

We begin our freefall.

"Give me your hand."

My booming command resounds through the living room.

She complies without hesitation, exactly as I suspected.

"And your other hand."

Again, she obliges without question, and it makes my blood sing.

I slowly lift her arms until they're extended straight up. The air between us sizzles and sparks with anticipation. Time stands still as my hands lingering on hers before slowly trailing down her arms and ribs to rest at her waist.

"Hold them there." My voice is as shredded as my restraint. Both raw with hunger for her.

I lower my gaze and feast on the sight of her pebbled nipples reaching for me through the snug fabric of her shirt. She notices my focus, but instead of yanking her arms down to hide herself, her chest expands on a heady inhale.

"Don't. Move," I breathe before slowly dragging her shirt up and over her head. She's not wearing a bra, bare from the navel up.

The rush of her submission is dizzying.

She's incredible.

And I'm man enough to admit I'm not just attracted to her.

I'm fucking famished for her.

"What is this, DiAngelo? What's happening?" The tenderness in her voice has my dick swelling to the point of pain. Because I know the truth. Her show of vulnerability isn't weakness; it's trust and courage. She's trusting me not to hurt her, and there's no more precious gift that a man can receive.

"This is me showing you that it's not my job to touch you. It's my duty because your body belongs to me."

CHAPTER 30

Terina

PRESENT

It's the most brazen thing a man has ever said to me, yet I don't balk. I stand with my arms in the air, my bare chest exposed because DiAngelo told me to, and I want to know what he'll do next.

Your body belongs to me.

How can I argue when my body responds to him in ways I don't understand?

I don't understand any of this, if I'm honest. Fear and excitement play a vicious game of tug-o-war deep in my gut. I don't like how much I want his touch, yet the craving is undeniable.

"Is this the way you feel when he touches you?" DiAngelo's hands take a possessive sweep up my sides, his touch claiming and sure.

I shake my head.

"I want to hear you say it."

"No."

"Mmm ... that's right," he almost purrs.

Pride unfurls in my chest, and I have no idea why. I've done nothing beyond answering a simple question. Yet bringing him the smallest of pleasure sends me soaring.

He trails his thumb along my jaw to my mouth. My lips part, sparking a fire in his eyes. The thrill of his approval cascades in a waterfall of tingles down my spine.

"Who's the only one who makes you feel like this?" He lowers one hand to graze a thumb across my nipple.

A whimper slips past my lips before I answer. "You."

It's the truth, too. I haven't felt lust like this ... ever. It's all-encompassing. And while I'm not sure where it's coming from, I can't deny it either. Something about his manner is speaking to my body on a molecular level. His presence shuts out the world.

When his attention is trained on me, there is only him.

No regrets or guilt.

No duty or expectation.

DiAngelo fills every nook and cranny of my awareness until there is no room for anything else. There's only one other way I've experienced this sort of peace...

No. You are not going there right now.

I slam the door on those thoughts before they can ruin the moment. I'm so sick of the past haunting me. And if giving myself to DiAngelo gives me a reprieve from the shame, would that be so bad?

It would just be this once. D isn't the relationship type. Like Isa said, it would only be scratching an itch. This doesn't have to change anything.

The internal debate flashes through my mind in a millisecond. Hardly enough time to truly consider the ramifications, but that may have been intentional. I want this too much to talk myself out of it.

When the thumb of his other hand grazes my mouth again, I circle my lips around the tip of his thumb in invitation.

"Fuck." His exhale is a benediction and a curse rolled into one. "Spread your legs." His voice unravels with each passing second, and I love hearing the effect I have on him, though a sliver of worry snares my enjoyment.

I can't get naked. Please don't ask me to get naked.

I step my feet out, opening my legs to him and praying this doesn't backfire. To my relief, he slides his hand down my yoga pants rather than undressing me.

My heart beats so erratically, a doctor would probably whisk me away to a hospital. There's nothing wrong, though. Only right.

"Put your hands on my shoulders."

I'm relieved to lower them but don't have time to think

about it because the second my hands take hold of his muscled frame, his fingers find my entrance.

"D..." I moan as my eyes flutter shut.

"Eyes open, little firefly."

I do as he says, losing myself in the mottled colors of his rainbow hued eyes. Hazel doesn't begin to describe them. It's too flat. Too monotone, as though all the colors have bled together to form some muted anti-color. DiAngelo's eyes aren't like that. Distinct patches of gold fracture the rusty-brown centers, all surrounded in a kaleidoscopic ring of greens from a soft moss to dense forest.

The intensity and variation of color serve as the perfect manifestation of the man himself—too intricately complex to be categorized by one simple descriptor.

As though proving my point, his fingers begin their magic.

"*Fuck*, you're so wet for me already."

My mouth opens on a gasp. He tries to use the opportunity to bring his lips to mine, but I turn my face before he can. Even in the foggy haze of my lust for him, I know that kissing will be too much. Too intimate. Too permanent.

His eyes narrow, expressing his disdain for the wall I've erected, but he lets me keep my boundary, and I'm grateful.

"*D...*" I moan, my fingers clutching his shirt. I need the leverage. Something to ground me against the swelling storm inside me.

"That's it. Rock your hips against my fingers while they fuck you. Show me how much you want it." He nips at the skin of my neck while his free hand massages my breast. When he twists my nipple, he looks down and rumbles with satisfaction. "Do you know how perfect these would look pierced? Platinum bars with my initials engraved in them so that you think of me every time these perfect peaks get hard."

I don't have the wherewithal to process his words, but my body devours them, glowing its approval in radiant fluorescents. Before long, I'm perched on the precipice of a torrential orgasm.

"*Yes*, keep going. Just like that."

"Mmm ... normally, that's not how this works. I decide if and when your pretty little pussy comes all over me, but you've been such a good girl today. I'll let you have your reward." He brings his lips to my ear and grazes his teeth over my lobe. "Come for me, firefly. Soak my hand with your creamy goodness."

His guttural command detonates the explosives deep in my core, sending shock waves of pleasure into every molecule of my body. I cry out and cling to him as my legs shake and tremble.

"Ohhh, *fuck, yes*. Give me every last drop." He slows his movements but doesn't stop until my knees begin to buckle. "I've got you."

I lean into his huge frame, my hands hooking around the back of his neck while I recover. Once my head begins to clear, I pull back, meeting his gaze shyly. It's been a long damn time since I orgasmed in front of a man.

My hands slide down the front of him and begin to fumble with the button on his pants. I'm not sure what I'm planning to do, except reciprocity only seems fair. And I'd be lying if I said I wasn't insanely curious to see the monster cock behind the enormous bulge in his pants.

Before I can get anywhere, his hands stop me.

"Get on your knees," he instructs in a soft but firm tone.

I drop instantly.

DiAngelo brings his hand beneath my chin and lifts my gaze with a gentle caress. "You think you like to be in control, firefly, but I know better. What you want and need is surrender. Someone you trust enough to allow you to let go."

He begins to undo his pants as he talks. Despite thinking his words sound a touch cocky, I don't argue because damn if they don't resonate. The prospect of setting aside my worries is beyond tempting. Five minutes of absolution from my responsibilities and a chance to just be me.

"You think you're the right man to do that?" I ask in return.

His eyes flash with an unnamed emotion. "That's not what I said, but I'm damn sure not the wrong man. I can respect the value of what you're giving me down there on your knees, and I won't abuse it."

It's not the most romantic promise, but I don't want romance, right?

This is physical. Purely physical.

His cock pops free and the sight erases my thoughts. As suspected, it's enormous and thick with bulging veins. My tongue swipes across my parches lips, and I swear I can already feel him bobbing at the back of my throat.

"Tell me what you want," I breathe, desperate for instruction.

His eyes light triumphantly. It's a simple statement on the surface, yet it stands for so much more. It's consent. It's an agreement to surrender and see where this takes us.

"Fuck, I've been blind." His hand caresses my cheek while the other fists around the base of his cock.

The sudden ring of his phone startles both of us.

DiAngelo curses and takes the phone out of his back pocket, silencing it and tossing it onto the sofa.

"Hands behind your back, and they better stay there. You hear me?"

Instantly, I'm back in his thrall. His hand cups the back of my head as he guides his cock to my lips. I open for him and feel the corners of my mouth stretch.

Fear of inadequacy escapes me in the form of a quiet whimper.

"You can do it—I know you can," DiAngelo says in a low murmur.

His voice is so gentle and reassuring, I desperately want to give him exactly what he wants. I try relaxing my gag reflex and welcome him inside me.

"*Fuck*, yeah. Take me in all the way, baby." He starts to move himself over my tongue.

I want to wrap my hand around his heavy balls where they're pulled tight with the need to come, but I won't move my hands from behind me. Not unless he tells me to.

"*Jesus*, Ree, your face was made to be fucked."

DiAngelo's words fill me with warmth. Strain lines his face as his movements grow faster and more erratic. I try to keep up, following his lead. I wrap my tongue around the head if he pulls back and only gives me the tip, then hollow my cheeks and suck him deep when he plunders my mouth. Saliva coats my lips and drips down my chin but makes me feel oddly beautiful when the sight brings such intense satisfaction to his face.

It doesn't take long at all before he pulls out and trails head of his cock across my chest with one hand and plucks at my nipples with the other. When he starts to pump himself, eyes still glued to my chest, I know what he's thinking.

"Tell me you want it. I want to hear the words," he says raggedly, his control shredding.

"Please, D," I beg. "Please come on my tits." My voice is husky and raw from his cock and my own crippling lust. As if I didn't just have an orgasm, my insides are throbbing with need all over again. The ache to touch myself is so great that I moan in an effort to keep from releasing my hands.

"*Jesus fucking Christ, stop before I vomit!*" The muffled scream slices through the room like the scratch of a record.

We both stare at one another in a moment of horrified confusion before DiAngelo darts for the sofa and fumbles with his phone.

That's when I realize. The phone hadn't been silenced.

He'd accidentally answered it instead.

Someone has been there on the other end, listening.

A geyser of horror erupts in my stomach, threatening to surge up past my throat and all over DiAngelo's living room rug.

Please, please don't let it be anyone I know.

"Tommy?" D asks breathlessly.

I make a mad dash for the bathroom.

CHAPTER 31
DiAngelo

PRESENT

I PRIDE MYSELF ON MY ABILITY TO KEEP A COOL HEAD. I may be intense or act like a dick, but I rarely lose my shit entirely. I can't remember the last time I hit an inanimate object out of frustration, yet here I stand opposite a fist-sized hole in my guest bedroom wall.

My chest expands and contracts with rapid breaths as I try to calm myself.

I could have gone to the room I use as a home gym. I could have hit the heavy bag. The problem is, that wouldn't have satisfied this intense need to destroy something. I'm so fucking furious with myself that I can't see straight. I can't believe I compromised Terina so recklessly. What an epic fuck-up.

That's what happens when you forget your priorities.

Lightning fast, I put a second hole in the wall next to the first.

I don't even let myself shake out my hand afterward. I don't deserve relief from the pain. Especially when, after everything that just happened, I desperately want more of her. Have I lost my fucking mind? Am I so damn selfish that I'd rather hurt her beyond repair than deny myself?

I'm not sure I want to answer that question because seductive whispers in the back of my mind already threaten to twist reality with acrobatic rationalizations.

I want to think I could keep her safe from the world *and* myself. That if she were mine, pain would never touch her. But those are bold proclamations.

Are you willing to risk her life on that gamble?

Her physical and emotional well-being are at stake. No matter how naturally she responds to me or how desperately I want to possess her, I don't want my mistakes to harm her. I already care for her too much to risk her like that.

If you care so much, maybe you should get your head out of your ass and check on her.

Shit.

That's exactly what I should be doing. I had to take a minute to calm myself after the call with Tommy, but it's time to grow a pair and repair the damage I've caused.

I cross the house to the primary bedroom and see that Terina has shut herself in the bathroom.

I knock gently on the door. "You okay?"

That's it? That's the best you have?

I know I should apologize. I should do something, but my damn throat won't cooperate.

"Yeah, just going to get in the shower," she calls back. Her voice is thin and hollow. Despite what she says, she is not okay.

I wish I could punch myself in the dick. This is what happens when I make bad choices.

"Shae went into labor," I tell her. "Everyone is going to the hospital."

"Yeah, okay. I'll be ready to go once I take a quick shower."

I stare at the door and berate myself for being a chicken-shit coward. I should force the damn thing open and insist on showering with her. I should comfort her and make sure she understands no one will look down on her. I don't do either of those things for one main reason: it will only string along what never should have happened in the first place.

What if the phone screwup had instead been a life-threatening mistake? What if I'd missed clocking an attempt on her life because I was too busy admiring her evergreen eyes or giving her my coat so she didn't get cold?

She would be dead right now.

Holding back isn't cowardice. It's selflessness. I'm doing her a favor by not endearing myself. This can't continue.

"We'll head out in thirty minutes," I respond tonelessly. "That enough time?"

"Yeah."

I need to get my head on straight. And no matter how tempting it is to finish the raging hard-on that still hasn't fully calmed, there's no way in hell that's happening. Even if it means a case of blue balls so intense that my dick falls off. If she has to be hurt, I damn well should be in pain, too.

She doesn't deserve any of this.

She was sheer perfection—the way she presented herself for me. Her courage and trust.

And I fucked her over royally, proving that I am completely unworthy.

"I FUCKED UP, Terina, on a massive scale. I want you to know that it won't happen again." I force myself to say the words I've rehearsed in my head for the past half an hour. "I've realized what a huge mistake it was to cross that line with you."

The click of her seat belt buckling ricochets through the air.

"Definitely, I totally agree." Her ready reply should be a relief. Instead, irritation slithers under my skin. "Um ... do you know how much he heard?" she asks quietly.

Fuck, I hate myself.

"He only heard me." My assurance is a lie, but I can't bring myself to tell her the truth. As it is, she's already shrunken in on herself, her shoulders curved and arms wrapped protectively around her middle.

I swear, I will cut myself wide open before I hurt her like this again. It goes against everything I stand for. As a man, my sole responsibility is to protect my partner. To be trustworthy and safe.

I failed.

Epically.

I sit in silence with that truth the rest of the way to the hospital. By the time we arrive, Terina has rallied. Shoulders squared, she summons a ready smile for her family.

"Can you believe the time is finally here?"Azzurra cries excitedly before hugging her daughter. "I feel like we've been waiting forever."

"I know! And we'll finally get to find out if it's a boy or a girl. I'm so excited." Terina is a perfect reflection of her mother's energy. If I didn't know better, I'd have no idea she'd been achingly upset minutes earlier. The girl is damn good at covering up her pain. It makes me wonder what else she could be hiding. Someone so skilled in masking surely has extensive experience in the art. It's an observation I stash away for future evaluation.

Mrs. Donati ushers us into an interior waiting room in the Labor and Delivery area. "Renzo swears it's a boy. We need to all place our bets."

"Shae still refusing to guess?"

"Yup."

We pick a couple of seats—the room is nearly filled with Renzo and Shae's family members. Two large Catholic families, one Irish and the other Italian, which amounts to a small army of people.

A few minutes after we settle in, Renzo appears. He's got a hospital band on his wrist and a touch of mania in his eyes. I don't blame him. I can't imagine anything more stressful than standing on the sidelines while your wife is in labor.

"They finally got Shae in a room and assessed her. She's 4 to 5 centimeters dilated, so we still have a ways to go. We're happy for you guys to stay or we can text updates. Totally up to you."

"I'd like to see you try to drag me out of here," Azzurra jabs playfully.

Everyone laughs and sits back in their seats, clearly in for the long haul. Not how I planned to spend my day and night, but so long as we're all here together, I feel decent about Terina's safety. That's the most important part.

Well, that's not true. I have one other concern.

From what I've observed, I don't think Tommy has told anyone about what he overheard. I steal a glance at his wife, Danika, and the sudden bloom of crimson across her cheeks tells me I may have been mistaken.

Shit.

Tommy isn't one to blabber, but I have no clue about Danika. I certainly don't want to think about how Renzo would react if he got word. Fortunately, he has bigger things on his mind right now.

After an hour, I decide to grab a soda from a vending machine. "You want anything to drink?" I ask Terina.

"A bottle of water would be great, thank you." That same energy she shows the others isn't present when she answers me. I don't like it.

"No bathroom breaks or wandering while I'm gone, okay?" A note of contrition finds its way into my voice.

Walking this damn line between duty and desire is hard. At the end of the day, the most important part is not hurting her.

I weave my way toward the elevators, which is where I'm told the vending machines can be found. I stare at my options once I locate the machines, only for awareness to prick that someone has approached me from behind in an unusual way. I peer back and see Tommy glaring at me, daggers in his eyes.

"Don't you fucking dare think you can treat my sister like one of your whores." The man is livid. He's raring for a fight.

Thank God.

I'm more than happy to oblige.

CHAPTER 32

Terina

PRESENT

WHEN I SAW TOMMY SLIP AWAY AFTER DIANGELO, I HAD to follow. I wish I hadn't. The first words out of my brother's mouth drench me in ice-cold mortification.

I knew that Tommy likely assumed DiAngelo and I were screwing. DiAngelo is supposed to be guarding me twenty-four seven, after all. But a part of me had hoped Tommy might think DiAngelo had brought in another woman for sex. That little delusion has died.

If Tommy knows it was me, does that mean he heard me, too?

Oh dear God.

I'll never be able to look him in the eyes again.

I should go. I should walk right out of this hospital and bury myself under a rock where no one will ever find me. I want to, but I can't. I can't make myself budge when I hear DiAngelo's vicious response from where I stand, hidden around the corner.

"You're talking about things you don't know shit about."

"I know you, and I know what I heard."

"Oh yeah, what do you know about me?" DiAngelo's voice goes deadly calm, like a jungle cat quietly readying to pounce.

"I know you get off on dominating women."

Hearing him say that makes me feel so small and embarrassed, yet I never felt remotely belittled by DiAngelo, even when I was on my knees. Quite the opposite. Every second of his attention was founded in reverence and admiration. I felt cherished in his eyes, so much so that the implication of him doing those things with other women sends a jealous heat from my neck to my face.

"That right?" DiAngelo snaps back. "And here I was believing Renzo when he said you're the smartest man he knows."

"You saying you're not taking advantage of her just because she's weak and alone?"

My entire body recoils at Tommy's assessment of me, though I don't have time to dwell because next I hear sounds of a scuffle. The thud of a body slamming into a wall hits my ears. I can't resist a peek.

DiAngelo uses his impressive size to pin my brother up against the wall, balanced on his tippy-toes. "You say whatever the fuck you want about me. I can take it. But I won't hesitate to rip out your goddamn tongue if you talk about your sister like that again. You understand me?"

I'm stunned speechless.

Considering DiAngelo's cool demeanor since the phone call, I didn't expect such an ardent defense. It's oddly soothing. Nothing's changed, but knowing D doesn't think I'm pathetic helps.

The two men begin to talk quietly such that I can't hear them. And when DiAngelo lowers Tommy back to his feet, I decide it's time to disappear. I hurry back to the waiting area and start scrolling on my phone as though I'd been doing that the entire time DiAngelo was gone.

When he returns, he brings me my water, then sits on the opposite side of the room and doesn't look at me. I know because I keep checking. I can't help myself. His normally olive complexion is noticeably red, and his muscled shoulders look coiled with tension.

What I wouldn't give to eavesdrop on his thoughts right now.

His declaration that our sexy exchange was a mistake felt like a rejection. I had to agree because I didn't want to sound wounded and weak. Plus, a part of me knows it's probably for the best we're not together. But would I have said it was a mistake? I'm not so sure.

Is that truly how he feels?

Does it matter? This is for the best, remember?

Ugh, I don't know. It's definitely embarrassing for my family to know. And I don't want anyone to think I've degraded myself, including me. But if what we did was wrong, why did it feel so right?

I don't have any concrete answers, though I do obsess over the questions between updates on the progress of Shae's labor. Being the badass that she is, she has the baby surprisingly quickly. We should have known.

Liora Aine Donati is born at 8:55 p.m. at 6 lbs, 5oz.

She's absolutely perfect with jet-black hair and a round, cherubic face that brings tears to my eyes. The new parents are blissfully happy and equally exhausted, so we don't hang around for long.

Back home at DiAngelo's apartment, I'm suffocated by a flood of emotion. Something about being alone with him again, and the haunting lack of distractions, has a rising panic constricting around my chest.

What happens now?

Will he ignore me?

Do I want him to?

Has Tommy told the rest of my family?

Am I forming feelings for DiAngelo?

What if I am, and something happens to him?

Don't forget, it's almost the anniversary of Craig's death.

What if DiAngelo ends up dead because of me, as well?

Would his murder be just as gruesome?

My ears begin to ring, and nausea roils in my stomach. Before I know it, I'm in the bathroom with the door locked. The closet light shines into the room, but I keep the main overhead light off. It feels safer that way. Tucked away in the back of the apartment, sitting on the woven shower mat, I stare at the candle I retrieved from my suitcase.

I told myself I wouldn't do this.

I want to be strong enough to weather the storm, but the walls are closing in on me, and I need to make it stop. When desperation hits like this, there is nothing I wouldn't do to escape it.

I need the burn.

I need to believe that everything will be okay.

I need relief from the crippling fear.

The scrape of my lighter rips through the silence. As the flame takes hold of the wick, tingles of anticipation dance from my scalp down my spine—the same sort of tingles DiAngelo brought on.

I haven't done this in a while. A part of me hoped it was a thing of the past. I should have known better. I'm too messed up to be miraculously normal.

As the words float across my mind, I scoot my butt away from the wall and lean back with my legs extended so that my body is curved. I roll my shirt up and tuck it under my bra and push my leggings down to expose my lower belly.

My breathing hitches.

Two hushed voices hiss in my mind, one pleading with me to stop, the other insisting that I need this. While my mind argues with itself, my hand holding the candle tilts, and the wax drips onto the discolored skin below my belly button.

I've learned this is the easiest place to hide the marks. I've also learned that the higher I hold my hand, the less it burns.

Sometimes I need it to burn. But I try to start light, hoping to assuage the urge with minimal damage. This time, my hand is high enough that the trail of drying wax won't blister, but I still hiss from the sting.

My head drops back as relief washes over me.

However, like the ocean waves on a sandy beach, the sensation quickly drains away, leaving me dry and empty. Empty enough to be filled with a brand new serving of shame at my weakness.

I hate that I do this to myself.

I hate that a part of me revels in the pain.

All of it makes me wonder if I don't deserve everything that's happened to me. My husband's murder. The threats on my life.

I am weak and pathetic, just like Tommy said.

Tears pool in my eyes, and I align my hand over my stomach again when a quiet knock sounds at the door.

"Rina?" DiAngelo's voice is gruff but soft. Almost tender.

"Yeah?"

"I ordered us a pizza—you okay with meat lovers?"

The shift in gears takes me a second. "Yeah, yeah, that's good."

There's no response at first, and I wonder if he's left before he continues. "Also ordered one of those big cookies they make. I know you like cookies and thought you might want one."

"You know I like cookies?"

"Noticed you had one of those tubs of dough in the fridge back at your place."

I wonder what else he noticed.

"Yeah, that sounds great, actually. Thanks."

There's a muffled grunt, and then he's gone.

I can't deny the sense that this was some sort of apology. He didn't have to come tell me what he'd done, after all. I would have figured it out soon enough when I returned to the living room, but he felt the need to come tell me.

The gesture is especially impactful considering DiAngelo doesn't exactly go out of his way to be sweet. He's loyal, honorable, and probably has some other glowing qualities that I've yet to experience. However, his edges are sharp enough that his softer side is hard to find. He does have one, though. That much is more evident every day.

It makes me want to know how deep that well runs.

And why he keeps it locked away.

Looking down, I realize my hand has lowered and is now resting on the base of the candle on the stone floor. The flame, still flickering, doesn't hold the same allure as it did moments ago. The wave of panic is no longer crashing over me. DiAngelo's distraction worked almost as well as the candle.

Maybe even better.

I lift the candle and extinguish the flame with an easy breath. I need to get ready for the pizza and cookie. My stomach is still a little woozy, but it's feeling better by the minute.

I clean up the wax and change into lounge pants and a camisole with a built-in bra—comfortable, casual, and even a little cute—not that I need to be cute. It just makes me feel better. I assure myself that DiAngelo has nothing to do with my clothing choices. I don't care what he thinks.

When I see him in the living room, warmth radiates off my skin at the way his eyes rake over my body.

You're such a liar. You care.

Nobody's perfect, least of all, me.

I know I shouldn't want him to want me, but I do. I crave it with every irrational bone in my body.

"Thanks for taking care of dinner," I offer softly.

He looks down at the beer in his hand as though my words snapped him out of a trance. "Yeah, uh. You want one?" He raises the brown bottle.

I take a seat on the opposite side of the sofa from him. "Nah, I'll probably just have some water."

"That juice you wanted is in the fridge," he tells me. "It accidentally got put in the pantry when the order arrived. I can pour you a glass."

"Thanks, I'll get it when the pizza's here."

He nods, then taps the remote, and an action movie flicks back to life on the screen. We watch in companionable silence until the food arrives, then move into the kitchen. I pour myself a glass of apple juice and am turning to get pizza when I bump him while he's getting paper plates, sloshing the juice out of my glass.

"Oops! Sorry!" I squeak.

"I'll get it." He takes the glass and sets it on the counter, then gets paper towels.

I bring him the cleaning spray from under the sink. "You don't want the floor to be sticky."

He cleans the floor and wipes down my glass before returning it to me. Our hands touch in the process when he doesn't immediately release the glass.

Time stretches thin like caramel off a freshly dipped apple.

I'm utterly lost in the landscape of colors in his eyes when his lips part.

He's going to say something.

My heart stutters.

Please, please don't push me away.

CHAPTER 33
DiAngelo

PRESENT

Fuck, I hate seeing Terina so out of sorts. She's practically skittish, and that's not at all like her. That's not the same woman who stuck her finger in my chest while railing at me about what I do and don't know. That Terina demanded to witness a snake being killed and welcomed a growling Rottweiler into her open arms. This new Terina is timid and uncertain.

I'm responsible for that shift, and I hate it.

Fuck what I should and shouldn't do. My conscience won't allow me to leave her flailing.

I set down the glass, then, with the tactfulness of a blind gorilla, I wrap my arms around her and crush her against my chest in a hug. It's not exactly romantic. I want to comfort her without tempting myself, and this is the only way I know how.

She's still at first, then I feel her hands loosely wrap around my waist.

I take a long, steadying breath. "Rina, everything's going to be fine. What happened today changes nothing. Your family loves and respects you. And trust me, they wouldn't want their private lives broadcast to anyone else and won't judge you for yours. It'll blow over. I promise," I say as soothingly as possible. I have to. I can't stand to see her so rattled by something I did.

Her fingers curl ever so slightly tighter into my shirt.

Relief loosens the knot in my stomach.

"That's better. Now, you good to eat? I'm fucking famished." I pull back.

Pleasure like liquid sunshine in my veins fills my chest when she gives me her eyes and nods with a small smile. I'm blindsided by the urge to get her back on her knees, or even better, naked and cuffed in my bed.

I don't want to lose her.

I want to simultaneously destroy whoever is threatening her while dragging out the situation just so I don't have to let her go.

The craving is loud enough that I have to wonder if fighting it isn't more of a distraction than simply giving in and claiming her. I want her safe. How can I protect her properly when I'm mentally at war with myself?

I'm not sure, but I have a sneaking suspicion I've been looking at this all wrong. It's an entirely new angle I'll have to consider.

After pizza, because fuck, I'm hungry.

WHY THE *FUCK* is this guy here? I thought he only taught afternoon classes, but it's ten in the morning, and fucking Chase is Terina's class instructor. I'm fairly certain that when we were in this class before, it was led by an Aussie woman with an obnoxiously high-pitched voice. I'd prefer that over Captain Tentacles, who has to touch every person he sees.

People gather in the room and ready their spots as he walks around welcoming them one by one. I watch as he gets to Terina and places his hand on her arm. I nearly crush the water bottle in my hands when this asshole slides his hand down her arm instead of simply letting go.

You can't fucking tell me that's normal. *That* was a caress, and I'll be goddamned if he touches her like that again.

The second he heads for the lobby, I'm in motion.

"Hey, Chase, can I talk to you for a minute?" I ask without inflection, motioning to the back hallway as I set the trap.

"Yeah, but I only have a second. Class is about to start." His smile doesn't erase the wariness in his eyes. Smart. My motives aren't at all friendly.

"Definitely won't keep you."

The second he rounds the corner, I pounce, crowding

him. I'm a good foot taller and have at least fifty pounds on him. I don't touch him, but my features harden.

He pales.

"Here's the deal, Chase. I see you're a hands-on kind of guy." I lean in a tiny bit more. "Every time you consider putting your well-meaning fingers on Terina, I want you to pretend it's me you're touching. And if you're not comfortable doing it to me, then you better not fucking do it to her. Am I understood?"

Eyes wide, he swallows. "Yeah ... uh, yeah. Got it."

I give a curt nod. "Then I suppose you should get back to class." I wait for him to realize he's got to squeeze past me if he wants to escape.

It's the most fun I've had in weeks.

Miraculously, Terina's form must be perfect because Chase abstains from giving her any pointers. As if she needed any to begin with. She eats, sleeps, and breathes yoga—her body bends and folds as though she were a circus performer in a past life.

Well, fuck.

I may have just unlocked a new kink because seeing her work her subtle curves on center stage for me might be my new favorite fantasy.

I chide myself to focus and manage to keep from getting a hard-on during class. After that, I take Rina to her place to check on things and let her pick up anything she might have forgotten.

"We should probably empty the fridge. I completely forgot about that, and there's no telling what might be rotting in there," she says after piling a bunch of random toiletries into a tote bag.

"Already took care of it last week. I had one of the guys come by."

"Oh," she says, surprised. "Thanks."

I nod, holding her stare while a myriad of questions pass inscrutably behind her eyes.

"I guess that's it, then. I think I have everything."

We lock up and head back to my place. She cooks shrimp scampi for dinner while singing along to music playing on a mini speaker. I work on my laptop at the table, as though I don't have an office a few feet away. I don't want to hide away in my office. Not when I can be endlessly distracted by the goddess in my kitchen, though I try to hide my fixation.

Our evening together is an odd mix of comfortable yet awkward. We're polite but distant—as though we're both dancing around the elephant we've silently agreed to ignore. We're back on that knife's edge as if we haven't learned a thing. I'm not sure the two of us can exist together with the intensity of our chemistry without giving in or combusting.

Nevertheless, we try.

An entire week passes in a holding pattern. We are planes circling the airport with fuel levels inching dangerously low.

Each passing day, pressure builds in my head with every empty word we exchange and incidental touch. I wonder if she can hear the ticking time bomb in her head the same way I can every time we're in a quiet room together.

Tick. Tick. Tick.

Counting down the seconds to something cataclysmic.

Whatever this is between us won't survive much longer in its current state. Will the new order lead to something beautiful, or will it devastate all it touches?

I fucking wish I knew.

And on top of it all, that's not the only obstacle to cross our path. Over two weeks have passed since the snake, and we still haven't confirmed the source of the threat or which dealer obtained it.

The best news of the week was the return home of Renzo, Shae, and the new baby. All are doing well. We have security detail on their house night and day. I suggested they seclude themselves in a safe house for the next month or so, but Shae insisted she wanted to be in her own home with the new baby. And when Shae makes up her mind, there is no changing it.

Aside from that, the week has been utterly unremarkable, which makes me especially hopeful when I see Renzo's number flash on my phone.

Please, tell me you've had a breakthrough.

"Hey, man. How's the new family?" I ask before jumping into business.

"Tired but good. Who knew that a baby who sleeps all the time could be so exhausting?" He sounds like he's just finished his first triathlon. I have to laugh.

"Not sure you're allowed to complain about being tired, seeing as how you didn't push that baby out and aren't waking up to feed it."

"Just wait. You'll see one of these days," he grumbles. "Listen, I called because we got a message from Reaper. Says he's not responsible."

I sit taller, my eyes narrowing with concentration. "What kind of message?" We'd put out some feelers on the street, hoping to get word to the guy, but had no idea if or how we'd hear back from him. He's not the sort to make a call or send an email.

He's a fucking phantom.

"You wouldn't believe me if I told you."

"Try me," I urge.

"Asshole shot an arrow into the pergola on my back patio with a note tied to it. Even sealed the damn thing in wax."

"You fucking kidding me?"

"Told you, you wouldn't believe me."

"What is he, fucking Robin Hood?"

"Hell, I don't know." Renzo's exasperation is audible. "Maybe. According to the cops, he's shut down a number of child trafficking operations."

"He's also bootlegging and running guns, as far as we can tell. Dude's not a saint."

"Either way, no real reason to trust him, but if we did take him at his word, he's not responsible for the snake."

I grumble. "Shooting arrows isn't exactly the way to convince me you're not the one sending venomous snakes. Those two tactics seem equally odd."

"Good point." He takes a slow, deep breath. "Simeon still insists any threats expressed by Pasha aren't shared by him. I think Pasha blames us for his father's death, not out of loyalty, but because it led to his downfall. Right now, our best guess is it's Pasha out for revenge."

"Makes sense," I agree. "Also makes him that much more unpredictable. Do we have any idea where he's hiding?"

"No. You're better at that sort of thing than anyone, and while I hate to pull you away from protection duty, I think it might be necessary."

My hackles rise. "What exactly are you thinking?"

"Nothing major. I just thought it would be good to have someone fill in for a few hours so you can put your ear to the ground."

I exhale my relief that it's not a permanent shift. For a second, I thought he might assign someone else to protect her, and I'll be damned if Terina moves in with some other asshole.

"Yeah. I can take a few hours, and maybe then we can put this to bed."

I'd like nothing more than to get my hands on the man who thinks it's fun to send deadly snakes to innocent women. I have one particular acquaintance who could be helpful, but I have held off on reaching out. It's never good to ask for favors unless necessary. In our world, help always comes at a price.

# CHAPTER 34
DiAngelo

Miracles do happen. After resetting the breakers to the abandoned factory, I was able to get power flowing. And on top of that, I was able to power up the industrial meat grinder to dispose of the dead kidnapper.

God hasn't completely abandoned me.

Though he might after all of this.

I start five small fires strategically placed throughout the building, using whatever flammable objects I can find, and douse them with oil meant to lubricate the machinery. I watch the fires build from inside, at first. When the smoke is too intense, I head outside, but I don't leave.

I think it's the guilt that keeps me there.

Not my guilt about the fires or the murder. It's guilt over the loss of my brother that roots me to the spot. I sit cross-legged in the middle of the parking lot with his necklace in my fist while angry flames lick the outside of the building. That's where the authorities find me when the wailing fire trucks arrive.

Watching.

Waiting.

I go with them peacefully. I don't admit my guilt, but I don't deny it either.

The hardest part is seeing my parents at the police station.

They demand to stay at my side at all times. They're sitting next to me when I admit on the record that I burned down the old factory. I never mention the man I killed, and they never ask. Dad tries to explain about Elio's kidnapping. Mom sees the grief in my eyes and recognizes that Elio's never coming home. It's her heart-wrenching cry that I'll never forget.

It'll haunt me until the day I die.

I almost wish my parents would forsake me, but they never do. They fight for me. They love me. But they don't understand that I'm not me anymore.

It's an unexpected relief when I finally sign the paperwork agreeing to a no-contest plea deal for two years in prison for arson. Despite being a minor, the crime was severe enough, and my age old enough, that I'm considered an adult with adult consequences. I'm glad. I don't want any part of my old world. It'll only remind me of what I've lost.

To that end, I begin a frigid December day walking into my new home at Queensboro Correctional Facility.

"Y'er big, but y'er nothin' but a baby, ain'tcha?" A middle-aged man with a scraggly red beard and a heavy Southern accent sits down at the table across from me. My first dinner in my new home.

I continue to eat the so-called food on my tray.

The chatter in the room around us softens, and I know this isn't a friendly chat. I expected something like this to happen upon my arrival. I've seen prison shows and heard rumors about what it's like. While this is a minimum-security state facility rather than a federal penitentiary, it's still a prison. This man is testing me to see where I fit in the hierarchy.

His test should terrify me.

If I'm honest, there's a sliver of fear somewhere down deep, but it's been buried by a mountain of grief and self-loathing so heavy, it has no hope of surfacing. This guy wants to taunt me? Make me fear for my life? I have news for him.

My life's already forfeit. Killing me would be a mercy.

He swipes his finger through what I think is supposed to be mashed potatoes and sucks his finger in and out of his mouth with a pop. "Don't suppose you'd mind sharin'? We could be friends, you and me. It's good to have friends in a place like this." He sounds country in a way that his mama might have also been his sister.

Not ideal friend material.

"Hey!" He flicks my tray, irritated at my lack of reaction to him. "I'm talkin' to you."

When his hand comes toward my tray again, I quickly shift my fork to a fist hold and stab it into the back of his hand with lightning speed. Before he can react, I stand and yank my tray up, sending food flying everywhere, then use both hands to slam the lightweight metal across his head. It's too flimsy to cause real damage, but it sends the proper message.

Don't. Fuck. With. Me.

The entire mess hall erupts into chaos. Some people take trays and scurry to the far walls. Some abandon their food to get a closer look at the scene, and a guard over the intercom issues a warning. The man across from me stumbles backward off the bench seat, his hand held tight to his chest, and a savage snarl on his face.

"You fuckin' *cunt.* You'll pay for that," he spits at me.

I glare back at him unmoving, keeping my senses open to detect movement at my back. I don't expect a bully like him to admit defeat easily. As if on cue, two men sidle up to the redneck across from me so that all three can attack on a unified front.

My hands ball into fists.

The chatter all around us swells then swiftly recedes, allowing a single cackling laughter to rise to the surface. Before long, the entire room is silent, save for an old white-haired man sitting in a corner. If I'd thought the redhead's beard was scraggly, I'd been mistaken. Not compared to the leathery-faced geezer who is now the central focus of every pair of eyes in the room.

What the hell is going on here, and why are they all staring at him?

I watch warily as inmates scatter to get out of the way when the old man stands and crosses the room toward me. Once he reaches me, he pauses, his eyes sweeping the room.

"Eat your fucking food. Show's over." His grizzled voice lilts with a heavy Eastern European accent. "You, too, Miller," he adds with an edge of disgusted irritation. When he looks back at me, he flashes a wide grin of crooked, yellowing teeth and claps a hand on my back. "Sit, my new friend. My name is Grisha, and that was the most I've laughed in months."

The room slowly returns to normal around us.

While he seems agreeable, I'm not about to assume anything. My shields are all still on high alert.

Grisha chuckles. "Good, good. You're no fool. It's good to be wary in life. Tell me, what is your name?"

"DiAngelo."

He nods, bushy white brows drawn in concentration. "A strong name—Italian?"

"Yes, sir." My upbringing sneaks in before I can catch myself and leave off the sir. It's a show of respect and, in a way, submission, which is something I'm not sure I'm ready to concede, but what's done is done.

The old man's response surprises me. He seems to sober thoughtfully before giving me a single nod. "Yes, you interest me a good deal, DiAngelo. I think you and I could learn much from one another."

He unleashes an ear-piercing whistle from his lips without using his hands and nods after making eye contact with a man across the room. The next thing I know, a new tray of food is placed before me, and Grisha's tray is brought to him.

I have no clue if this guy's interest in me is good or bad, but one thing is certain: he's royalty among these men.

"Eat." He nudges me. "It tastes like shit, but it's better than being hungry. We eat, and you tell me how it is you ended up joining us here, yeah?" He lifts his fork and takes a bite, signaling my turn.

With nothing better to do, I oblige him and quietly recap my life's rapid descent into hell.

ELIO and I were ten when our parents took us to Atlantic City. They weren't the gambling sort, but they took us to check out one of the big casinos while we were in town. I remember being stunned by the flashing lights and constant barrage of sounds. I also remember being so damn confused. It was impossible to tell your way around in that place, and with no windows, time seemed to disappear. We went in midafternoon, yet it was dark when we left. I remember thinking, *How on earth has so much time passed so quickly?*

Prison is the same way.

Two years fly by faster than I imagined possible.

"In six months, when I'm out, we will drink to freedom." Grisha grins.

"So long as you don't fuck it up and do something stupid to prolong your sentence." It's a joke. The man works the system better than the warden himself. He'll be out in six months, and I'll absolutely drink with him to our freedom. He's the only reason I've survived the past twenty-four months, after all. I've learned some hard lessons from him, but I've also learned to let go.

I'll never fully forgive myself for my carelessness that caused me to lose my brother. Those actions, no matter how innocent, are unforgivable. But they are also tools that can be used to refine my purpose in life. My mistakes have molded me, and I'm ready to carve out a place for myself in the world.

"Go on." Grisha motions with his head. "Get out of here. Your pretty face is making me sick."

I chuckle and make my way to processing. It's time to go home, wherever that is. I'll stay with my parents at first, but only because I have no other option. I'm dreading that house more than I ever dreaded going to prison.

They were generous with their visits, and I couldn't bring myself to tell them to stay away, but seeing their faces guts me every single time. I don't know how I'll handle being with them day in and day out. And on top of that, Elio's absence will be that much more prominent when I'm sleeping in my childhood bedroom, hearing the phantom calls of a voice that sounds the same as my own.

As expected, they're both waiting for me when I step outside with my plastic sack of belongings. They grin from ear to ear and envelop me in a crushing group hug. It's not as uncomfortable as I expected, but that niggling voice won't allow me to fully enjoy the moment, either.

They probably hate you for what you've done. They may not say it, but you know it's there.

I take a deep breath and force a smile. "Thanks for coming."

"We've been counting down the days." Mom beams up at me. "And my goodness, you've grown, and not just in height. You must lift weights every day." She's seen me plenty of times and knows exactly how big I am, but I agree, seeing them beyond the confines of that building feels different.

"Not much else to do in there." I smirk, trying to keep things light.

"Now, the world is your oyster. Let's get you home." Dad claps his hand on my back and leads us toward the car. His sentiment is right, though I doubt he interprets it the same way I do. I have plans for myself. They're just not the plans he'd likely have wanted for me.

I don't worry about that now.

Today is about enjoying my family as best as I can and giving them the solace my return allows. Tomorrow, I track down Cosimo Costa and express my desire to pledge myself to the Moretti Family.

I've had plenty of time to consider my options. The straight and narrow doesn't suit me any longer. I've seen behind the curtain and know the facade of civility in our world is meaningless. We're governed by the law of the jungle just as much now as we were thousands of years ago—eat or be eaten—and I was made to devour.

CHAPTER 35

Terina

PRESENT

At what point do you start charging rent from the elephant in the room? Is ten days enough? Because that's how long it's been since Tommy's call. I've grown so accustomed to the elephant's awkward presence that I feel like I should at least do her the decency of naming her.

Day in and day out, DiAngelo and I go about our lives, pretending we're completely unaware of the behemoth pachyderm munching leaves in the corner.

Is that an elephant in the room? No way.

Did DiAngelo say my body belonged to him? Of course not.

Did I suck his cock and tell him to come on my tits? That's absurd.

Nothing of the sort happened. It's all a figment of my imagination...

Except it isn't.

We both know it happened, and the knowledge is maddening. A hysterical voice in my head is constantly screaming all the things I want to say but can't. Not when he is so adamant that it was all a big mistake. Instead, every conversation is civil, distant, and shreds at my sanity with poisonous talons.

I should be glad he pulled away. My logical mind knows I'm better off this way. But my heart keeps manufacturing excuses to be around him—interrupting him in his office to ask about dinner plans, or getting a glass of water after we've both gone to bed just so that I can walk past him on the sofa in the living room.

It's not healthy. I shouldn't be so drawn to him, but I can't help myself. Even now, I walk back to his office to ask him if he's already put in the next grocery order. I don't actually need to add anything, but I will if it means chatting with him about it.

"Yeah, delivery is scheduled for tomorrow morning. You need to add something?" DiAngelo sets his phone on the desk and gives me his full attention.

His penetrating stare puts me on a pedestal, strips me bare, and worships at my feet.

Even when he's distant, he makes me feel more seen than I've ever felt in my life. And if that wall between us were to come down? Would life ever be the same again?

"No, that's fine. I was just curious." I flash a weak smile and start to turn.

"Hold up."

His words hook me around the middle and spin me back toward him. Has he changed his mind about us being a mistake? Is he going to beg me for more?

Anticipation lights my eyes as I bring my gaze back to his. "Yeah?"

"I have to go out on business for a while. I have someone coming over to stay with you while I'm gone."

And just like that, the heart-shaped balloon in my chest deflates, sputtering against the walls of my rib cage until all that's left is a stretched-out piece of empty red rubber.

"Yeah, okay," I say in an artificially high voice, then disappear down the hallway in record time.

The next hour is spent berating myself for being such an idiot. By the time the elevator buzzes to let us know someone is on the way up, I'm emotionally exhausted, which is why the sight of my temporary babysitter is such a welcome relief.

"Rina Banina, long time no see!"

"Ciro!" I beam at my old friend who lifts me plumb off the ground in a crushing hug.

CHAPTER 36

DiAngelo

WHAT THE FUCK JUST HAPPENED HERE? MY HEAD IS filled with strategies for tracking down intel on the threat to Terina when I'm suddenly feeling like I walked onto the set of *The Bachelor*. Not that I watch that shit, but the commercials are hard to escape.

I didn't realize Ciro knew Terina. Dickhead didn't say anything when I called and asked him to come by. Now, I'm wishing I'd asked someone else. Anyone else.

I slam the door shut, startling the two out of their hug.

"Come on in," I say dryly. "Sounds like introductions aren't necessary."

"Yeah." Ciro grins. "Rina and I went to high school together."

"He was a year ahead of me but was sweet enough to take me to senior prom even though he'd graduated." She's radiating happiness as she tells me this asshole probably took her virginity, and all I can do is listen as she continues. "Dad was super protective and told me the only way I could go was if it was with someone he trusted."

"You say that like it was a hardship," Ciro says. "We had a great time that night." He dips his chin conspiratorially, and she giggles.

Jesus Christ, I'm going to break this fucker's neck.

"Yeah, well, a lot's changed since then." My harsh words are a bucket of black on their rainbow reunion.

Ciro looks at me for a second, trying to read the situation. "That's true." He looks back at Terina. "I hear you've attracted a bit of trouble recently."

"Eh, it comes with the life, right?"

"Suppose so. I'm just glad I can help out." He puts his arm around her, tugging her into his side in yet another hug.

That's it. I gotta get out of here before I do something I'll regret.

"I need to go," I blurt, sounding like a surly ass. "No one steps foot in or out of this place. Call me immediately if there are any problems." I grab my wallet and bolt.

I'm so fucking irritated that I punch the metal wall of the

elevator with my bare fist. Pain radiates up my arm, but not in a bad way. I didn't break anything. I'm too experienced a fighter for that. It was just enough to get my goddamn head cleared.

Shit. That's twice now I've lost my cool in a week.

I shake out my hand, flexing my fingers as I remind myself I'm supposed to be a professional. My relationship with Terina should be purely professional. None of the shit that just happened should matter.

You can say "supposed to" and "should" all you want—it doesn't change how you feel.

The elevator doors open before I can dent another wall panel. Good for my wallet, since I'll get stuck paying for the damage, but it's an ominous start to my mission.

Here's hoping I don't launch a war while I'm out.

"A GIFT." I set the bottle of vodka on one of the wooden crates stacked on the pier.

"Never arrive empty-handed when you want something." The old man across from me hardly spares me a glance as he uses a dirty switchblade to cut a slice of apple. His voice is as rough as the weathered boards below our feet and heavily feathered with a Russian accent.

"It's a good rule to live by. I was taught well."

His eyes, silver as the fish in his nets, peer up at me. "You going to suck my cock while you kiss my ass?"

My old friend draws a reluctant chuckle from deep in my

chest as I take a seat. "Good to see you, too, Grisha. I can always count on you to keep me humble."

Humble and alive. He took me under his wing those two years in prison and taught me to fight and to listen. He's the reason I made it out without severe emotional and physical trauma.

A grin breaks out on his face, unleashing a yellow, crooked smile. "Hand me those glasses, and we'll drink to humility."

I do as he suggests. Pushing him for information before he's ready will only result in frustration, so I allow him to take the lead. We go through three rounds of drinks while catching up before he brings us back to the purpose of my visit.

"I suppose we should talk business before you end up passed out on my pier." He takes a long draw from his cigarette, mirth in his eyes.

"I won't pretend to be your equal where vodka is concerned, so that would be appreciated." I'm a big guy and can handle my liquor, but Grisha breathes vodka. The fact that he's still alive is a medical miracle.

"Someone sent a nasty snake to my boss's sister," I tell him.

Another long puff of a cigarette. "Not very friendly."

"No, it's not. Simeon has denied his involvement."

He nods thoughtfully. Even if he knows who I'm after, he wouldn't give anything away until he decides to do it. Grisha isn't part of the New York Russians. He goes back to the old country—did time in a Russian gulag and swears his loyalty to no man these days. Decades ago, Biba insisted Grisha either swear an oath to him or label himself an enemy. Grisha refused to do either. Every attempt to kill him failed until Biba finally gave up. The two maintained an uneasy truce thereafter.

Despite being independent, Grisha has his finger on the pulse of the Russian community. Biba's family doesn't take a piss without Grisha knowing.

"The Reaper has also denied his involvement," I continue.

As expected, this draws a reaction from the old man. The ever-so-slight lift of his chin is the equivalent of any other man dropping the F-bomb.

"I've been very interested in this Reaper man," he admits. "They say he's quite skilled with a karambit blade, those who survive."

"I've heard the same. You're not the only one seeking information on him." I wait, emphasizing that I have intel he wants because I know Grisha. I arrived with a gift, but I know better than to expect a free handout.

Finally, a sly smile splits his face. "I did teach you well."

"You did."

"Well, go on, then."

"He sent a message via an arrow, shot into the wood siding of a house. It had a note wrapped around the shaft, sealed with wax."

"Interesting," he muses slowly, eyes unfocused on the horizon.

"We don't have a reason to trust him, or Simeon, for that matter. But with Pasha being edged out of power, he's looking like the most likely culprit. I imagine he blames us for his ouster."

"I can't tell you what's in a man's head."

"No, but you could help me find him."

Again, he studies me. "There's someone you haven't mentioned."

Every muscle in my body tenses as I rack my mind for who I could have forgotten about.

"Misha Savin," he continues. "He's known by you Italians as Michael—cozied himself up to the Lucciano family."

"What about him?"

"He rose in the ranks over the years. Biba favored him almost as much as his sons. Some thought he might inherit the whole organization."

I'm stunned. I had no idea another player was so involved. "Where is he now?"

He gives a slight shrug, palms up. "No one knows. He disappeared the day Biba died."

Holy shit.

My brain races to catch up and figure out how this information might change things.

"Simeon?" I ask, wondering if he could have taken out the man he saw as a rival.

"No, he was a mess when it happened. Never could have moved so quickly to take out a rival."

I know Michael wasn't responsible for Biba's death, but I won't breathe a word of that to Grisha. Some things are too dangerous to share. Michael ran, but why? Fear of Simeon coming after him? Could Michael lead me to Pasha? Would the two be together?

"You think I'm better off chasing Michael than Pasha?"

"Who's to say? But if you wanted to think on it over a good drink, you could visit The Half-Mast. I hear it's good for people watching."

Bingo.

"I always enjoy a bar with a good atmosphere." I extend my hand. "It's good to see you, my friend. Our talks are always greatly appreciated."

He shakes my hand, making note of the recent blood on my knuckles, and chuckles to himself. "Always a pleasure, Moy mal'chik. Always a pleasure."

I DECIDE to stop at Terina's apartment on the way to The Half-Mast to check on things again and get her mail. The first thing I notice is that the security system isn't armed when I enter. While nothing seems immediately amiss, a lingering odor draws me farther into the apartment. Gun drawn, I enter her bedroom and have to fight back the urge to gag at the stench.

Set in the center of her bed as if on display is the rotting remains of what appears to be a heart—animal or human, I have no idea—with a large knife through the center stabbed into the bed.

The words "eye for an eye" are written in dried blood on the wall.

The scene is grotesque and unsettling, even for me. I can't imagine how horrified Terina would have been if she'd seen this. I'm so fucking grateful she's not here.

I'm grateful and enraged.

But this sort of anger isn't explosive. This is the sort of deep-rooted fury that goes white-hot and silent like magma ready to pour down a mountain and annihilate an entire city with slow and steady totality.

No survivors.

No mercy.

The thing that bothers me most is knowing whoever came here knew Terina wasn't here. They came prepared to stage this scene with the intent to terrorize an innocent woman. They're playing with us, and I hate games.

This motherfucker's days are numbered.

I make a couple of calls to get cleaners sent up—the professional kind who handle this sort of stuff under the radar —and let Renzo know what I've found. While I wait for the crew to arrive, I scour the hallway security footage from the cameras I installed. I didn't use motion sensors because they can malfunction, which means I'll have to go through hundreds of hours of footage.

I haven't spotted the perpetrator entering by the time the crew arrives, so I put that on the back burner to continue once I return home. Once I'm comfortable leaving, I set out late afternoon for the dive bar known as The Half-Mast. It's located in the outskirts of Little Odessa in Brooklyn, which houses the largest concentration of Russian immigrants.

The bar is a locals-only joint. Not that tourists wouldn't be allowed, but it's doubtful any would walk through the door voluntarily. The exterior isn't exactly inviting, with its unlit metal sign bolted to the orange brick building and its blacked-out windows revealing nothing about what goes on within.

The interior is an eclectic mix of tarnished old-world relics and smoke-stained modern conveniences. It suits the handful of individuals currently patronizing the establishment like a worn leather recliner molded to its owner's body after decades of use. They're a hardened, rugged lot who don't look at all pleased with my appearance.

Zero fucks given, I make my way to the bar and order Grisha's favorite vodka because it's a niche make that might gain me a tiny bit of goodwill.

"You new to the area?" the bartender asks, paying particular attention to the tattoos on my arms. The Russian underworld uses tattoos more than the rest of us to signal status and allegiance. He's likely looking to discern whether I've been sent by a rival from out of town.

I down the shot and motion for another. "Not exactly."

The heavyset man, about ten years older than me, refills my glass rather than dirtying a clean one. "Maybe you're not new to the city, but you're new here."

"I am." Keeping my eyes on him until the last moment, I down the second shot. "I'm looking for a man named Misha Savin. Ever heard of him?"

No reaction. He doesn't even blink. And the rest of the room seems to have gone noticeably silent as well.

Excellent.

I've come to the right place.

The man takes the vodka bottle and sets it on a shelf

below the counter out of sight. It seems the bar has closed where I'm concerned.

"You're brave to walk in here asking questions," he says with an amused tilt to his head and steel in his eyes.

The scrape of chairs sounds behind me.

I've found over the years that men seem to find my size a personal challenge, as though by merely being tall and built that I have insulted their masculinity. People fucking love to fight me. Most of the time, it's a pain in my ass. Today, it's a welcome relief. I have a shit ton of tension I'd love to work off while rearranging some faces.

I stretch my neck from one side to the other, then turn to face my opposition.

The two men flanking me don't even give me a chance to fully turn before one throws a punch. The only problem is, my arm is already in motion to block. I deflect his strike and nail him with one of my own. As he flails backward, his buddy tosses a punch with a roar, but he's not positioned well to get any real heat behind the strike. My head pops to the side briefly before returning my pissed-off attention to him. His eyes widen and nostrils flare.

That's right, asshole. You're in over your head.

Both are young and smaller than me. They probably thought they had the advantage since it's two-to-one. They were mistaken.

I backhand the shit stain with my fist, sending him crashing to the wooden floor, where he stays motionless.

The first guy is a better fighter, and now that he's recovered from my right hook, he's snarling for more.

"Fuckin' mutant, need to be put out of your misery."

I huff wryly. "That the best you can do?" That's when I notice one of the men still seated at a table glance over my shoulder. I move to duck and swerve, but I'm not quite fast enough to avoid a glancing blow from the bottle the bartender uses to swing at my head. It hurts like a motherfucker, but at least I'm still conscious.

Conscious and pissed.

I kick my leg out behind me into the young guy's gut, sending him flying into a table, then deck the bartender with a right-left combination. While he's reeling, I slam the other guy's head into a post and let his body collapse to the floor alongside his friend's.

When I go back to the bartender, he tries to scurry away but is too dazed to be effective. I yank him close with my hand fisted in his shirt and sneer.

"You see Misha, tell him the Morettis want to talk."

He nods rapidly.

Message received. It's time for me to go, anyway. Every second I waste here is a second Ciro and Terina are spending laughing it up in the land of fond memories.

I shove him away from me and walk out, pleased at a nice day's work.

CHAPTER 37
Terina

PRESENT

TODAY HAS BEEN EXACTLY WHAT I NEEDED—A PERFECT distraction. Catching up with Ciro has been awesome, and an impromptu dance party with hits from our childhood has my spirits higher than they've been in ages. He showed off his Stanky Leg while we both nailed the Crank That dance.

He's a great guy, and I'm sad to realize what I missed by losing touch. When I met Craig, everything else ceased to exist, and after his death, there was nothing. I withdrew from the world as a whole.

Ciro's a great reminder that I'm not as immune to the isolation as I'd like to think.

"Oh, thank God. A slow one. I forgot how exhausting this stuff is." I take a long drink from a bottle of water as piano strains from Alicia Keys's "If I Ain't Got You" fill the air.

"You need to hit the club more!" he says, pulling me into his hold.

"No way, those days are done for me."

We sway, and I rest my head in the crook of his neck, allowing myself to fully embrace the moment.

"I'm so sorry you're in the mess, Rina," Ciro says softly. "I've been worried ever since I heard there were threats on Renzo's family."

I pull back and smile up at him. He's a handsome guy and goofy in the best way. "We'll get through this. We always do," I assure him.

He pulls me close again and spins us in a circle, drawing a giggle from me.

"The fuck is going on here?" DiAngelo's furious words crack like thunder all around us. The music was so loud we didn't hear him come home.

We instantly release one another and turn to face him while Bonny comes to my side and gives a low warning growl. I pat her head and try to settle her despite my head spinning when I see the blood splattered all over DiAngelo. It looks like he's tried to wipe it off the side of his face, but it's still caked in the hair above his temple and staining his T-shirt.

"Oh my God. Are you okay?" My hands press themselves

over my mouth as though to hold back the panic rising in my belly.

DiAngelo ignores me. Instead, he crosses to Ciro until the two are face-to-face and grabs a fistful of Ciro's shirt. "I leave you for a few hours, and you try to fuck her?"

My old friend blanches, his hands rising at his sides. "Hey, man. We were dancing. That's it."

"D, what on earth is wrong with you?" I grab his arm and try to get him to let go.

He releases his hold with a disgusted growl and turns around as though trying to calm himself.

"No worries, man, okay? Looks like you had a rough day. I'll head out and let you two sort it out." Ciro gives me a thin, apologetic smile, then leaves.

I stop the music, and suddenly, it's just the two of us and a storm of emotions raining down on us. He's obviously pissed. I'm a little dumbfounded, but more than anything, I'm horrified to see him covered in blood.

Fear wraps a bony hand around my throat and squeezes until tears spring from my eyes.

Photos from the scene of Craig's murder flash through my mind one after another.

"What happened?" I'm barely able to force out the words.

He catches a glimpse of his reflection in the window. "Shit, I should have cleaned up first." He goes to the kitchen and wets some paper towels. "It's not as bad as it looks. It just bled a lot."

"Bleeding is bad," I say, the words sounding distant to my own ears. They're drowned out by a voice screaming in my head that someone tried to kill him. DiAngelo was being attacked while I was up here dancing like a silly little girl.

It's going to happen again.

This man is going to end up dead because of me.

Something in my voice must register with him because seconds later, he's in front of me, coaxing my gaze up to his.

"Look at me, Ree. I'm fine. I promise. Just a little fight, okay?" His attempt at reassurance bounces off me like rain on a tin roof.

I shake my head, dazed. "No, it's not okay."

None of this is okay. My growing feelings for him. His willingness to die for me.

It's going to happen again. He'll die because of me.

"I don't know what the fuck is going on in that head of yours, but I need you to stop, right goddamn now."

Eyes wide, my gaze flits back to his.

"I was wrong," he says in a ravaged voice tinged with the scent of liquor. "I've known it since the minute I said being together was a mistake. I was wrong." His hands lift to cup either side of my neck while tears pool in my eyes. "The only reason I look like this is because I was so goddamn mad that someone wants to hurt you. Today has made me realize I need to get my head out of my ass."

I'm stunned. Trying to process what's happening. "What are you saying?"

"I'm saying you're mine, and I'll bleed this city dry until you're safe." Then his lips are on mine.

Terina's body melts into mine. As a result, the cacophony of worries constantly vying for attention in my head seems to harmonize in a way that cancels them all out, gifting me with a peaceful sense of rightness.

This is where I need to be.

This is life's purpose.

Her body pressed against mine. My tongue tangled with hers. Our breaths giving and taking in shared communion. Everything about the way I feel right now confirms my suspicions.

I belong with Terina.

When I saw her in Ciro's arms, I knew I couldn't fight this need any longer. Refusing to admit how much I want her will compromise my ability to keep her safe more than being with her ever will because in that scenario, I'm waging a war on two fronts.

I can't fight myself and the enemy.

Now that I have her in my arms, I can see clearly that fear was holding me back.

I've been terrified of failing her. But if I hurt her emotionally in the process of protecting her physically, I've still failed. I want her to feel safe relying on me in every way, and I swear to God, I'll make it happen. One way or another.

When my hand slides under her shirt to rest on her ribs, she startles, pulling back and breaking the kiss. I'm surprised to find her eyes wide with panic.

"I can't do this," she hurries to say, peeling herself out of my hold.

"What are you talking about? You're an adult. You can be with whoever you want."

"No, I can't." Her words are firm, even a touch exasperated, as if it should be obvious.

I coax her back toward me, not wanting to let her put distance between us. "Little firefly, you want this. I know you do. The way your body responds to me—there's no faking that."

Distress creases her forehead and draws her brows together. "No, DiAngelo. I don't want this. I don't want you because I still love Craig." She gulps in a breath of air as though she's fighting something, but I have no idea what it is. I'm too busy recovering from a proverbial punch to the gut.

She's still in love with her dead husband?

Could that be possible when she responds to me the way she does? We've never talked about him. My eyes drift to the empty ring finger on her left hand. She doesn't wear her wedding band or have the hint of a tan line. On top of that, I've only spotted a single photo of the two of them together in her apartment. Those don't seem like the actions of a woman who's clinging to the past.

I think it's fear, not love, that's stopping her.

She's afraid of being hurt, which means I need to prove to her that I'm safe. That being with me is worth the risk.

I'm the home she's been looking for. I know it.

"Come here." I gently take her hand and pull her into my arms. I cup her head against my chest and wait until I feel her accept me. Once her heart rate calms and her arms are soothingly wrapped around my middle, I lay out a map of what's going to happen. She needs certainty, so that's what I'll give her.

"It's been a long day. Neither of us needs to be making any big decisions at the moment. We're going to shower and eat, then we'll see what tomorrow brings. Okay?"

She nods against my chest.

"Good girl." I press a kiss to the crown of her head before ending the hug and taking her hand again. I lead her back to her bathroom. Bonny is close at our heels. I start the shower water for Terina and hang a clean towel on the rod next to the shower, then instruct Bonny to lie down and stay. "When I'm done with my shower, I'll get started on dinner. Take your time."

I start to turn when her fingers snag in the waist of my shirt.

"What about your head?"

I peer in the vanity mirror and try to angle my head to see the wound. "It stopped bleeding, so it's probably fine."

"Let me have a look," she says softly.

I'd topple a building for her if she asked in that voice. Letting her look at my head is a no-brainer. I rest my butt against the vanity countertop and fold myself enough that she can get a good look.

Her fingers gingerly sift through my curls to identify the source of the blood while I try not to stare at her incredible chest inches from my face.

"Looks like a chunk of skin was gouged out, but I don't think it's deep enough to need stitches." She pauses as I lift upright again. "Make sure you clean it out really well despite the burn."

"Yes, ma'am," I tease lightly.

Amusement creases the corners of her eyes. She crosses her arms over her chest as she waits for me to leave and give her privacy. I oblige, heading to the guest bathroom to take a quick shower. The cut stings like a bitch but doesn't bleed much once it's dry.

After I'm done, I get dinner started, calling Renzo while I'm at it.

"Michael Savin? The name is familiar," he muses after I tell him about the bar scene. "If I recall, he has some personal connection with the Genoveses who run the family, rather than the Lucciano Family in general. We could reach out to them if we need to."

"Let's see what comes of my visit to the bar. He may come to us. I'd rather not go asking for favors unless necessary."

"True. Hey, how's Terina holding up?"

He must be a mind reader because at that very moment, she appears in the living room with her wet hair piled on her head, wearing sexy-as-hell pink pajamas. Not the kind meant to be racy. The long, flowy pants paired with a camisole top are sweetly feminine, making her look almost edible.

My eyes hold hers captive as I delight at the way her cheeks blush from my devouring stare.

"Your sister's doing well. She's stolen my dog, in fact." A smirk teases my lips as Bonny shadows Terina, her red nails clacking on the hard floor.

"Huh, didn't see that one coming."

"Yeah, funny how things happen sometimes when you least expect them."

Please don't hate me when I tell you I'm falling for your sister.

He's quiet for a second as though trying to decipher my cryptic message. Little Liora starts to wail in the background, drawing a sigh from him. "I gotta go."

"Good luck, man."

He grunts before the line goes dead.

"That Renzo?" Terina asks as she joins me in the kitchen.

"Yeah."

"They okay?"

"Think so, just tired."

"I'll bet." She peeks at the pan of Italian sausage I have browning on the stove. "Need any help?"

"You want to grab some garlic from the pantry? I was about to start some orzo."

"Sure." She sets the bulb of garlic on the counter by the milk, butter, and parmesan.

"I'll chop it if you can keep an eye on the sausage." I don't want her to have to handle the garlic and get it on her fingers. If one of us has to smell like garlic all night, I'd rather it was me.

"Yeah, no problem. Also, I forgot to mention it before, but tomorrow is the anniversary of Craig's death. I usually go out to the cemetery. Is it okay if you take me out there tomorrow?"

For a second, I feel like utter shit for pushing her about us on the eve of her husband's death. Then I realize that she forgot to tell me. She forgot. If she was truly still harboring feelings for him, wouldn't that date be in the forefront of her mind?

We've had a lot of shit going on, so I can't say for sure, but it's something to consider.

"Yeah. When do you want to go?"

"Whatever works for you, so long as I get a chance to go by."

"How about eleven, then we can pick up lunch on the way home?" I offer.

She nods with a smile. "That works. Thanks."

"Of course."

We finish cooking together and eat at the kitchen bar. I

tell her about Grisha, even delving into our past at the prison, since she seems eager for more information.

"Can I ask what you went to prison for?" Her voice is hesitant as though she's worried she'll upset me.

I make sure to answer openly so she feels comfortable asking me anything. "Arson. I burned down an old factory when I was seventeen after my brother was taken."

"Isa told me a little about it," she whispers. "He was your twin?"

"Yeah, identical." I smile, happy to share his memory with her. Despite my shame, I try not to diminish his life by refusing to talk about him. It doesn't come up much, but when it does, I want to make sure people know how amazing my brother was.

"I can't imagine two of you. I bet your mom had her hands full."

"Always." I grin, and I'd swear Terina's breath catches. "She did her best to raise us in the church." I fish out the two silver cross pendants I wear on a single chain beneath my shirt for her to see. "Gave us these for our first communion, but we were still little hellions."

"What was his name?"

"Elio."

"Elio," she says softly, testing the word on her lips.

My heart contracts at the sound. What I wouldn't give to introduce her to him. He would be so happy for me. He'd also kick my ass if I hurt her, not that I plan to, but I never thought I'd hurt my family either.

"I should visit him more," I admit quietly.

"I know how you feel. We could go by tomorrow while we're out, if you want. No pressure," she hurries to add.

"Another time, when things are safer."

Her nod morphs into a mighty yawn.

"You ready for bed?" I ask.

"Not yet. I think I'll watch a little TV first."

"Sounds good to me. I have some computer work to do."

We put our dishes in the sink to deal with in the morning, and I grab my laptop from my office. While she watches TV on the sofa, I sit on the adjacent loveseat and continue scanning hours of video footage from her apartment building. I wanted to sit next to her, but I didn't want to have to explain what I'd found earlier today. Some things are better left in the dark.

I eventually find the culprit entering her apartment, but the footage offers little to help us. The man is wearing a ball cap with a jacket and long pants. I can't see his face or even hair color, nor do his clothes bear any distinguishing markers.

I separate a small clip of him in the hallway and email it to one of our tech guys, asking him to see if he can gather any other CCTV from that day tracking the man.

"Okay, it's getting late," I announce.

"Yeah, I'm ready to conk out." She turns off the TV and heads toward the bedroom. When she turns back to say good night and sees I'm following her, her brows knit together.

I turn her shoulders back toward the bedroom hallway. "Keep going, or did you forget where the bedroom is?"

"What are you doing?"

"Going to bed."

"With me?" she squeaks.

"Yes, I'm going to sleep in *my* bed."

"I can move to the guest room, if you want."

I raise my brow. "That's not happening. You're staying in my bed ... with me."

She opens her mouth to argue.

I hold up a finger to stop her. "There's no pressure or expectations here, Rina. We're simply two adults sleeping in a single bed. Now, keep moving."

Her jaw snaps shut. She does as I say, but damn if she doesn't shoot me a haughty look over her shoulder in the process. It takes everything I have not to give her ass a swat.

I know I'm walking a fine line, so I refrain. But once we're in bed, I pull her close until she's nestled against my side.

"I thought this was just two people sleeping in a bed," she reminds me pointedly.

"It is, firefly," I whisper. "Just you and me and our dreams."

Slowly, her body softens against mine. She lasts all of five minutes before her breathing signals she's fallen asleep. Safe and secure and all mine, whether she knows it or not.

CHAPTER 39

Terina

PRESENT

I TRY TO THINK OF THE GOOD TIMES WHEN I'M HERE visiting Craig at the cemetery. The months before we were married. Before he took the job on Wall Street. We were so blissfully happy. Dwelling on the struggles during our one and only year of marriage feels like a dishonor. That Craig wasn't the same man I fell in love with.

The man I agreed to marry was funny and spontaneous and full of life. It was easy to get swept up in a whirlwind romance with him. And who knows, maybe my parents were right about us not knowing one another yet. Maybe the darker side of Craig was closer to reality than I wanted to think. Regardless, he didn't deserve to be murdered.

Standing at his grave, my eyes trace the letters etched in his tombstone. I wonder what went through his mind when he was faced with threats against my life. He wasn't a fighter like DiAngelo. I can't see him confronting dangerous men. He must have felt compelled to give in to their demands.

Did he ever consider going to my family for help? I know they wouldn't have refused, which is how I know he must not have asked. I think he desperately wanted to make a name for himself and handle matters on his own. But he got in way over his head.

And it never would have happened if our paths hadn't crossed.

Unlike Craig, DiAngelo leads a dangerous life, with or without me. That doesn't mean I don't worry about him or that he can't still be hurt because of me. Seeing the blood all over him last night was an all-too-real reminder. The sight reminded me of the photos of Craig. So much blood.

I'm terrified something just as awful will happen to DiAngelo.

And despite those fears, I can feel myself falling for him anyway. It's happening even though I've tried to distance myself. Does that mean I'm setting myself up for history to repeat? I'm falling just the same, but he's not Craig. Not even a little.

I sneak a glance at him over my shoulder, where he's respectfully stationed himself to give me privacy. He's so dang sweet but in a totally different way than Craig. DiAngelo is a grizzly, whereas Craig was all panda—funny and playful and totally incapable of surviving in a world of predators. D could savage most any opponent, but when he's not in fight mode, he's surprisingly adorable.

How does a girl not develop feelings for a man like that?

He even wore a suit today. I told him he didn't have to. He did it anyway—a deep charcoal gray with a crisp white shirt beneath. It's a traditional, classic style with a modern cut that fits his athletic form perfectly. He looks just like the Secret Service with his black sunglasses on. Sweet and strong and delicious in every way.

That's why I had to lie to him and say I was still in love with Craig. I didn't know what else to do. And even so, his compassionate response has only made me want him more.

Every time I consider giving in, though, I remember what that means. Revealing all of myself. My struggles and scars, inside and out.

What if I let down the last of my walls only to face his rejection?

I sigh. "I'm so scared of the pain. I don't want to make more mistakes in my life." I finally lay the bundle of flowers I've been holding on Craig's grave. "Maybe if I hadn't bumped into you that day at the park so many years ago, you'd still be alive. I know it's bad to play the what-if game, but it's hard not to wonder. What if I'd pushed you harder for an explanation about your stress? What if you'd asked my family for help? What if I'd listened to my parents and delayed the wedding?"

Voices behind me draw me from my one-sided conversation. Kristi is here, and she's squaring off with DiAngelo. He has his arms out wide, preventing her from coming any closer, and she's not happy about it.

"Hey, D. It's okay. That's Kristi, Craig's mom. You can let her by," I assure him despite my dread. I've wondered if she stakes out the cemetery this day every year, waiting for me. No matter what time of day I come, I always manage to run into her.

"You keeping me from my son, even in death now?" she snaps quietly once she's tiptoed close enough in her heels. She's so dang skinny, I don't think there's enough weight to push the pointy heels of her shoes into the ground, but she tiptoes anyway. Her wavy brown hair looks amazing, but it always does. It's a wig. Her thick eyelashes are fake, as well. And her makeup—so much makeup. She and I have never had much in common, inside or out, except for Craig. Unfortunately, that tie is enough to bind us for life.

"No, I'm so sorry. He's just making sure I'm safe." I wish I could gobble the words back into my mouth the second they emerge.

Her head slowly swivels in my direction. "So you've found a replacement? It wasn't enough that you sacrificed my son for your safety? More have to die?" Her voice rises as she speaks, flushing my cheeks bright crimson because I know DiAngelo has probably heard.

Sure enough, when I peer back, all six-foot-five of his suited fury is charging toward us.

"What *the fuck* did you just say to her?"

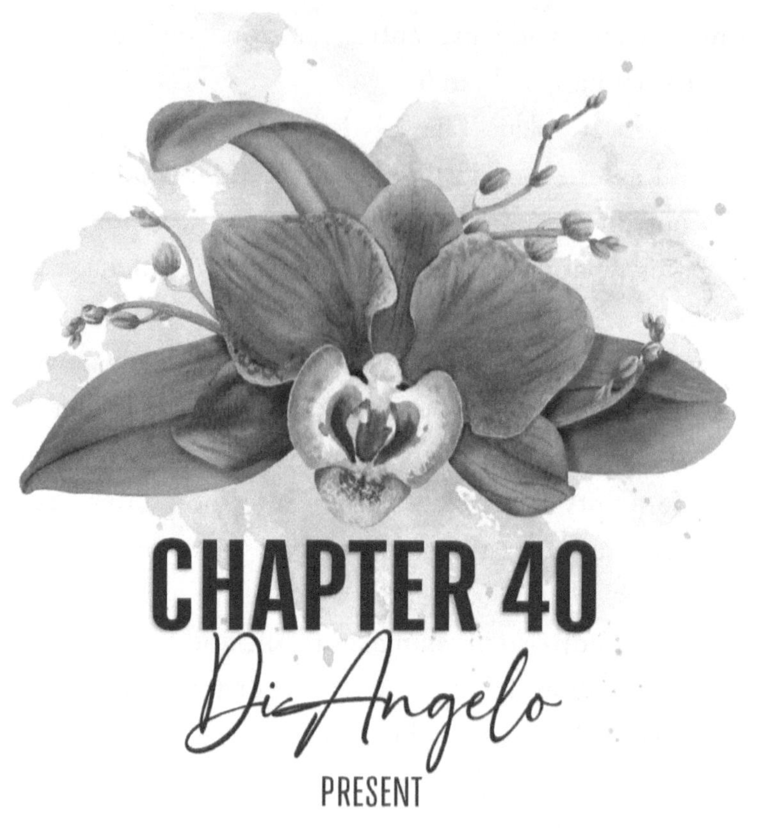

CHAPTER 40
DiAngelo

I knew the second this woman walked up that she was trouble. First, she's made up of enough plastic and chemicals that just touching her is probably a cancer risk. That's revolting enough as it is, especially for a woman in her sixties, but something else about her is off.

The dress she's wearing has a faint stain at the hem just above her knees, and the paint on two of her fingernails has completely chipped away. The juxtaposition of vanity alongside neglect sends mixed signals that raise questions. Is she simply clumsy, or perhaps she lacks attention to detail? Or is there another, more nefarious issue, such as a drinking problem?

I don't know the answer, but something doesn't add up.

Already on alert, my feet are in motion the second I hear her vile words to Terina, blaming her for Craig's death. Fuck if I'm going to let that shit happen on my watch.

"What *the fuck* did you just say to her?" I demand.

Rina spins to face me, but my attention is centered on the cosplay hag beside her.

I know how hard it is for Rina to be here. God knows I don't visit my brother's gravesite often enough because of the guilt. The last thing she needs is some psychopath spouting bullshit accusations.

The woman Terina called Kristi places her hand over her chest as though taken aback by my question. "I was speaking to my daughter-in-law *privately*. No one involved *you*."

I position myself next to Terina but slightly in front of her, inserting myself between the two women. "I don't care who she is to you. If you speak to her like that, you'll answer to me." I lean forward and lower my voice. "And if you think you've got a nasty temper, just wait until you see mine."

Her jaw drops in offense. "Are you *threatening* me?"

"It's not a threat. It's a promise. Keep your fucking thoughts to yourself, or I'll erase your thoughts entirely." I place my hand on Terina's lower back. "Time for us to go. I can't stand the stench here any longer."

Rina obliges, leading us swiftly back to the car while I try to tamp down my fury.

What a fucking cunt. Who says shit like that to family?

Terina didn't do jack shit to cause Craig's death. Has that cigarette with legs been spewing venom like that for the past five years? Probably. And if so, it's no wonder Terina has assumed some fictional role in the guy's murder.

I drive us out of the cemetery with a strangled grip on the steering wheel. I only wish it were that bitch's neck instead.

"The anniversary is always hard on her. She's lonely without him. Craig was her only family." Terina's defense of her ex-mother-in-law has the opposite effect of its intent, amping up my irritation rather than quelling it.

"You can't make excuses for people like that," I say in a clipped but level tone, trying not to take my anger out on her.

"I know," she says softly.

The broken words chip away at my heart. Fuck, I don't want her to hurt, but I need to know more about this situation.

"Is she in contact with you beyond the chance cemetery encounter?"

Terina is slow to answer. "She texts sometimes," she finally admits.

Not anymore. I'll be goddamned if Rina ever hears from that woman again.

"Renzo know about her?"

"It's not a big deal."

"I didn't ask if it was a big deal. I asked if Renzo knows."

"No, okay. I've never said anything, and there's no reason to," she says forcefully, growing more defensive. I have to wonder why. Why would she want to keep this from her brother?

According to Renzo, Rina is under the impression that her

husband's death was a mugging gone wrong. If that's the case, why would Rina and Crispy Kristi think Rina was to blame? Did they know about his shady extracurriculars? Even if they did, why would that implicate Rina?

"You keeping something from him aside from that?"

"No." She crosses her arms, a clear sign that she's closing herself off.

I spend the rest of the trip home mulling over the facts. Nothing seems to add up, but I'm not sure where the disconnect enters the picture. This would be so much easier if she'd just talk to me.

Is she truly still in love with Craig?

Why does she blame herself for his death?

Why can't I shake the feeling that she's lying to me?

I want to demand an explanation. What I *should* do is give her space until she's comfortable enough to trust me with her story. That's going to take time. I've always thought of myself as decently patient. Today, I'm proving myself wrong.

We're halfway up the elevator to the apartment when my frustrations hit a boiling point. Using the side of my fist, I hit the emergency stop button, sending the elevator to a lurching halt. Terina gasps, clutching the handrail to steady herself.

"What's going on?" she asks, wide-eyed.

I close the distance between us, crowding her against the wall. "It's time for some new rules between us."

She peers up at me through thick lashes, her lips slightly parted, and her chest rising and falling on rapid breaths.

She's so damn beautiful.

"From now on, you're going to do exactly as I say, without

hesitation." I place my palms flat on the wall, caging her in. "You're going to start trusting me with your body and your truth."

"What are you saying, DiAngelo?"

"It's D. You call me D when we're alone."

"D..." she breathes, sending a jolt of lust straight to my swelling dick.

"That's right. When you call me D, I know there are no barriers between us. No lies or judgment. Only trust. Because I don't want any harm to come to you—physically or emotionally—and the only way I can ensure that is if you open up to me."

"You don't know what you're asking." Her face crumples.

"I tried so damn hard to keep myself away from you, Rina. Then I told myself we could take things slowly so that I didn't rush you, but I can't do it. I want you too damn much. I don't care that I'm too old for you, or that my best friend is your brother. I don't give a shit that the things I want to do to you will send me straight to hell. I've never wanted to possess a woman more than I crave you. I need you. All of you."

"You want ... to possess me? What does that mean, D?" Her wariness is palpable. I'm going to lose her if I'm not careful. I have to word this in a way that won't send her running.

"It means you give yourself to me, firefly. Tell me you'll trust me to take care of you."

Temptation shines in her eyes, but she's scared. Fear holds her back.

"Why do you call me that? Why firefly?"

"Because you're my light in the darkness." I bring my lips

to her neck and jaw, peppering her skin with reverent kisses. "Please, Rina. Try to trust me. I swear you won't regret it." My ragged plea is fraught with desperation.

Thudding heart beats pulse in my ears as I wait.

Finally, she breathes the one perfect word I needed to hear.

"*Yes.*"

CHAPTER 41
Terina

I'M NOT SURE WHAT JUST HAPPENED. D WAS SUDDENLY everywhere at once—in my lungs and on my tongue, filling my vision and wrapping himself tightly around my heart. He's weaving his way into the fabric of my soul, and I'm powerless to stop him because that's exactly where I want him.

The problem is, I'm more broken than he knows. What he thinks he wants isn't real. Yet I said yes because I want to give him what he wants. I desperately want to trust him.

I want to know what it's like to be his.

That's the only thing I know for sure in all of this. I need to know what it feels like to have this warrior of a man devote himself to me, even if it means catastrophic heartbreak at the end of the day. Because that's what might happen when he learns the truth—that I'm not the fighter he thinks I am.

I never meant to mislead him. I made every attempt to keep up my boundaries, but that battle has failed miserably. This incessant pull between us has only intensified.

There will be a reckoning.

I can't hide my scars forever, but I can try to savor what time we have together. If I'm going to be heartbroken regardless, I should earn that pain with as much joy as I can muster.

So that's what I do.

I surrender and allow my fate to carry me where it will.

D kisses me for endless seconds. His claim brands me on the inside, etching his initials into my soul with every masterful sweep of his tongue.

When he pulls away, we're both breathless.

"Take off your panties and give them to me." His gravelly words shock and arouse me to the point of freezing.

"What?" I glance up over his shoulder at the security camera.

He brings his cheek to mine so that his lips are close to my ear. "Trust me, firefly. I won't ever expose you or harm you. But I will give you instructions, and I expect you to follow them without question. Is that understood?" Each word oozes with reassuring authority.

Desire pulses like a bass drum in my core.

I reach under my dress and slide off my black satin panties, then hand them to him. "I knew you'd be perfect," he murmurs. To my amazement, he brings the scrap of fabric to his nose and takes a long, languorous sniff of my panties, his nostrils flaring.

My heart trips and stumbles.

"What happens next is," he continues, "I'm going to feed you lunch, then have you for dessert. And you're going to be my perfect angel and do exactly as I say. Are you ready?"

I nod because I'm incapable of speech.

I knew D liked control when it came to sex. That was easy enough to tell when he had me on my knees the first time we were intimate. This side of him feels like more than that. I've read about Dominants. I'm not sure that's what this is, but it feels like something along those lines. It's not at all what I expected, yet I'm starving for more.

A predatory smile teases his lips as he restarts the elevator, his arm reaching out at the last second, pulling me into his side to steady me from the sudden movement. Having my body pressed against his has me famished for something, and it's not food. Regardless, he's true to his word and takes us right to the kitchen once we're home. He washes his hands, piles a single plate full of leftovers, then leads me to the dining table.

"Wait." His command stops me as I begin to pull out a chair for myself. "You're sitting here." He sits in his chair and pats his lap.

A rose gold sunset of color heats my cheeks.

He wants me to sit on his lap while we eat ... without any panties?

Holy freaking hotness, yes.

I scoot myself into place across his legs. His hand rests on my thigh, inching ever so slightly up beneath the edge of my dress. The touch feels taboo and naughty in the very best way. D has me feeling like a college student being seduced by her professor.

I wonder at first if this is some sort of fantasy play, but I get the sense this is the real D. He's not pretending to be in control. He is the embodiment of authority. This is who he is behind closed doors when he's most comfortable.

I'm utterly spellbound.

His absolute confidence puts me at ease in ways I've not experienced.

So long as I am his, I am safe.

"Pasta or fruit?" he asks, his voice a mesmerizing rumble of distant thunder.

"The grapes, please."

He holds a single grape between his fingers. I wrap my lips around his offering, slowly pulling the green globe into my mouth.

"Jesus, you do things to me that shouldn't be possible." He adjusts in his seat, accentuating the ridge of his thick cock as it presses against my hip.

"I think I know how you feel," I reply in a husky voice.

A primal growl rumbles deep in his chest.

"Eat first."

The stilted words amuse me. His control is frayed to the nubs, all because of me. Knowing that makes me feel like a queen. Powerful and ethereal. DiAngelo has a way of making me feel regal, even when I think I don't deserve it.

He feeds himself a bite, then scoops up pasta sauce on his finger to bring to my lips. I eagerly suck his finger into my welcoming mouth.

"Fucking Christ, knew I shouldn't have done that." His other hand lowers the zipper at the back of my dress before he eases the garment down over my shoulders, exposing my bare chest.

A sliver of worry trickles down my spine.

I don't care if he sees my top, but I'm not ready for him to see my belly. I want to enjoy whatever this is between us without marring the moment.

Please, God. Let me have just this once with him.

"My turn." He scoops up another finger full of sauce, then paints my nipples with it. When his mouth latches onto me, my eyes roll back into my head.

"Oh ... D ... that's so good."

He pulls himself free of my flesh with a pop. "Fuck eating. It can wait."

The next thing I know, he's pushed the plate aside and set me on the wood table, laying me back with my feet on the edge, my knees bent in the air. My black dress is pooled around my waist. I discreetly place my hand on the wadded fabric below my belly button to make sure it stays in place.

Towering over me, he is a vision of masculine rapture.

While his golden-green eyes devour the sight of me, his

hand cups his straining erection through his pants. He rakes his teeth over his bottom lip as he lays his palms flat on the table.

"Keep those knees wide for me. I want to see you open and weeping for me."

He slowly lowers himself, kissing and nipping a trail down my inner thigh toward my center. The anticipation sucks the air from my lungs. And when his strong hands take hold of my thighs, and his mouth closes over my core, my entire body spasms with the intensity of the sensation.

I let out a moan worthy of Aphrodite herself.

DiAngelo's devilishly talented tongue teleports me to another dimensional plane. Nothing exists but him and the crescendoing orchestra of pleasure singing in my veins. He works me until I'm so close that my legs quiver and shake. My back arches, and my heart beats without rhythm.

Until suddenly, he's gone. Everything stops.

"Wha—" I start groggily.

"Little firefly, I want to know why you feel responsible for your husband's death."

His words fight to penetrate the blissful haze fogging my mind. "You what?"

"I want to know..." He slowly licks from my entrance to my clit, making my body jerk alive. "Why do you feel responsible for Craig's death?"

I don't know why he's doing this. And why now?

"Please, D. Please don't stop," I beg him.

He gives one more languid lick. "Answer the question, and I'll let you come. The truth, remember?"

"I ... I know Renzo lied to me. I know it wasn't just a mugging." There. I said it. I didn't think I'd ever admit to that because there was no point, but this is just another example of the many ways DiAngelo is changing me. I hardly recognize myself, and I'm not sure if it's for better or worse.

Another lick.

Another wanton moan.

"His bad choices aren't your fault, Rina. I want to hear you say it."

I can see where he's coming from, but at the same time, I don't fully believe it. Craig would probably still be alive if he'd never met me. That's just a fact.

"It's not my fault," I say, aware of the dull ache that pulses in my chest.

"That's my girl. One more time." He licks again, then slowly circles my clit.

"It's not my fault." The words are sinfully guttural.

DiAngelo rumbles his approval against my heated flesh, ravishing me until my orgasm splinters my body into thousands of tiny light fractals. I scream through the ecstatic torrent of pleasure.

"So fucking responsive. So fucking perfect." He drops tender kisses along my inner thighs as he stands. "We're going to finish what we started last time. I want to see my cum dotting your perfect tits."

The clink of his belt buckle coaxes my eyes to open. This is a show I don't want to miss.

His shirt is already off. I have no idea when that happened. The sight is mesmerizing—muscular pecks lightly feathered with dark hair. Rippling abs leading down to a sharp Adonis-V. He's so perfectly sculpted that he doesn't seem real. Like he's a Roman gladiator who's lost his way from some faraway field of gold. Except he is real. Every delicious inch of honeyed skin and protective strength.

Real and *mine*.

This will absolutely crush me when it's over, but I can't seem to care. I want him too much to resist.

D has me sit, then helps me to a chair, having me sit crossways so the chair back is to my side. "Hands behind your back," he commands quietly, freeing his monster cock from his boxer briefs. My mouth waters while I do as he says. He then uses his belt to secure them together before rounding the chair to face me again.

I stick my chest out even farther than needed for my shoulders to be comfortable. I do it for him. I desperately want him to want me. To be as maddeningly addicted to me as I am to him.

His hand trails a finger along my jaw. "Who do you belong to, firefly?"

"You, D."

"Mmm..." The sound is pure satisfaction.

He fists himself, bringing his cock to my lips. "Show me, Rina. Let me fuck your face and feel my dick bob all the way to the back of that delicate throat of yours. *Show me...*" The last words are spoken on a hissed breath as I do exactly as I'm told.

I sway back and forth as I lavish his thick sex with attention, my breasts bouncing as I do. The movement tugs at my sensitive flesh, stirring even more need within me.

I moan and swallow with him deep in my mouth.

DiAngelo's abs flex and strain. He grunts and works his hips, holding the back of my head cupped in his hand.

"Jesus, you're going to suck the cum from me." He gently tugs on my hair to separate us. "Spread your legs for me."

I don't know what he's planning, but I do it anyway. He brings his hand to my entrance and slowly inserts a long, thick finger. My head rolls back on a groan.

"You're so damn tight. We'll have to be careful when I finally fuck you." Carefully, he eases a second finger in with the first and gives them a couple of easy pumps inside me.

I arch from the stretch.

"Gooood girl." He slips out, holding out the fingers now drenched in my arousal. "Beautiful," he muses. "Now, spit." He motions to his cock in his other hand.

I spit and watch as he strokes himself, using my cum and saliva as lubrication. It's so fucking erotic, I have to squirm in my seat.

"None of that," he warns in a strained voice. "You sit still for me like a good girl and show me where you want this cum."

I preen, pressing my chest outward.

God, what I wouldn't give for just a little nipple pinch or a bit of friction. How could I be so damn aroused after having one of the most devastating orgasms of my life only minutes ago?

The answer is DiAngelo.

The sight and smell and feel of him chemically alter my DNA.

When he's close, I'm no longer Terina.

I'm his.

"Fuck, yesss." His knuckles whiten with an iron grip as he relentlessly flogs himself.

My legs part of their own accord, wanting to give him all of me.

"Please, D. Collar me with your cum. Make me yours." I don't know where the words come from, only that they are spoken from somewhere deep within me. Somewhere raw and real.

DiAngelo roars as his release seizes him. Jets of hot cum shoot onto my chest, claiming me. Marking me in a way eyes can never see, but I will always know is there.

He inches forward, chest heaving, and begins to drag his heavy cock through the sticky globs on my chest, painting me his.

It's done.

This thing between us is now an unspoken pact that can never be unwritten. Whether he knows it or not, I have handed over a piece of my mottled and scarred heart. What if he examines my offering and changes his mind after seeing the extent of the damage?

The possibility hits me like a wrecking ball.

Not just a possibility—he will see what a mess I am. How could he ever feel the same about me after that?

My lungs collapse in on themselves.

I need to escape so he doesn't see me fall apart, yet if I do, he'll know something's wrong.

Tell him. Tell him now and get it over with.

My lips remain sealed. I can't do it. I can't force out the words that will destroy the way he sees me.

D releases my hands, then leans in and places a reverent kiss on my lips. "Stay there."

I watch him cross to the kitchen and wet some paper towels before returning to gently clean off my chest. Only after he's wiped away all physical traces of himself from my body does he tend to himself. After he's done, my skin is heated and raw from the scrape of the paper towel. I cling to the feeling so that when the red irritation fades, the memory of his touch will remain.

This won't end well. You need to go. Go now.

I can't. If I can just hold on a little longer…

D has me stand and helps right my dress, zipping me in. "As much as I'd prefer to keep you naked at all times, we both need to eat, and that will never happen with such a distracting temptation."

He has me sit in my own chair this time, though he ensures we're no more than an inch apart. We eat from the same plate. He feeds us both. I desperately try to keep it down.

The room slowly shrinks around me, pressurizing the air. I don't have the capacity to wonder if he feels it, too. Every ounce of my focus is concentrated on acting normal. Buying time.

The moment I feel an escape is viable without drawing suspicion, I seize the opportunity.

"I think I'm gonna go rinse off," I say lightly.

"You okay?"

I plaster the happy mask I've worn so many times before on my face and smile. "Yeah, just still feel a little sticky."

He studies me for a second, then nods. "I'll get this cleaned up. You go."

He doesn't have to tell me twice.

CHAPTER 42

Terina

PRESENT

I'm falling for DiAngelo. Every minute I spend with him hoists my heart higher and higher in the sky, and if the rope tethering me to him should snap, I have no parachute. My heart will plummet to the ground and shatter beyond repair.

I can see it playing out in my head, and I don't know how to prevent it. How do I keep myself from falling for such an enigmatic man?

His all-consuming presence is too overpowering.

The complexity of his boorish nature, offset by a selfless,

compassionate side, ties me in knots with the need for more. No matter how much I want to tell myself a fling with him would be purely physical, it's a lie. If I hand him a part of me, the rest will follow. He already owns enough to do irreparable damage, should he choose to.

Even if he doesn't choose to, it can still happen.

It's true. Someone else could take him from me, and the result would be the same.

Decimating heartbreak.

I can't breathe.

My diaphragm is seized up so tight, I have to rush to the toilet as soon as I've sequestered myself in the bathroom. One look at the empty toilet bowl, and my stomach revolts. I throw up every bite he fed me and gag until only acrid saliva comes up.

A thin layer of perspiration coats my body.

Did you forget where you were today? Do you want to lose another man in your life?

God, no.

I don't want that. I don't want any of this.

The ceiling looms over me as the entire world feels like it's caving in on me. I need an escape from this feeling. I know my fears aren't necessarily rational, but that doesn't make the feelings go away. This haunting terror. The unavoidable certainty that something terrible is going to happen.

My stomach roils again, but instead of the toilet, I go to the closet and fish out my candle and lighter from my suitcase.

I shouldn't, but I have to.

I don't know how else to make the horror stop.

Needing to hide, I take the bath mat and my supplies into the shower and sit. My entire body is twitching and cramping—that's what it does when these spells get especially bad. It makes me feel so out of control. Like I'm a prisoner in my own body.

I hate it.

I hate this so much.

I transfer the flame from the lighter to the wick and feel a trickle of relief ease the tension in my chest. My body melts against the shower wall. When the first beads of wax form, I hold the candle over my belly and allow the drips to fall one after another onto my skin.

The burn brings tears to my eyes.

I've broken my own rules and started the drip mere inches from my skin. This will leave marks. It may even blister.

Good, maybe then you'll stay away from him and save yourself.

Shame leaks from my eyes in salty streams.

I am so broken.

D would be disgusted if he saw this side of me.

I don't even want me when I'm like this, so I let the wax drip...

and drip...

and drip...

CHAPTER 43
DiAngelo

I spend my afternoon looking into Kristi Kirkland. She supported herself and her son, who has no father of record, as a licensed cosmetologist doing nails at a small salon. Life in the city as a single mother would have been difficult, yet Kristi managed to rent a two-bedroom apartment on the Upper East Side. On one small income? I don't think so.

The discrepancy can likely be explained by the prostitution arrest record I found buried in her file. It happened when she was much younger and was never prosecuted, but it's telling. I have to wonder what else she got into through the years.

I've known plenty of shitty people in my life. Kristi fits the mold. I doubt she has a moral bone in her body, which makes me wonder what kind of person Craig was. He didn't have a record and managed to graduate from NYU with honors, but I can't find much online about him as a person. I'll have to continue my search on the ground at a later time.

While I'm focused on the Kirklands and Rina is napping, I take a moment to get into her phone and block Kristi's number. The vitriol she texted Rina was inexcusable. And more to the point, it was unnecessary. I'd say she's been torturing her ex-daughter-in-law over the years for the pure joy of it. It's no wonder Rina latched onto the fucked-up belief that she's responsible for Craig's death.

I'd say it pisses me off, but that doesn't adequately capture my feelings on the matter.

I'm a shaken soda bottle full of indignant rage and ready to blow. The fury coiled in my muscles has me so tense, I've actually considered doing fucking yoga to relax, and that's how I know shit's out of hand.

Yoga is incredibly beneficial. Look at what it's done for Terina.

Fuck, I'm well aware.

Her supple body is the perfect balance of feminine strength and grace. And the way she presented herself for me? A man could die feeling fulfilled after receiving a gift like that.

I've imagined being with her dozens of times since that phone call interrupted us. Reality surpassed fantasy in every way, except for after. I can't escape the feeling that something was off when she left to shower. She seemed more distant, but I don't know her well enough to read between the lines.

I may bring it up later after yoga, once she's had some time to process. The gravesite visit and the shift in our relationship were a lot for one day. I could understand if she needed a little room to adjust.

The mid-afternoon yoga class passes unremarkably. She seems more relaxed when it's over, and I resolve to keep things light this evening.

"Ready?" I ask after she collects her water bottle, rolled mat, and bag from a cubby.

"Yeah."

I guide her into the cool lobby toward the entrance with a hand on her lower back. A mix of people, mostly women, crisscross into and out of the classroom. When we exit the studio into the dusky evening air, a woman with a rolled mat strung over her shoulder follows us.

It occurs to me that I don't remember her being in the class just now, which makes it odd that she'd be leaving. It's a passing thought that doesn't trigger an alert, though it does snag in my consciousness.

"Excuse me," the woman calls from behind us after we've rounded the corner onto another street. "I think you dropped this."

We both pause to look back and see she's holding up a small towel. She continues to walk closer, the towel extended, and a smile on her face.

"I'm afraid that's not mine," Terina says warmly.

Time slows.

My mental alarms finally wail as I catch a flash of silver hidden beneath the towel.

She's got a knife.

The thought is barely formed when the woman lashes out, her blade aimed at Rina.

CHAPTER 44

Terina

PRESENT

One minute, I'm smiling at the woman on the sidewalk, and the next, I'm being shoved out of the way as DiAngelo flings himself between us. I'm stunned and confused as I try to figure out what on earth is going on.

That's when I see the knife.

Adrenaline rockets into my system, sending my heart into overdrive.

The beautiful, petite woman with bright blue eyes and lovely blond waves has transformed into a snarling monster, and her sights are now set on D. She attacked me. He jumped between us.

Oh God. He's bleeding.

Her knife must have made contact with his arm when he launched himself into the fray. I only have a second to assess how bad it is, and it's not enough time to tell before chaos descends.

"Back up, Rina," D growls at the same time the woman snarls. She drops, sweeping her leg out to take DiAngelo's feet out from under him.

He stumbles from the attack but is able to grab her wrist in the process and drag her with him so that she can't make a move for me.

All I can do is watch in horror.

They grapple with one another, inching into the shadows of a nearby alley. I'm dumbfounded at how the woman overcomes the enormous size difference between them. She is all over DiAngelo, climbing him like a tree and making it hard for him to get his hands on her. One second, he has her wrist in his grasp, then she twists herself and spins until he has to let go.

I know I should probably run back to the yoga studio, but I can't. I'm frozen in terror that I'm about to witness DiAngelo's violent murder. Not only is he going to die protecting me but it's going to happen right in front of my eyes.

I'm going to lose him before I ever had a chance to truly know him.

Please, God, no.

I start to look around for something I could use to hit her

with when a sudden burst of movement ends in the woman staggering away from DiAngelo's fist to the head. While she's disoriented, he takes her to the ground with swift efficiency, then looks back for me.

"You okay?"

"Yeah," I nod, blinking away tears as I walk closer. "I'm fine. Are you ... you okay?" My breathing hitches as I grapple with a surge of emotion.

"Yeah, but I need you to get out your phone and call Renzo." He holds the woman secure with both hands. While she isn't fighting against him, he's not taking any chances.

I dig my phone out of my yoga bag with shaking hands and dial.

"Hey, Rina. What's up?"

I've never been so damn grateful to hear my brother's voice.

"We were leaving yoga, and a woman attacked us. DiAngelo has her on the ground, and his arm is bleeding, and I think we need help." The words are jumbled and chaotic as they roll past my lips.

"Tell him we need three guys and a van," D adds, which I pass along.

"Got it," Renzo responds in full tactical mode. "I have your location and will have men there shortly. Hang tight."

He wasn't kidding. We don't have to wait a full five minutes when a black van pulls up at the entrance to the alley. Four guys roll out and secure the blond, finally freeing DiAngelo to stand, which unveils a river of blood staining his jeans from the thigh down.

"Oh, God. You've been stabbed in the leg, too." I move closer and try to determine the severity of the wound.

D stops me, forcing me upright. "Rina, look at me," he says in a steady, calm voice.

I give him my wide stare.

"Breathe, firefly. Everything is going to be okay. The arm is just a graze, and the leg isn't too deep. I know there's blood, but it's not bad. Okay?"

"How do you know?" I ask, my chin quivering.

The maddeningly gorgeous man flashes a boyish smirk as though he's not bleeding out in front of me. "Because I've seen worse. I'm going to be just fine."

I nod and tamp down the fear. If he's so sure of himself, he must know. And I want to believe him. I want to believe that everything's going to be fine.

"She's secure. You guys need a ride to the doctor?" One of the men asks DiAngelo.

"I can make it there. Thanks for the help on short notice."

"Appreciate you keeping life interesting." The guy grins before heading back to the van.

D huffs and places an arm around my shoulder. I wrap my arm around his middle and try to help support him as he limps toward the main street. The car isn't far away. He takes me to my door first, then retrieves a towel from the trunk and takes his place behind the driver's seat.

"You sure I shouldn't drive?" I push.

"Right leg's fine. I can drive."

Of course, he *can*. But should he?

I swear these men around me are beyond mystifying.

"Stubborn ass," I mutter under my breath, finally starting to feel more like myself now that we're safely back in the car.

DiAngelo cuffs his hand behind my neck and brings my lips to his for a possessive tease of a kiss. "That's my Rina," he breathes against my lips. "I wondered where you've been."

His words wrap a warm, fuzzy blanket around my heart.

"Just tryin' to deal with all this the best way I know how," I whisper back.

He drops a tender kiss on my forehead. "I know, baby. And you're doing amazing."

What's amazing is how a few simple words like that can bolster a person long after they're said. We spend an hour at a doctor's apartment getting DiAngelo's leg stitched up. As he said, the cut on his arm wasn't bad enough for stitches, so that is a relief.

I don't freak out once. And even after we get home, the fortified connection I feel with D keeps me grounded and feeling secure.

The worst of my struggles almost always hit in the evening, after the day's activities have ended. When the world quiets. That's when my thoughts are the loudest.

Today would be a perfect day for my anxiety to rear its ugly head. Except D doesn't let me out of his sight, aside from a quick shower. He allows me privacy, but doesn't request the same when it's his turn. I'm surprised to find how normal it all feels. It's companionable. Comfortable.

We're just two people who've had a long-ass day and are ready to go to bed.

There's no pressure or expectations. And while I can't

deny sneaking a few glances at him in the shower, it's more to reassure myself he's okay than anything else.

And once we crawl into bed, he pulls me snug into the crook of his body.

"You did really well today, firefly," he murmurs into my hair.

"It was pretty terrifying," I admit.

"Told you I'm not easy to kill."

"I'm glad," I say softly.

He gives me a little squeeze, and within minutes, his body grows lax with sleep. I'm glad he's resting. He fought hard today. Seeing that side of him is quite the revelation.

He doesn't just look like a warrior; he is one.

DiAngelo was skilled at defending himself against the assassin—and that's what she was. It was like watching the Black Widow character from the Marvel movies. She was everywhere at once, yet he took her down in a matter of minutes. It felt like an eternity, but in reality, he bested her in no time.

Witnessing something like that changes the way you view a person. How can it not?

I still worry about him being hurt on my behalf, but I have a greater appreciation for his skills. I'm starting to trust that he actually does know what he's doing. And maybe that means, just maybe, there's a chance that everything truly will be okay.

Thinking something so contrary to what I've told myself for years is a scary proposition.

What if I'm wrong?

What if I let my guard down and end up more devastated than ever?

Yeah, but what if you're right, and D gives you the security you've been longing for?

I have to decide which eventuality I'm prepared to invest in. And from where I'm lying snug against his warm, slumbering body, I want to choose optimism. I want to believe I won't lose him. That he'll keep himself alive, and that if he sees my scars, he'll still want me.

Hope has been a scarce commodity for me. I gobble it down and pray more is to come.

I'm not foolish enough to assume I'll never have doubts again, but if this is a taste of how things could be, there may be more light at the end of my tunnel than I ever realized possible.

"Tommy's going to come by in an hour to stay with you while I head out for a bit."

DiAngelo is shirtless and eating eggs in the kitchen when I get up after sleeping later than normal. No matter how many times I see his beautiful body, it has the same effect of muddying my brain. I have to physically shake off the spell to make sense of his words.

"You're leaving?"

"I'm gonna go talk to our new friend, see if she'd like to tell us who sent her."

I take a seat next to him at the bar, making sure to get a

closer look at the bandage on his arm while I'm at it. He's got joggers on, so I can't see his leg, but nothing seems to be bleeding, so that is reassurance enough for now.

"She was really impressive."

He scowls and shakes his head. "She was damn good, and if I hadn't trained with Shae over the past couple of years, she might have taken me. Those two women are cut from the same cloth. And I'm a goddamn idiot to have dismissed the possibility of a female assassin. Not that I actively dismissed it, but I wasn't as guarded when she approached as I would have been with a man. It's a mistake I won't make again."

"Everybody makes mistakes," I offer quietly. "That's how we learn. That's how we grow stronger."

His penetrating gaze lifts to mine, and the torment swirling in those depths winds me. My hand reflexively goes to rest on his.

His gaze drops. "The problem is, some mistakes have permanent consequences. No lesson I could learn would ever make up for that." His sorrow is so palpable, the pain bleeds into me until my chest physically aches.

Is he talking about losing his brother? God, I hope he hasn't experienced more than one horrific loss like that in his life. If it is his brother that haunts him, where does the mistake come into play? How could he possibly think his actions had anything to do with someone kidnapping and killing his twin?

I'm not sure, but it helps to explain why he takes protection duty so seriously. He's terrified of losing someone again.

Just like you.

Dear God, I feel bad about giving him hell at first. He was

simply doing his best to keep me alive, putting his own soul at risk while knowing he could fail and strap himself with another lifetime of guilt.

D takes his hand from beneath mine and leans back in his chair. "I wanted to talk to you about yoga. I don't think it's a good idea for you to leave the apartment until we resolve this." His brows are drawn together, creasing his forehead with worry.

"I agree," I quickly assure him.

His eyes cut from his plate back to me. "I appreciate that. I know none of this is easy for you." His tone is adorably gruff. I think he expected me to put up more of a fight.

I give him a small smile. "It's not forever, right?"

"I suppose not." He takes his plate to the sink. "Want some eggs?"

"I'm not hungry yet, thanks."

"Let me know if you change your mind. I'm gonna get dressed—don't forget Tommy is on his way over."

"Yes, sir," I say playfully.

His eyes grow hooded as he returns to my side, cupping his hands against my head. "Sir is good, but D is better." He slants his lips over mine, seducing me with a passionate kiss that fills the cracks and crevices of my heart in a way I wasn't sure was possible.

I told myself no kissing, but that rule never stood a chance with DiAngelo. The first time I experienced the soaring joy of his lips on mine, addiction was born.

Eventually, he pulls away, despite my body listing forward in resistance. The golden starbursts in his eyes blaze with heat. "Eat, firefly. You're going to need your strength." He gives my jaw one last caress, then heads to the bedroom.

I stay at the bar for a moment, in awe at how much has changed in the past days and weeks. I'm realizing the changes might be for the better, but it's no wonder I've struggled.

My hand moves to rest protectively over my lower belly, careful not to press on the blistered skin. I went too far the last time. Too hot, too soon after the previous time. Showering last night was painful.

I hate that I'm so weak that I can't cope without falling apart.

That's grown into my biggest fear—that D will learn how damaged I am and walk away. The moment of truth is coming. I can't hide my body from him much longer, and I'm terrified of what he'll think about my shameful secrets.

It's a collision course I can't avoid.

A chill wraps its icy fingers around me until I'm cold to my bones.

I'll eat, but first, I have to grab a hoodie to stave off the cold settling in my bones. I head to the bedroom but pause when I hear D talking in the bathroom.

"Eleven works, but not my place this time. I'll come to you." His voice is low and even. I'd guess he's dictating a text rather than talking on the phone. Making plans to meet with someone. It could be anyone.

Sure sounds like a booty call.

Stop! Do NOT go there. You are reading into things that you know nothing about.

Hearing that after dwelling on my existing fears drags me

deep into muddy waters, despite the pleas of my logical mind. I spin around and march myself back to the living room, where I wrap up in a blanket and sink into the couch.

Every time I take a mental step forward, something pulls me back by half a step. I'm making progress, but it's a fight, and the constant battle is exhausting.

I get dressed after DiAngelo, and not long after, Tommy arrives. I've been so preoccupied with D that I forgot to stress about seeing my brother. It's the first time we've been alone since the phone fiasco.

This day keeps getting better and better.

To my relief, he's quick to give me a hug, which isn't exactly his MO. He's making an effort to show me I have nothing to fear.

"Hey, Mr. T," I say with a shy smile, using the nickname I gave him as a kid after seeing an old episode of The A-Team. We're the two youngest of four, so we spent a good amount of time together growing up.

He raises an aristocratic brow. "Oh, really?" No one plays the comedic straight man like a neurodivergent. Tommy has a wicked sense of humor if you're adept at deciphering it. Knowing that, it doesn't take much for him to tickle me.

My giggles trail off when I notice DiAngelo securing Bonny's leash.

"You're taking her with you?" I ask, surprised. He's been using a dog walker while I've been staying with him so that he doesn't have to leave me alone, and otherwise, he's kept Bonny at the apartment.

"I am. Hopefully, you two can manage to be apart for a few hours."

"I suppose I'll manage." Surely, taking the dog with him is a sign that he's not meeting up with another woman while he's out. I latch onto that reassurance and give him a smile.

DiAngelo leans down and plants a possessive kiss on my lips right in front of Tommy.

My stomach cannonballs into my feet, then soars high into the sky. D knows exactly what he's doing—nothing he does is without purpose—and that is especially evident when he pulls away and shoots a glare at my brother.

"I'll be back as soon as I can."

Tommy nods, then locks the door behind him. When he turns back to me, my cheeks flame a bright crimson. I don't need a mirror to know. The heat is telling enough.

"It's a relief to know I don't need to put a bullet between his eyes," Tommy says flatly.

I smack his chest. "Tommaso Donati! He's your family— you swore an oath."

Tommy doesn't flinch. "You're my blood. You come first. Always have, always will."

Emotion clogs my throat as love swells in my chest. I'm not sure I can take much more without bursting into tears, and judging by the increasing worry in his eyes, Tommy has reached his capacity for feels as well.

I grin at my little brother and take his hand. "Come on, let's play cards."

"You know I hate cards."

"Yeah, but I'm your big sister, so you're gonna do it anyway."

He rolls his eyes but allows me to drag him to the living room. We play two boisterous rounds of war, and by the time we call it quits, I almost feel like a kid again.

Life truly is all about the people we love.

I've spent years depriving myself of that essential connection. I learned a lesson when Craig was killed, but I'm starting to realize I may have learned the wrong lesson. I thought I needed to protect people by keeping them away from me. Maybe the lesson I should have learned was to cherish the ones we love at every opportunity.

Rejecting Craig might have saved him, but maybe love was all he truly needed. Love from me but also his mother. Grappling all alone with the dangers he was facing was a choice that very well may have had nothing to do with me. That decision could have been purely tied to his own pre-existing struggles.

The realization stuns me.

How had I dismissed the possibility that his issues might have stemmed from childhood with that wretched woman rather than my arrival into his life? Maybe his ingrained need to prove himself would have been his downfall regardless of threats to my safety. I have to consider that his death might have truly had nothing to do with me.

My conscience isn't wiped clean, but this new perspective changes things. The blinders I've been wearing have shaken loose, and suddenly, the world looks full of possibilities.

CHAPTER 45

DiAngelo

PRESENT

My first stop is to drop Bonny at the groomer. She usually comes to us, but I don't want any unnecessary visitors close to Terina. I've already seen how desperate these assholes are to take her from me. I'm not making assumptions anyone is safe at this point.

Walking on my injured leg is against doctor's orders and hurts like a bitch now that the good drugs have worn off. I'd love to do as he said and plant myself on the sofa. That would be great if we weren't under siege. Eliminating the threat to Terina is too important for me to sideline myself. Someone needs to interrogate the assassin, and that someone is going to be me.

When I arrive at the isolated warehouse we use for this sort of thing, a group of three guys are playing cards while a small speaker plays metal music into the dusty air. Not far from them, the woman sits bound to a chair in her bra and underwear.

We're not rapists, so I know they haven't crossed that line, but that doesn't mean our captive hasn't had a shit night.

"How's it going, fellas?"

My answer is a chorus of complaints—one's blaming another for cheating at cards, someone hates the music choice, and the last one thinks his buddies are whiny bitches.

I chuckle. "Sounds like it's all good, then. She have anything to say yet?"

"Nah," says the oldest of the three. "We didn't give her much of a chance, though."

I glance at the duct tape over her mouth and nod. "Good, time to let her sing." I walk toward her, careful not to limp. I don't want her getting any satisfaction from knowing she hit her mark with that knife of hers.

I peel up a corner of the silver tape, then rip off the rest. She pulls against the pain with a growl, then glares at me.

"You know, as a rule of thumb, I don't hurt women." I grimace and shrug. "But ... rules are made to be broken."

"*Fuck you*," she spits. "Why should I tell you anything when you're just going to kill me?"

"That's the thing. I don't actually feel a need to hurt or kill you. You're not the problem." I close the distance between us and stare down at her. "What I want is the name of who sent you."

"I start ratting out clients, and I won't work again."

"You don't start talking, and you won't breathe again." Each lethal word is laced with malice. I need her to know I'm not bluffing. I turn to my guys. "Bring me the pillowcase and hose."

Her chest starts to expand and contract with rapid breaths. She's right to be worried. This isn't going to be fun for her. I don't enjoy this sort of thing, either, but it's necessary.

Eat or be eaten.

"You two angle the chair back," I instruct while placing the thin white pillowcase over her head. "Let's get started." I'm handed the garden hose, which is pouring a steady trickle of water. "What's your name?"

"*Fuck you*," she spits through gritted teeth.

"Alright, Fuck You. Who paid you to kill Terina?" I don't actually give a flying fuck what her name is. What I need is for her fear to hit override levels so that her Amygdala takes over. The fight or flight part of the brain will easily deem answering a question a better option than letting herself drown. Drawing out the dread amplifies her fear and gets me where I want to be that much faster.

I've studied these things not because I love torture, but for the opposite reason. I taught myself so that I could be effective at getting what I want with minimum damage because no sane human enjoys inflicting pain.

I do it because it's necessary.

"I told you, I can't give names."

"Wrong," I say matter-of-factly, then hold the hose over her face. She tries to escape the water by turning her head from one side to the other as it soaks the fabric and trickles into her nose and mouth, but she's fighting a losing battle. She coughs and sputters, her arms and legs straining against the zip ties rendering her helpless.

I don't leave the water over her for long. It doesn't take long to feel like you're drowning. After she has a second to catch her breath, I return to my questioning.

"Who paid you to kill Terina?" I ask again evenly.

Her answering scream is feral with rage.

"Wrong." I return the water to her face, this time continuing for a few seconds longer than before. When she starts to gag, I allow her to breathe again.

"Protecting him isn't worth it, trust me. Tell me who paid you to kill Terina, and we can all go home."

"You won't let me leave here alive."

"Then you might as well end it quickly rather than prolong the inevitable."

"Agree to let me go, and I'll tell you."

"Or, you can just tell me *who the fuck paid you to kill Terina!*" I roar the final words, dousing her head in water yet again. This time, I let it continue twice as long as before.

When I turn the hose away, she begins to vomit inside her waterlogged cocoon.

"Pasha ... it was Pasha Mikhailov," she sputters hoarsely.

"You part of his outfit?"

"No," she snaps adamantly.

"And where is he hiding?"

"I don't know, okay?"

I give her the hose again. Her body jerks away from the seat of the chair, her wrists beginning to bleed beneath the zip ties. When I remove the water, she shudders from head to toe as she coughs and sputters.

"Dead ... animals. That's all I know. There were dead animals ... everywhere."

I'm not sure what to make of this revelation. "You mean like a crematorium?"

She shakes her head. "Stuffed. I forget what they call it."

I envision the Modern Museum of History with all its animal exhibits. "Taxidermy."

"Yeah." Her head lists forward in defeat. "That's it. Don't know where. We only talked on video conference, but there were dead animals all in the background."

I can tell we've gotten all we're going to get from her. I take out my gun from its holster in the back of my pants and release the safety. I don't drag it out, nor can she see the gun with the pillowcase still over her head. My gift to her. One quick bullet to the head, and it's over.

"Take care of that," I instruct the guys before walking back to my car. I call Renzo on the way.

"That was quick," he says in answer.

"The desire to keep breathing is a powerful motivator, even if only for a short time."

"No shit. She confirm what we needed to hear?"

"Yeah, it was Pasha. We also got another bit of info that may fill in some missing pieces."

"What's that?"

"Sounds like he might be holed up at a taxidermist's shop."

"Huh, did not see that coming," he muses.

"Me either, but it might explain how he'd get access to the snake without using any of the known dealers in the state." We'd checked them all and got nowhere.

"I suppose a taxidermist might have connections for procuring live animals."

I nod to myself. "Yeah, and to animal parts."

"The heart in her apartment." Now, he's catching on.

"Exactly."

"Great work. There can't be that many taxidermists in the city."

"If you're good with it, I'd like to have a couple of guys stake them out."

"Yeah, set that up. Let's hope this gives us a lock on him."

I pause before asking the next question, knowing I may not like the answer. "And if we do?"

Renzo sighs. "I'm not sure. Assassinating him could be a dangerous escalation. I don't want to risk starting a war with Simeon."

"You fucking kidding me? He's made two attempts on your sister's life." I was worried that would be his response. I should be respectful of my boss's opinions, but I can't stay silent on this. Too much is at stake.

"Calm the fuck down," he snaps at me. "I'm not saying we won't deal with him eventually; I'm just asking you to hold off until I can work things out with Simeon. I don't want to cross off one threat just to create a new one. And while I'm doing that, I'm also going to reach out to the Genoveses and see what we can learn about Michael's disappearance. I don't like the uncertainty there."

Okay, that's not so bad.

"The guys will probably need a few days before we get anything with surveillance," I concede. "This needs to end, though." I need to watch it, or he's going to wonder why my feelings are so strong about it. He doesn't know about things between Rina and me, and I don't feel like I can tell him when I don't even know where we stand.

Renzo's silent for a handful of seconds. "I get that, and I appreciate all you've done for my sister, which his why I'm not going to rip you a new one for thinking you can give me an ultimatum. She's my fucking sister. I want this guy finished as much as anyone, but I don't want to rush into it and lose more good people in the process. Understood?"

"Yeah, I got it," I murmur back.

Irritation chafes, but not because he's wrong. He's spot-on, and I'm glad he's doing this right. My emotions are trying to cloud my judgment. He's keeping me in check, and I'd do the same for him. It's what Elio and I used to do for one another.

As much as I resist letting people in, I have to admit that having a team at your back is an advantage in life. One I probably should have been utilizing in my personal world, and not just professional.

It's something to consider.

For now, all my focus goes to Terina. First, to keep her safe, then to make her mine.

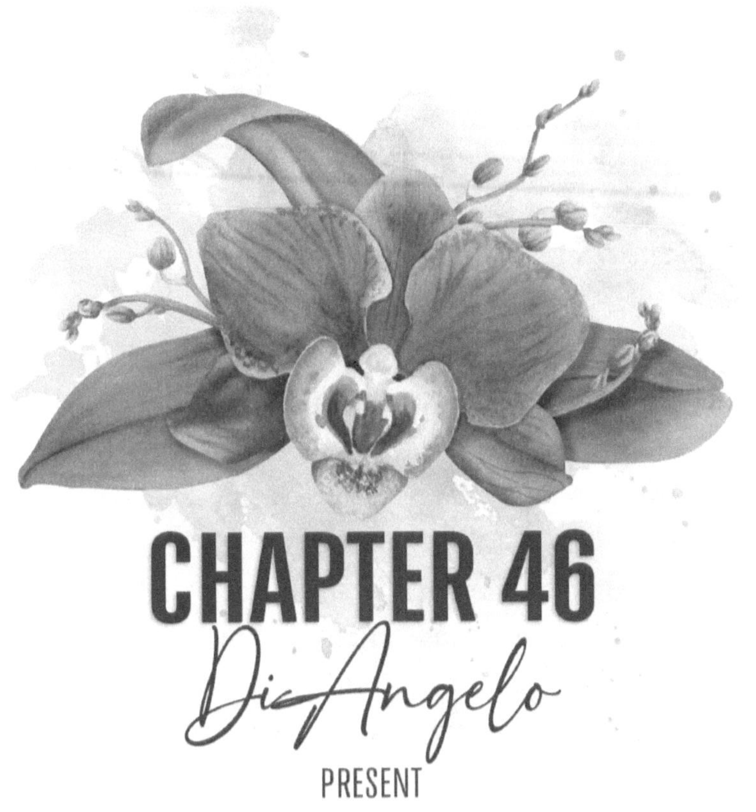

CHAPTER 46

DiAngelo

PRESENT

Terina reminds me of a willow tree, the way she bends and sways. Watching her do yoga on my balcony is my new favorite hobby. Much more relaxing than a crowded yoga studio. And the way her skin glows in the morning light? She's radiant.

I'm realizing after nearly six weeks spent together that her flexibility isn't exclusively physical. The light and energy she carries despite the trials she's endured fortified her with a strength few possess. I don't know how I didn't see it before.

She got Tommy to play cards with her while I was gone.

Cards. With *Tommy*. I can't even picture how that would work. But that's Rina. She gets her mind set on something and makes it happen. Calling her a bull in a China shop was an ignorant way of minimizing her ability not to let life hold her back.

She doesn't have a cowardly bone in her body.

Terina is all survivor.

I was an ass for making assumptions and doubting her. She and I don't think the same, but that doesn't make her any less astonishing. And despite the way I treated her at first, she's been nothing but appreciative of my help and worried about me.

Last night, she wouldn't even let me stand to come eat dinner. My leg was acting up after being on it more than I should have. She damn near threatened me with violence if I even thought of getting up off the couch, and instead, brought me a plate. We ate together, watching TV, while Bonny lay below, monitoring the ground for fallen crumbs. I'm pretty sure Rina intentionally accidentally dropped more than one morsel.

And the strangest part is, I don't actually care what she does, so long as she's safe and happy.

Paint my dog's nails? Sure.

Rom-coms on the TV at night? That works.

If it means seeing her squirm and giggle with joy, I've fulfilled my most important job. How could that not be satisfying?

And in the case of yoga, my satisfaction is twofold because

god*damn*, her body is a work of art. Lithe and soft and supple in all the best ways.

As though reading my mind, she sneaks a glance over her shoulder and catches my eyes roving over her. A coy smile spreads across her kissable lips before she abandons her mat and joins me inside.

"You watching me like a creeper?"

"Absolutely." I snag her hand and pull her closer so that her thighs are between mine. She turns and sits on my good leg, wrapping an arm around my shoulders.

Fuck does it feel good.

"Have you heard from any of the taxidermy guys?" she asks with a note of curiosity. I told her about the interrogation when I got home last night. She wanted details and didn't shy away from the ugly parts.

"I checked a few minutes ago. They're all in place, but no sightings yet."

"Let's hope it happens soon." Her fingers trail distractedly through the short hair on the back of my head, and it feels incredible. Makes me want to pleasure her as well but in a very different way.

My hand caresses up her thigh. "If not..." I gently nip at her jawline. "I'll just have to..." Nip, then kiss. "Keep you ..." More kisses down her neck. "Locked away here."

"Mmm..." Her husky reply has me grinning.

I have her stand and start to strip her leggings down, but her hand clamps down on mine.

"Oh, ummm ... I really need to shower. I'm all sweaty."

"Just wait until I'm done with you," I rasp, resuming my efforts.

She pulls away out of my reach. "No, I'm gross. Really. I just..." She motions behind her toward the bedroom. "I'm just gonna take a quick shower." Faster than a squirrel on crack, she bolts out of sight.

What the fuck was that?

Did Rina just run away from me? Why? It wasn't like she'd been laying fertilizer or something.

Curious, I head back to the bedroom and find the door to the bathroom closed. I quietly test the door and confirm that it's locked.

Huh.

While I'm not sure about her motives, wanting to clean up isn't all that crazy, so I let it go and head to my office to get some work done, including checking in with the tech guys on whether they've been able to identify the guy from the apartment break-in on any other security cameras. So far, nothing. Another dead end, just like the snake, but hopefully, not for long.

The next thing I know, it's nearly time for dinner.

I rub my face to wake myself up and stand, wincing from the pain. I've been sitting too damn long. After grabbing some painkillers, I join Terina in the living room.

"I see you two have been up to no good again."

Bonny leaps off the sofa and prances toward me, showing off her new pink collar and matching pink toenails.

Rina beams. "Isn't she adorable?"

"Are those skulls?" I look closer at the collar after I sit, and Bonny bounds onto the couch between Rina and me.

"Skull and crossbones! It's a pink pirate collar for Bonny the pirate—isn't it perfect?" She's so tickled with herself, you'd think she found the cure for cancer.

I'm starting to realize that sort of radiance is a gift.

I think if more people had such a deep appreciation for the little joys in life, this world might be a tad more tolerable.

"I think you're right," I concede with a smirk. "The look suits her, and she obviously loves it."

"Oh, I'm so glad you think so. We were a little worried you'd fuss about it." Her teeth graze her bottom lip.

"If my girls are happy, I'm happy." I pat Bonny's rear. "Now, what are we going to eat tonight? I'm thinking it'd be a good night to order in."

"That works," Rina says quietly, her eyes soft and sweet as a fresh-baked cinnamon roll.

We decide on Italian—cliché, I know—and I put in the order. While my phone is still out, I get a call from my mom.

"Hey, Mom. What's up?"

"Hey, sweetie. How's all that work stuff going? You still have a house guest?"

Shit, I forgot about scheduling our monthly dinner.

I grimace. "Yeah, actually, not much has changed."

"Oh, man. I'm sorry to hear that." She pauses. "You think there's any way you could squeeze in a visit? We sort of need to talk to you."

"Yeah, um. We can make that happen." I glance at Terina,

who's watching me closely. "What about tomorrow afternoon?"

"That would be wonderful, thank you." The relief in her voice sends a trickle of unease down my spine. I'm not sure if it's just guilt or something else bothering me, but her reaction seems odd. Whatever the reason, I'll find out soon enough.

"Sounds good. I'll see you tomorrow."

"Looking forward to it. Love you."

"Love you, too." I hang up and stare at my phone.

"Everything okay?" Rina asks gently.

"Yeah, just need to drop by my parents' place tomorrow. I'll have to see who can come by to be here with you."

"I'd love to visit Isa and get out of the house for a bit. Would it be okay if I met up with her at her dad's place?"

I lift my gaze and meet her hopeful stare. "Yeah, if Cosimo will be around, we could do that." I make the call and set it up, then Rina calls Isa. By the time we're done, dinner arrives. We eat and watch a little television before calling it a night.

When I see her brushing out her rich auburn hair in the bathroom, my eyes snag on her movements. The long strokes of the brush. The way her chest presses forward, accentuating her nipples pebbled inside her snug camisole.

I'm suddenly ravenous.

I walk up behind her and gather her hair in the three sections, careful not to snag any remaining tangles. She watches raptly in the mirror. I begin to weave the sections into a braid until I reach the ends.

"Rubber band?" I ask, palm out.

She takes one off the counter and hands it to me. "You know how to braid." Her breathy words go straight to my cock.

"I do. I'm also good with knots ... and rope."

Her chest swells on a jerky inhale. I ease my fingers beneath the hem of her top and slide it upward until the curves of her heavy breasts peek beneath the fabric. We both watch the scene unfold in the mirror as though looking in on someone else. Her sultry reaction has me just as hard as the sight of her luscious body.

I allow the shirt to rest where it is and trail my hands seductively along the underside of her breasts toward the inside and back out. Rina lets out a moan and leans backward into me.

"The things you do to me should be illegal," I rumble in her ear while pulling her ass snug against my throbbing erection.

"D." Her breathy plea undoes me. I want to pledge my life to worshipping her body.

I return to her camisole, lifting it enough to fully expose her perfect, round tits. God, I need them in my mouth to lick and suck and flick with my tongue. Her pink nipples are already pebbled tight and begging for my touch. I'm just as eager, but force myself to tease a path all the way around, then back before finally twisting those greedy peaks.

Terina cries out, arching her chest hungrily.

I wrap one arm around to knead the far breast and use the other hand to hold her middle snug against me. "I wasn't kidding when I said I wanted to pierce them," I rasp close to her ear. "Would you do that for me?" I hold her wanton stare in the mirror. She doesn't keep me waiting. She nods readily.

"Give me words, firefly."

"Yes."

"Yes, what?"

"Yes, D. I'll get my nipples pierced for you."

"*Fuuuck.*" I grind against her again, this time bringing my hand to the waist of her pajama pants.

Terina's hand clamps over mine for the second time today. "Wait. Um..." Her gaze drops. "I, uh, I've started my period."

Ah, so that's the problem.

"That doesn't bother me if it doesn't bother you."

I swear fear flashes in her eyes for the briefest of seconds, and I don't understand why.

"I don't think it's a good idea. I'm actually a little crampy. I'm sorry." She tugs at her shirt to lower it, her shoulders rounding protectively.

I turn her to face me and force her gaze to mine. "I want you, Rina, but I'm never going to push you into something you're not comfortable doing or be upset if you're not in the mood. No need to apologize."

I mean every word, though a niggling thought snags in my mind.

I could have sworn I saw a tampon box on the counter two weeks ago. I'm no expert in women's cycles, but that seems awfully fast.

Is something else going on here?

I suddenly remember her claim that she still has feelings

for her dead husband. Could that be true? Is she struggling with guilt?

Or maybe it's Ciro. She could have resurrected feelings for him when they were together.

She's been so receptive in every other way that neither of those options seems right. If it's not about someone else, what then?

I don't have any idea, and I don't like the feeling of being shut out. She's keeping something from me when I specifically asked her to be open with me. Doesn't she trust me?

Frustration claws at me to demand an explanation. I tamp it down. Logic tells me I need to give her time instead of being a dick and pushing her. It's not easy, though, because as she pointed out early on, I'm an expert at being a dick.

CHAPTER 47

Terina

PRESENT

Tormented thoughts made it hard to sleep, then followed me into my dreams. They started out well enough. I was given a beautiful new home set beside a river with huge windows to let in the sun. Everything was decorated to my taste, and I instantly felt at peace within its walls.

That's when the dream began to morph.

Large chunks of drywall started to fall from the ceilings and walls. Mold crept up from the baseboards, and sewage belched up from the sinks and toilets. While I'm panicking about how to stop the house from falling apart, a city official arrives with a demolition notice, claiming my own actions have rendered the house uninhabitable. I'd been running water in the yard for so long that the foundation had shifted, mold had infested the walls, and the plumbing had ruptured.

My beautiful new home was going to be torn down, and it was all my fault.

The obvious parallels to my current reality aren't lost on me. I've stressed about it all morning.

After Craig's death, I didn't think I'd ever want another relationship, but DiAngelo has changed everything. My heart feels whole around him. The thought of losing him and going back to the way things were turns the contents of my stomach rancid.

I fear that's exactly what will happen if he learns about the wax and my scars.

I also don't see how I can continue hiding the truth. He knows something is off—that much is obvious. If I want to try to make this work and truly give us a chance, I have to come clean.

A part of me wants to end it so that the separation is on my terms. I'd rather walk away than know he saw my darkest parts and rejected them.

But then I'd never know the what-ifs.

What if he doesn't reject me in disgust?

What if D sees all my ugly and wants me anyway?

Wouldn't the risk be worth finding a love like that? Probably, but the uncertainty is terrifying. That's why I couldn't bring myself to show him my mottled skin last night or earlier in the day. I resorted to lying about my period, instead.

God, what a mess.

I've run on this hamster wheel of worries all morning, and after a bad night's sleep, I'm exhausted. I'm so tired of the shame and loathing. I'm sick of the secrets.

In the end, it's weariness rather than bravery that leads me to unburden myself to Isa shortly after arriving at her father's house. I lay everything on the line.

My marital struggles.

The truth about Craig's murder.

His mother's blame.

I tell her the whole awful story, and she listens with compassionate warmth.

"Oh, honey, I'm so incredibly sorry," she finally offers. Her voice is reed thin, tears pooling in her eyes as she squeezes my hand in hers.

"But there's one more thing," I whisper, unable to give voice to the words. I close my eyes to gather strength, sending tears running down my cheeks. "After learning my role in Craig's death, the shame weighed on me so heavily that I had these episodes of horrible panic. I would feel like I was drowning with no hope of air until one day, something happened that finally gave me some relief."

I pull my hand from hers, the touch magnifying my vulnerability.

"I know it sounds awful, and I don't want to make you feel awkward, but I'm so tired of hiding. I needed to tell someone."

"Rina, honey, I told you that you could tell me anything, and I meant it."

I nod and swallow back my nausea. "It was an accident the first time it happened. I was up in the night and had lit a candle. The wax ... accidentally dripped onto my thigh. I don't know if it was the adrenaline or what, but the sudden burn sort of cleared my head. For the first time since Craig's death, I could breathe."

"And you've done it again since then?" she prods.

I nod again. "Not often anymore, but when I get overwhelmed, it's the one thing that gives me peace."

"And does it leave marks?" There's sorrow in her kind blue eyes, and it guts me.

"*Yes*," I breathe, eyes closing. "I know it's awful—"

Her hand returns to mine, prompting me to reopen my eyes. A gentle smile tugs at her lips.

"Rina, I'm so proud of you for telling me. I can't imagine how hard it's been living with all this for so long."

There's not a trace of horror or disgust in her words. No judgment in her eyes. She's accepted the absolute worst of me without a hint of rejection.

The relief pours out of me in a burst of violent sobs.

I press my hands over my face and surrender to the emotions. My sweet friend Isa wraps her arms around me and holds me tight.

"You are so strong, Rina. There's absolutely nothing wrong with you." She whispers soothing words of encouragement until my torrent of tears settles to a gentle sprinkle.

"I've been so worried that if anyone knew, they'd think I was broken," I admit once I've recovered.

"Anyone who knows you at all knows how strong you are.

Admitting you're struggling is a strength. You're not broken. You're a survivor."

Her choice of words strikes a chord in a good way. "I am." The threat of more tears burns the back of my throat, but I resist with a sniffle. "Do you think ... do you think DiAngelo would see it that way?"

Her gentle smile is a warm blanket around my shoulders. "You have feelings for him, don't you?"

I bite on the inside of my cheek as I weigh my answer, then nod. "It wasn't supposed to happen like this, but I can't seem to stop it. He means a lot to me, and I'm terrified that if I tell him what I told you, I'll lose him."

"I'd say that if he's dumb enough to walk away, then it wasn't meant to be. The right person for you will love you exactly as you are."

My breathing hitches, then morphs into a laugh. "God, you're good at this stuff. Why didn't I say something sooner?"

Isa's wide grin softens before she responds. "We've all got our demons. Recognizing that makes accepting those around us that much easier. No one's perfect."

Her own struggles reflect in her eyes, locked away where I can't reach them. I wish I could convince her to tell me so that she can experience this newfound freedom I've discovered, but she knows I'm ready to listen. She's simply not ready to share. And that's okay. I'll be here when that day comes.

I squeeze her hand. "Thanks, Isa."

"Have you ever considered talking to someone like a counselor?" she asks gently.

"Yes and no. I've always been worried I'd say something that would get my family in trouble."

"What if it was your mom who was struggling? Would you want her to get help or stay quiet?"

I blink, her question so simple yet so profound. "I'd want her to get help, of course."

Isa smiles. "I bet she'd say the same for you."

I nod and sniffle. "Well, then. I guess if that's decided, it's time for some chocolate. What are the chances there's any in the house?"

"Are you kidding?" She beams. "Daddy always keeps some Ferrero Rocher in his office. Come on." We walk hand in hand in search of chocolate like two little girls without a care in the world. My heart feels ten years younger and lighter than it has in years.

I can't guarantee that DiAngelo will welcome me with open arms once I tell him the truth. But I think that even if he doesn't, I might still be okay. Hopefully, that gives me the courage I need to finally lay myself bare.

The time for secrets is over.

Fear and shame have no home here.

CHAPTER 48
DiAngelo

PRESENT

"It's so good to see you!" Mom gives me a hug that borders on aggressive, coaxing a smile from me.

"I know, I know. That was way too long between visits. I'm sorry about that."

Dad waves his hand before giving me a hug of his own. "That's life sometimes. We're just glad you're here."

"Dad has ground hamburger all seasoned, and I made potato salad. There should also be some cut-up watermelon in the fridge, if your father hasn't eaten it all," she adds with a playful jab.

"That sounds perfect," I say. "What can I help with?"

Dad motions to the fridge. "How about you grab us a couple of beers, and we can sit on the patio for a few minutes while the grill warms up?"

"Sure, you want one, too, Ma?"

"Nah, I'll stick to my soda today." She raises a purple insulated tumbler and makes her way outside.

My parents have a nice little single-family home in the Bronx with a patio out back and a small patch of grass. I offered to upgrade them when I started making money. They insisted they didn't need more than what they had. I can only assume a large part of their desire to stay had to do with keeping Elio's memory alive. It's understandable.

I sit at the glass patio table in one of the four swivel deck chairs. Considering it's almost mid-September, the temps are still high, but the aquamarine awning overhead keeps the sun off us. Between that and the undulating fan Dad installed years ago, it's surprisingly comfortable outside.

"How have you guys been?" I ask after taking a sip from my beer.

They look ever so briefly at one another before Mom plasters a smile on her face that doesn't quite reach her eyes.

"We're mostly good—"

"Mostly?" I'm not sure what is going on, but I already don't like it.

"Let me finish," she chides me. "I was in for my annual checkup a while back, and my mammogram showed an abnormality."

My stomach lurches, then bottoms out in my feet. An abnormality? What the fuck have I missed here?

She continues as my mind races. "They aren't sure that it's cancer," she says as if that's supposed to reassure me. "But Dad and I have talked, and we decided it's safest to just do the double mastectomy and eliminate the risk."

"You have breast cancer?" My ears ring so loudly that it's hard to hear my own words.

"They'll biopsy the tissue after surgery, so we won't know until then. We could biopsy now and discuss treatment options based on the type of mass, but we aren't interested in dragging it out. I'd rather have the surgery and give myself the best possible chances."

Best chances of survival.

While I've been self-absorbed with my own issues, my parents have had to wrestle with the knowledge that Mom could die.

I've lived my entire life under the false assumption that my parents would always be around. Obviously, I knew their time would come eventually, but never so soon. I thought I'd have plenty more time.

God, please give me more time with them.

"If they do the surgery, you'll be okay?" I sound like a kid again because I feel like one. Helplessness and fear attack from both sides, bringing me to my knees.

"They can never guarantee that they'll get all the cells, but the chances of a recurrence are very small. The prognosis is really optimistic, sweetie, I promise." She gives me a sad smile, then stands and rounds the table to hug me where I sit, stunned.

I cling to her.

I cling to a life I wish I'd known. A life with family that I turned my back on out of self-loathing and shame. My parents didn't deserve that. They didn't deserve to be collateral damage in my war against myself.

How can I ever possibly make up for all the hurt I've caused?

It feels impossible, but I have to try, or I'm no better today than I was yesterday.

"When is the surgery? I want to be there."

Mom gives one more squeeze and goes back to her seat. "It's in two weeks."

"Two weeks?" I blurt, my incredulous stare dancing from one to the other. I don't know what I expected. When there's cancer involved, things probably move pretty quickly, but I've never dealt with this before.

Dad puts his hand over Mom's in a show of unity, his eyes apologetic. "We knew you had a lot going on and didn't want to bother you until we knew the plan."

"Jesus, Dad. You guys aren't a bother." I shouldn't take my frustration out on him. I'm the one I'm mad at. I'm the one who led them to believe they were an inconvenience.

Fuck, I've been selfish.

"Well, now you know," he says in his dad voice, warning me to calm down. "We can get you all the details, but for right now, we'd love to just spend some time together, okay?"

I exhale out years of frustration and nod. "Yeah, that

sounds good. How about I grab the meat so you can get those burgers cooking?"

They both beam at me.

The fact that I was the reason Elio was taken never darkened their view of me. I wasn't able to save my brother—I never even found the other man who was responsible for Elio's death—and I got myself thrown in prison for arson in the process. None of it mattered.

I truly can do no wrong in their eyes, and it's the one thing that gives me hope that I might be able to redeem myself someday. They would say I already have—hell, they would say there's nothing to atone for—but I'm the one I need to convince. The question is, how?

As much as I'd like to wallow in my shortcomings, I do the right thing for once and give them what they've asked for. We have burgers, and they update me on news of extended family. Mom rats out Dad's home repair mishaps, and we all have a good laugh.

The time we spend together helps, but the lingering melancholy resurfaces on my way home. I know that berating myself won't help. I try to lock those thoughts away, though my efforts are lackluster at best.

Terina is all smiles when I pick her up from Cosimo's house. A few minutes in the car with me sucks the joy right off her face. I ask her questions and try not to bring her down, but a woman's intuition is too adept to avoid. She senses my discomfit and retreats inside herself. That only spurs on my frustrations.

By the time we get home, I decide it's best to be alone and

sequester myself in the gym. I hit the heavy bag until my back and legs ache. It's a punishing workout, and I deserve every minute.

I sit on the weight bench when I'm done, elbows resting heavily on my thighs, and do something I rarely let myself do. I think about my brother.

It's no wonder I fall short so often when the best half of me died years ago.

I miss him every goddamn day. I've never truly learned to live without him. I try, but the man I pretend to be is just a shell of the man I was.

Elio wouldn't want me to give up.

He would want me to keep trying and live the best life possible, so for him, I'll do it. I'll keep fighting and hope that one day, I'll feel worthy of the love my family feels for me.

PRESENT

I SIT IN THE LIVING ROOM AND LISTEN TO THE FAINT sounds of DiAngelo working out at the opposite end of the apartment. The yawning emotional distance between us makes me feel like he's on the other end of the planet, and I hate it.

After talking with Isa, I feel a tiny bit more confident about opening up to him, so when the room goes silent, I head back to find him. My heart contracts at the sight of him sitting on the bench, his head hung low. He's worked himself harder than usual. And that's saying something, considering it's his second workout for the day, and his leg is still healing.

Something's eating at him. That wasn't the case last night before I shut down his advances. Ever since, he's been withdrawn. It's safe to assume I'm at least part of the reason he's upset. I want to do what I can to fix this, but holy crap, am I nervous.

"Hey," I say softly from the doorway to announce my appearance.

He lifts his gaze just enough to see me through his thick lashes. "Hey."

"Not sure if you have plans for supper. I'd be happy to make something for us."

D stands and wipes his face with a hand towel. He's wearing athletic pants with no shirt, and my eyes are desperate to follow the droplets of sweat as they trail down the dips and curves of his taut muscles. He is truly magnificent to behold.

"No need to mess with it. I'm good with making myself a sandwich or something simple tonight." He doesn't comment on my wandering gaze. He hardly looks at me.

"You sure? I really don't mind."

"I'm sure. I need to get some work done after I shower." He comes closer, elevating my heart rate, but instead of intimacy, he's looking for escape. His hand on my lower back coaxes me to the side enough for him to squeeze through the doorway without touching him.

He's sweaty, so the gesture is thoughtful, except it feels like more than that. It feels like avoidance. And that's what it is because after our short exchange, I'm now standing alone in an empty room.

Is this his way of telling me he's changed his mind?

Has he decided I'm not worth the bother?

Fear hollows out my chest and rings in my ears. I'm going to lose him if I don't do something. There was a time when I might have preferred the safety of isolation to exposing my vulnerabilities, but I'm quickly realizing I want DiAngelo more than I want to be safe.

I want DiAngelo. Period.

And I want DiAngelo to want me. Every broken piece of me.

Go now, while you have the courage. Hurry.

My legs are in motion of their own volition, carrying me through the apartment to the primary bathroom. D stands at the vanity with the broad expanse of his tattooed back in full view. We lock eyes in the mirror. He must see the desperation on my face because he immediately turns to face me.

"Kristi told me someone was extorting money from Craig and using my safety to control him." My rushed words sound random, but it feels like the right place to start. I don't exactly have a speech planned. All I can do is let my heart do the talking and hope it comes out right. "I went to the police station and demanded they tell me the truth. I saw the photos. I saw the quarters and know they were a message related to the money he owed. I know he died because of me—trying to keep me safe."

"Rina—" DiAngelo takes a step toward me, but I raise my hand to stop him.

"Let me finish. I need to get it all out, then you can say whatever you want." I regroup my thoughts for a second before I continue. "The guilt I felt about that was compounded by the fact that I was already contemplating leaving Craig. He was always gone. All he seemed to care about was making more money, but once I learned the reason for that, I hated myself for being so blind. I've spent the past five years keeping everyone at arm's length to avoid ever feeling that pain again."

My hands worry at one another, the nerves of my impending confession building to a frenzied state. I can tell D wants to interject. Concern lines his forehead and casts harsh shadows across his eyes. He listens, however, as I've asked, and I'm grateful because if I stop, I may not ever get it all out.

"I told you I was still in love with Craig, but that was a lie. I haven't been in love with him for a very long time. I only said that because ... because I'm so damn scared of what I'm feeling for you. Scared you'll get hurt because of me. Scared of falling for you ... then losing you. I've been so damn terrified that I've been pushing you away before we've even had a chance because there's something you don't know about me. Something you may not like."

I wipe my now sweaty hand on my jean shorts and unbutton them, letting them drop to the floor. With trembling fingers, I lift my shirt over my head so that I'm standing before him in my bra and panties.

D's concern has shifted to confusion as he tries to figure out what I'm trying to tell him.

He'll see soon enough, and then there'll be no going back.

I hook my thumbs in my panties and drag them down over my hips until they join my shorts and shirt on the floor. I nervously run my hand across the blotchy skin of my lower belly, and when I speak again, my voice is fragile and raw.

"I struggled with the guilt after Craig was murdered. One night, by accident, I spilled hot wax on myself."

DiAngelo's eyes clench shut.

His anguish feels like a door slammed in my face, stealing the oxygen from my lungs.

"I ... uh ... I know it sounds crazy," I force myself to continue. "But I felt better afterward. Like the pain reset my brain. I know it's fucked up, and I totally understand if this changes things. I just needed you to know that I wasn't rejecting you—I just didn't know how to tell you the truth. This doesn't happen often, but I was struggling after the cemetery when things shifted between us, and I got weak. I'm sorry," I breathe, my vision now swimming with tears.

I reach for my panties.

"*Stop.*" D's heavy command freezes me on the spot.

CHAPTER 50
DiAngelo

I CAN HARDLY BELIEVE MY EYES. SKIN THAT WOULD otherwise be naturally smooth and uniform beneath her navel is a rainbow of mottled shades of pink and brown flesh. Years of scarring in various stages of healing. The most alarming are the three patches of bright pink still in the process of peeling.

Agony is a serrated blade deep in my gut.

My strong, beautiful girl has carried so much shame that she's been hurting herself. Punishing herself for something that was never her fault.

I close the distance between us and drop to my knees, my

eyes fixed on the evidence of her pain. I gingerly take hold of her hips. "You did this here?" *Under my watch.* I feel horrible knowing she was suffering while I was oblivious.

"There was no way for you to know."

"I was supposed to be protecting you. If I'd been more understanding and less of an ass…"

"I still would have struggled." She cups my face in her loving hands. "I'm damaged, D, and that happened long before you entered the picture."

I close my eyes again, wishing I could do it all over. But I realize I'm making the same mistakes of the past by making this about me. Focusing on my failings is selfish. It's time to put others first.

I lean in and press a tender but ardent kiss on one of the healed scars.

An apology.

A promise.

"I'm so sorry, firefly." I peer up to see her chin quivering.

"You're not disgusted by me?" Her whispered words gut me.

She thought her admission might ruin my desire for her. The truth is far from it. Knowing the extent of her struggles only intensifies my respect for her. I am in awe of Terina. Her perseverance. Her compassion. She is a treasure, and the man who can't see that is either blind or a fool.

I want her to understand how I feel. I need to show her how committed I am to her.

I stand, keeping our bodies close, and my eyes locked on hers. "I'm in awe of you, sweet girl. And I want you to know none of it was ever your fault. Craig got into drugs and gambling. That's what killed him. You're right, he was murdered, but it wasn't for the reasons you're thinking. He owed a prominent bookie hundreds of thousands of dollars. That was the reason for the quarters. It was a message to other degenerates to pay their debts. It was never about you."

Her evergreen eyes search mine. "It wasn't ... it wasn't blackmail?" she asks on a shuddered breath. "But Kristi said—"

"I don't care what she said or why." I place my hands by her ears to capture her gaze again. "I'm telling you the truth. His death had nothing to do with you."

I won't dwell on that viper of a mother-in-law in front of Rina, but I damn well am going to get answers from the woman as soon as I have a chance.

Rina gasps as though she were close to drowning and taking her first gulp of lifesaving air.

"It wasn't me."

I turn my head from left to right in answer. "No, it wasn't. And even if it had been an enemy of the family coming after you that had ended his life, it's still not your fault. I said that from the very beginning, and I stand by it."

"Why did Renzo keep the truth from me?"

"He thought he was protecting you by not smearing Craig's name. He had no idea Kristi had let you believe the attack was part of some bullshit blackmail story."

A tear trickles down her cheek.

I bend and kiss the salty trail, noting the way her body lists toward me at the touch. It makes my cock stir in my pants. When I pull back, her heated gaze drops to my lips.

"You're not on your period, then?" My words are as coarse as a gravel road.

She starts to turn her head, then stills and gives me her voice instead. "No, D."

My nostrils flare on a heady inhale.

"And the sweat doesn't bother you?"

"No, D."

I trail my thumb across her full bottom lip as my dick attempts to burst from my pants.

"If I fuck you, firefly, you're mine. There's no going back." I hold her stare with unflinching intensity. "I need to know that you understand that."

Her throat bobs. "Please, D," she whispers. "Fuck me and make me yours."

I lift her against me, circling her legs around my waist while the beast in my head roars triumphantly.

"It's time to get out the cuffs."

CHAPTER 51

Terina

PRESENT

"Bonny, *out*." DiAngelo sends the dog out of the bedroom after dropping me on the bed, then closes the door behind her.

I sit with my legs under me, devouring his every move as he retrieves four black leather cuffs from a dresser drawer. They're wide with shiny silver buckles. His adept hands work them with skilled ease as he attaches one around each of my wrists and ankles.

He yanks the duvet and top sheet off the bed in one swift movement. "Bra off. Lie on your back, hands and feet out."

D the dominant is back, thrilling me to my core.

This is his domain, and within these walls, he reigns.

I move without hesitation. I trust him implicitly and want nothing more than to follow his lead. I'm so eager to do as he says that embarrassment over the visibility of my scars is only a passing thought. He's seen them. I have no reason to hide, though the echo of shame is hard to erase. It's going to take time.

Sensual music begins to play a seductive beat all around us.

"That's it, firefly. Wider." His hungry gaze surveys the banquet before him. He saunters to one corner and retrieves a black cord from beneath the mattress. One end is secured out of sight, while the other has a metal slide bolt latch.

"Was that there the whole time?" I ask, astonished. I've been sleeping in here for weeks and had no idea the bed was rigged for play. What else don't I know?

D attaches the bolt to my ankle cuff with a wicked glint in his eyes. "That and more."

More? Sparks fly as my brain short-circuits. What other sex-god secrets is he keeping? I want to know all of them. *Now.*

I've never been so turned on without a single touch.

DiAngelo's stare is so visceral, my skin heats in its wake as he prowls around the bed and secures each of my limbs until I'm fully secured spread eagle.

You're going to make a mess of the bed.

The thought flashes through my mind when I notice the

sensation of arousal slowly dripping from my entrance. With my legs open, there's no keeping it contained.

I squirm a little, but the tightening of my inner muscles only makes it worse.

"What's wrong?" D asks.

"Umm, I'm worried I'm going to make a mess," I admit quietly.

He rounds to the end of the bed so that he's standing directly between my legs. His stare locks on my center, amusement tugging at his lips. "I see what you mean."

He eases himself onto the bed, his gaze never deviating as he lowers himself between my open thighs. He draws his tongue in a languid sweep of my center, lapping up my juices.

"*Mmm* ... I could eat you out all fucking day. And while a mess doesn't bother me, I don't want you worrying about it." He rises, shifting farther up until our bodies are aligned, though he's careful not to touch my healing burns.

Before I can answer, he coaxes my lips apart and fucks my face with his tongue. That's the only way I know how to describe it—an erotic invasion that teases and titillates. The fact that I can taste myself on him only heightens the sensations because I can tell that's the point. He wants me to know how thoroughly he adores everything about me.

"Will you feel better if I get a towel?"

His voodoo tongue fuck renders me senseless, and I have to blink a couple of times before my brain catches up. "Yes, please."

He nips my bottom lip between his teeth before slowly releasing it. "Such a good fucking girl. I want you to tell me these things so that when the fun begins, you're not distracted. The only thing you should be thinking about when we're together is how good I make you feel."

A colony of butterflies takes flight in my chest.

This man is so much more than I ever could have imagined, and he wants me. Every neurotic, goofy, messed-up inch of me. He wants me so much that he didn't want my yoga instructor to even touch me. Not to mention, he practically fought my little brother for talking about me. He's seen the worst of me, yet his desire is unconditional.

He's protective and trustworthy and...

And I think I love him.

The words settle into my soul like marshmallows melting into steaming hot chocolate.

When he returns from the bathroom, he's carrying a towel and a toy. My gooey emotions take a back seat as arousal jumps back behind the wheel.

I lift my backside for him to insert the folded towel beneath me, then watch as he holds up the small blue device for me to see. It's not a dildo, nor is it like any bullet I've seen. It almost looks like a curved seashell, one end to be inserted and the other reaching around for the clit. I can already tell I'm going to love it.

"Before you start to worry, yes, it's brand new. I've been wanting to do this since that very first night when I heard the buzzing coming from your room."

My eyes bulge wide. "You could hear that?"

He clicks on the device in answer, a devilish smile creeping wide across his face.

"I did, then I fantasized about it a hundred times over, which is why I couldn't stop watching when I saw you in my bed. You were even more perfect than I'd imagined."

Embarrassment blends with pleasure to pinken my cheeks.

DiAngelo cycles through the toy's various vibration patterns until it stops. Except it doesn't fully stop. It suddenly buzzes to life briefly, then goes silent again for several seconds.

D grins, then eases one end of the blue shell into my pussy and aligns the other end over my clit. It bursts to life in the process, drawing a gasp and moan from me before going silent again. The sudden pulse is excruciating in the best way.

I can't tell if it's divine or diabolical.

Like D, I think it might be both, and I'm here for it.

DiAngelo wedges some of the towel behind the toy so that it stays in place, then goes back to the dresser. This time, he returns with something that scares me a little.

"Is that a ... ahhh ..." The vibrations derail me. "A flogger?" I ask breathily.

He holds the woven brown leather handle with one hand while leather ribbons glide along the other. "It is, but I don't want you to worry. And if this is too much, too soon, tell me. As you've probably noticed, I have particular tastes. Maybe not the norm, but nothing you should fear. I would never hurt you, Rina. Do you believe me when I say that?"

I nod my head, my nerves getting the better of me.

"Words, firefly."

"Yes, D."

"Have you ever experienced a flogger?"

"It's like a whip, right?"

"Not exactly. It can do a lot of things using both pleasure and pain." He gets close enough to kneel on the bed, then trails the ends of the flogger from my stomach up to my chest, moving it across one breast to the other just as the toy surges to life.

My body practically levitates from the bed.

"Oh *God*." It's part exclamation and part moan.

"See, it's versatile." He accents his words with a quick snap of the flogger. The leather ribbons bite at my breast, sending a bolt of lightning directly to my clit. D leans in and uses his tongue to lave at the stinging nipple. "I thought you'd like that. If today proves anything to me, it's that you were meant to be mine. I'm meant to show you how to utilize pain properly, without harming yourself." He trails the flogger down my side to my thighs.

My breath comes in shallow pants.

"I thought you didn't believe in fate," I tease.

He narrows his eyes playfully, then snaps the flogger over my pubic mons, careful not to hit the burns above. The vibrator buzzes immediately after.

My body writhes with sensation.

"I've learned the rules don't apply where you're concerned." He flicks the flogger against my inner thigh. One side. Then the other. It's not at all hard. The sting is just enough to distract from pleasure, which builds with every pulse.

"D, I need more," I cry when he continues to work the flogger back up my body. My arousal has reached devastating levels, but ebbs shy of release without a continued source of stimulation. This sort of delicious purgatory could drive a person to madness.

"Mmm ... we'll have to build up your tolerance. But not today. You've been so incredibly brave." He reaches between my legs and clicks the vibrator onto a steady setting, then uses his hand to rock the device against me.

My consciousness splinters from the world around me until I drift on a river of ecstasy. My body is engulfed in violent pleasure. Waves of radiant light flood my veins while flames consume me.

And in the wake, there is effervescent serenity.

I am undone.

"I will never tire of making you come," DiAngelo drawls in a ragged voice. He turns off the device and removes his pants.

I watch through slitted eyes, too sex-weary to fully open them. "Promise?"

Amusement flashes in his eyes. "That's a promise I'm happy to make." He unclips my ankle cuffs and coaxes my knees to bend so that my feet are up near either side of my rear.

His rough hands trail down my inner thighs. He slides his hands along the apex, pressing my swollen lips against themselves. I groan from the gentle massage that stirs to life a spark of need.

"You don't take birth control." It's a statement, but I know what he's getting at.

"I have an IUD."

"Thank God," he breathes. "I've never gone unprotected, but that's not gonna work with you. I need to feel what it's like to be inside you without anything between us. You okay with that?"

"Yes, D." It's the easiest question I've answered all day because I want the same.

His rumble of satisfaction gives my heart a gentle squeeze.

DiAngelo moves up my body, the sinew of his muscular shoulders visible as he supports himself above me. He brings his lips to mine at the same moment his scalding cock teases at my entrance. I lift my legs back, angling myself in invitation.

"Tell me if you need me to slow down—this might hurt." The strain in his voice is woven with worry. It's the sweetest damn thing I've ever heard.

"I will."

He rocks himself inside me, just an inch at first, then two. He's not only careful to go slowly but to keep himself suspended above me enough not to risk contacting my burns.

I moan at the fullness. "It feels so good, D. Keep going."

"*So fucking tight* ... scared I'll rip you," he hisses on a shaky breath.

He's not totally wrong. It does sting, but in a good way. And the pressure of him filling me is incredible—like he's burrowing a path straight to my welcoming heart. I don't ever want this sense of deep connection to end.

When his cock is fully sheathed inside me, his entire body shudders.

"This is where I belong. You're mine, firefly. All fucking mine."

"*Yessss*, D." I don't know if I'm responding to his words or his movements because he's begun to ease himself out of me, then slide home in commanding thrusts. Claiming me. Possessing my body and soul.

Electric need builds in my core as he fucks me with increased intensity. The sensitive nerves already stimulated by my earlier orgasm flare back to life.

My arms pull against their bindings, desperate to wrap around him. I want the connection but also leverage. I need more of him. I want to counter his thrusts until we're fucking with such violent abandon that our bodies become one.

DiAngelo reads my mind and inserts an arm beneath me, securing me in place to fuck me that much harder.

"*Oh God.* I'm going to come again."

"Give it to me, Rina. Soak my cock with your cum."

His filthy words send me over the edge. Blackness threatens the edges of my vision as pleasure consumes me. D moves faster and faster until he bellows his release with one final thrust, holding himself deep inside me where I can feel him pulse and throb.

Not once does he allow his body to even graze my healing skin. Even in the deepest throes of passion, he keeps his body curved to protect mine. That's no accident. It's devotion.

I wrap my legs around his waist since it's the only way I can hold him.

"You're going to marry me, Terina Donati. You're going to marry me and be mine."

CHAPTER 52
D'Angelo

Rina doesn't respond to my declaration that I plan to make her my wife. She probably thinks it's the sex talking. That's fine. She doesn't have to believe me for it to be true.

I lift myself back onto my knees, loving the sight of our mixed cum dripping from her body.

"Squeeze for me, firefly. Show me more." I don't have to explain. My intent focus makes it clear what I'm asking.

Terina contracts her inner muscles and abs, causing a fresh flood of moisture to drip from her.

"You like that?" she asks with a note of curiosity.

I run my hand along her inner thigh. "More than you could know. And as much as I'd like to make you stay like this for my viewing pleasure, I need to get you cleaned up."

"We could just use the towel for now."

"No, I don't want you getting a UTI. You're mine to look after, remember?"

She cracks a crooked smile when a long, pitiful whine sounds from beyond the bedroom door.

"Poor thing," Rina croons. "She's so lonely out there."

I roll my eyes good-naturedly, then remove the cuffs from her ankles and wrists. Once I'm done, I let my spoiled mutt in the room and watch as she shakes her back end so violently that she can't walk straight.

"You are the epitome of ferocious, you know that?"

Bonny beams at me, her tongue lolling out the side of her mouth.

"You've just made the classic blunder of underestimating her just because she's beautiful."

"I don't know about that," I chide, "but at least she doesn't stink now that she got bathed. Normally, the groomer comes here every couple of weeks so that I don't have to live with stinky dog smell everywhere."

Rina sits up, her head angling a fraction to the side. "The groomer comes here, but you went to her shop instead." She says the words as though the concept is novel, and I have no idea why.

"Yeah?"

She pulls her lips between her teeth, then grins sheepishly. "I heard you that day—I think you were dictating a text.

I thought ... maybe you were meeting up with someone ... for other reasons."

I tilt my head back in an exaggerated nod and close the distance between us. "You thought I was hooking up with another woman." I trail my thumb over her flushed cheek. "So my little firefly has a jealous streak."

"It's not like I'm the only one," she counters. "Don't forget your little meltdown over that poor yoga instructor." She places her hand in mine and allows me to guide her from the bed and toward the bathroom.

"Oh, I haven't forgotten about Chase."

"You remember his name?"

"Of course I do. He and I had words."

When I peer back at her with a smirk, her eyes are so wide I can see an entire forest in their depths.

"You didn't," she breathes.

"I absolutely did, and you can tamp down the righteous indignation. It's not like I beat the man senseless."

She props her hands on her hips. "Did you *threaten* to beat him senseless?"

I turn on the shower water and shrug. "I suppose that's debatable."

"DiAngelo!" Her attempt at outrage evaporates the second my lips connect with hers. She softens against me, her tongue tangling with mine. When I end the kiss, her hooded eyes are soft as velvet.

"That's better."

"Is that your plan for every argument? To sex me into submission?" Her tone tells me she's not entirely opposed.

"That, or I can just keep you sex drunk so there's no argument to begin with."

A sleepy smile teases her lips wide. "I suppose it's worth a try."

I step closer, my face inches from hers, and snap my teeth playfully. She yips and devolves into a fit of giggles.

I could hear that sound every day for the rest of eternity and never tire of it.

We step into the shower. I make sure the water isn't too hot because I'm sure the heat will feel extra intense on her burns. I still can't believe she's been living with that right under my nose. It's something we'll have to work together to overcome.

"There's something I need from you," I start while she allows the water to soak into her long auburn hair.

"What's that?"

"I need you to promise me you'll tell me if you're struggling."

She stills and opens her eyes despite the water droplets dotting her lashes. She doesn't immediately respond, so I continue.

"I need to know when trouble's creeping up so that I can be there to help. I ... I lost my brother because I was too blind to see that I put him in danger, and I don't want to make that same mistake with you."

Terina's hands come to rest on my abs before she hugs my middle. "I'll tell you if I'm struggling."

I gently hold her head against my chest and place a kiss on her crown.

"D, can I ask a question about your brother?" She pulls back to meet my gaze. "You don't have to talk about it if you don't want to."

"You can always ask me anything."

"Isa said it was a kidnapping, but you just mentioned putting him in danger—how could you be at all responsible for him getting kidnapped?"

I inhale deeply.

She's been so fucking brave telling me her truth. It's time I tell her mine.

I lather my hands with soap and begin washing her. "The night before he was kidnapped, I went out to a bar and lied to a bunch of random people about being on a yacht. I even showed photos. The problem was, I cleaned the boat—I wasn't a guest like I'd told them. I made it sound like we had money and connections.

"The next day, I was hungover, and Elio offered to go into work for me since he bailed on going out the night before. I let him pretend to be me. A man from the night before jumped him on his way to the marina, thinking it was me. Twenty-four hours later, my brother was dead."

"You were only seventeen, right?"

"Old enough to know better." I move her back into the spray to rinse off.

Rina hardly notices. Her attention is fixated on me. "You still blame yourself."

"Wouldn't have happened without my involvement, so yeah."

Her fingers trace the tattoo inked on my left pectoral—my brother's name over my heart.

"I've wondered a thousand times over if Craig hadn't met me if he'd still be alive. His death may not have been for the reasons I thought, but meeting me still could have been the instigator that sent him down that path. But when it comes down to it, you were right—the only one truly responsible is the person who actually murdered him. If I have no reason to feel guilty about the what-ifs, you shouldn't either."

My shame is so ingrained that I feel a visceral need to reject her argument, but I'm also wary of saying something that might imply blame on her part, so I weigh my words carefully. A funny thing happens when I consider my response in light of her perspective—a double standard emerges.

"I sound like a hypocrite if I argue, but I don't know how not to blame myself," I admit.

"I get that. It's going to take some work for me, too. But you have to consider, if he'd gone to a pharmacy to pick up meds for you while you were sick, and a hit-and-run driver killed him, would that be your fault? The only reason he was out was because of you, but no one would rationally say you were to blame."

I narrow my eyes at her and pull her chest flush against mine. "You are making entirely too much sense. I must not have fucked you thoroughly enough."

A radiant grin brings out the emerald shards in her eyes. "Sounds like you have work to do."

I have her spun around, hands on the tile wall, in two seconds flat. "Prepare to be fucked senseless."

"Yes, D." Her breathy reply has my already rock-hard cock throbbing.

I angle her hips and burrow my way back home, deep inside her. This right here is my heaven on earth, and it's not about the sex, per se. It's the trust and connection. The fact that this incredible woman is willing to give herself to me—her safety, her secrets, her very soul—she gives my life more meaning than I knew was possible.

I honor that gift with an orgasm that leaves her legs quivering, and her voice ragged from screaming.

I fucking love that she's a screamer.

It's just one of the many ways Terina embraces life with both hands. I can only imagine how vibrant she'll be without the shadow of guilt and danger looming over her. I will do everything in my power to see that day come. Sooner rather than later.

By the time we've finished showering, both of our stomachs are growling for dinner. We head to the kitchen and make sandwiches, too hungry to take the time for anything more complex.

"You seemed off in the car today, so I didn't want to press, but is everything okay with your parents?" Rina peers at me briefly before taking another bite.

The reminder of Mom's diagnosis settles heavily on my shoulders.

"Yes and no. My mom's got some kind of breast cancer and is going to get a double mastectomy in two weeks."

Rina gasps, her hand coming to her mouth in horror. "Oh God. D, I'm so sorry."

"She's in good spirits, and the surgery, from what they said, should take care of it, but it still scares me."

"Of course, it does."

I give a little grimace. "It's not just the cancer. I've been a pretty big dick to my parents over the years. They've always loved me unconditionally, but I've kept my distance out of guilt. I know what I stole from them, and seeing them reminds me of my failures."

"DiAngelo Farina. It's time to stop that sort of negative self-talk right-flipping-now. Do you hear me?" Her authoritative outburst is so fucking adorable, I can't help but smile.

"You giving me orders now?"

"If that's what it takes to get through that thick skull of yours. You are a good man who has done his very best to honor the people he loves. There is nothing to be ashamed of, and if you'd like to have a closer relationship with your parents going forward, then you make that happen. I'm sure they'd love it."

"Fuck, my mom's going to love you."

Rina visibly melts in her chair. "Yeah?"

"Yeah, now eat your food. You're going to need the energy." I arch a brow at her, pleased when she hungrily takes another bite because I'm definitely not done with her. I don't think I'll ever be able to get enough.

I want to make her mine in every way possible, but first, I have to make her safe. If that involves taking down the entire Russian operation, I'll make it happen. Every. Last. One.

CHAPTER 53
Terina

Sunsets bleed into sunrise as the world goes by outside our windows. One day. Two days. A week. Aside from the dog walker and deliveries, we exist for days on end in a timeless bubble. We eat when we're hungry, sleep when we're tired, have lots and *lots* of sex, and talk about everything under the sun.

It's the happiest I've ever been in my life.

I never imagined the risk I took in opening up to DiAngelo could yield such an incredible reward. I'd hoped it would be worthwhile, but the past week has been so much more than that. All because I chose to embrace D instead of fear.

I still get anxious, but I'm trying not to let it govern my decisions.

It helps enormously to know DiAngelo will catch me if I fall. He won't judge or criticize me. I think this might be what it feels like to have a partner—something I never achieved with Craig. Not with all his secrets acting as a barrier between us. I can see that now.

D has been keeping me updated on the hunt for Pasha. He's told me all about his time in prison and the years after when he tried to track down the man responsible for killing his brother. It's the one target he was never able to identify, but those skills have helped him hunt down other monsters like Pasha.

He's confident all of this will be over soon. In fact, he's taking me to Renzo's today so that he can follow up on leads. My job is not to panic that something awful will happen while he's out. That possibility feels especially real when he has me wear a bulletproof vest on the way. Bonny helps, though. I decide to take her with me. She makes an excellent distraction, bounding around in the back seat while D grumbles at her to sit still.

When we arrive at Renzo's brownstone home, Bonny puts on a good show of pretending to be all business. A real boss bitch, considering she still has her pink collar and nails. I'm totally smitten.

Mom is, too. She gives Bonny a leftover piece of sausage

from breakfast. After that, all pretense of badassery is dropped.

D just shakes his head. "You're the one who has to live with the consequences. She'll be farting sausage the rest of the day."

"Don't be silly." Mom waves him off. "She'll be fine."

"Who's farting sausage all day?" Shae rounds the corner with sweet little Liora asleep in her arms.

"Hell, did we wake you?" D grimaces.

"Nope, I was just changing her. Ah, I see what's going on. We get a furry visitor today, do we?" She lets Bonny sniff her, then scratches behind the dog's ears.

"I think we're both happy for a change of scenery," I explain.

"I hear you," Shae agrees. "Between the threats and the baby, I'm real close to going stir-crazy."

Renzo pipes up in response. "Just be patient a little longer. This will all be over soon enough. I should be hearing from the Genoveses any time now. They've been doing what they can to get intel on Michael to see what's happened on that front. And D, you've got a lead on Pasha, right?"

"Yeah, I'll show you what I have before I head out."

He nods, turning for the hall. "We can visit in my office."

While his back is turned and the others are looking in his direction, D leans in and places a quick kiss on my temple. At the exact moment his lips make contact, Renzo freezes, then slowly swivels back around to gape at us.

"What the fuck was that?" he demands.

Mom and Shae look from him to us, blinking cluelessly.

My gaze flits to the large horizontal hall tree mirror in the entry. The angle gives me the perfect view of the back of Renzo's head.

Uh-oh.

"We should probably talk in your office," DiAngelo mumbles.

"You think?" Renzo spins back around, pissed. D follows him, leaving me with Mom and Shae.

"What on earth just happened?" Mom asks.

Shae narrows her calculating eyes at me. "Nooo, surely not." A Machiavellian grin spreads wide on her face as she assesses my reaction. "Oh, hell yeah. This is way better than an outing. Zuzu, pour us some tea. It's time for Rina to spill the beans."

"Tea? Beans? What am I missing? And you're not supposed to have tea, it has too much caffeine."

Shae seats herself at the kitchen table. "If we don't have any decaf, then pour me some juice. Your daughter's about to tell us how she started bumping uglies with her bodyguard."

Mom gasps, her hand flying to her chest as she spins to face me. "Ree Ree, is it true?" There's so much hope in her eyes, I'm not sure if it's sweet or sad. I think she's been worried I'd never move on from Craig.

I bite back a shy smile and shrug. "Guilty as charged."

The next thing I know, she's shrieking and jumping around like a fool. The baby starts crying, Bonny begins to bark, and I'm doubled over laughing.

"Jesus, fuck. You three scared me to death." Renzo barrels

into the doorway, his frantic eyes wide. D is close behind him. "You okay?"

Shae and Mom assure him everything is fine. He runs a mystified hand through his hair, muttering to himself about lunatics as he ushers DiAngelo back toward the office.

Shae quiets the baby with a pacifier, then sits back at the table. "Sit. Spill."

It's a good thing I'm okay talking about it because judging by the look on both their faces, I'm not leaving this room without a full recounting of the past six weeks.

"Let's see ... I suppose it started that first night he was assigned to protect me..."

CHAPTER 54
D'Angelo

"How long?" Renzo demands as soon as we round the corner to his office.

"That's hard to say. It's sort of developed ever since the beginning," I admit.

"And you didn't think that fucking my sister was something I ought to know about?"

I try to keep calm because I understand why he's upset, but where Rina is concerned, my instincts are quick to defend and protect her. "I'm not just fucking your sister, Renzo. I wouldn't do that to you."

His hands go to his hips. "What then? You two are serious about one another, and still, you didn't say anything?"

Jesus, this is a clusterfuck.

"I was going to tell you right now. That's why I wanted a few minutes alone."

"And the past six weeks?"

I run my hand through my hair and sigh. "Things were ... complicated. It was hard to say anything when I didn't know where she and I stood."

He mulls over my words, his lips pressed into a thin line, but before he can respond, all hell breaks loose in the kitchen. Screaming, barking, crying. We crash into one another trying to race into the hallway at the same time.

He makes it to the kitchen first, stopping so that I have to peer over his shoulder to see what's going on.

"Jesus, fuck. You three scared me to death," he huffs. "You okay?"

All three women are pink-cheeked and fighting back grins.

"Yes, baby. I'm so sorry. We got carried away." Shae stands and tries to rock the baby back to sleep.

"We're fine, I promise," Azzurra chimes in.

Rina stares at me with wide, guilty eyes, and her lips pulled between her teeth. The secret is definitely out of the bag.

Renzo shakes his head. "Absolute lunatics acting like they don't know the danger they're in." His mumbled words carry back to me as we return to the office.

He drops into his desk chair. I sit opposite him and meet his level stare.

"You're the closest thing I have to a brother since I lost my own," I offer quietly. "I would never disrespect your sister or recklessly hurt her. Things just sort of ... happened. No, I didn't say anything, and I'm sorry for that. I love her, and if she'll have me, I want to marry her."

His chest expands on a long, deep breath. "Well, fuck. That was unexpected."

"You're telling me." I lean back in my chair and rub at the scruff on my jaw. "I can hardly believe it myself, but that's where we're at."

His eyes narrow a fraction. "I suppose she could have done worse."

Relief coaxes a smile from me. "You willing to keep me around as your brother-in-law?"

"Yeah, that could work." The levity between us dries up as worry deepens the creases on his face. "Before that happens, we have to end this threat, though."

"Agreed," I say somberly and get out my phone. "The team covering a place called Feathers and Fur has noted the same couple of guys coming and going. Not Pasha, but suspected to be his men. I think this is it. I'm picking up a floor plan from city records while I'm out today. We could be ready to raid tonight, if you're on board."

His face is grim. "I'm not rushing into this, D. Let's see what I hear from the Genoveses before we make any decisions."

I have to swallow back the argument that perches on the tip of my tongue. In my opinion, the time for patience is over, but he's my boss, and I have to respect that.

"There's one more thing I wanted to talk about." I adjust myself in my chair, unsure how what I'm about to say will be received. "Did you know Kristi Kirkland told Terina that Craig was killed because of her?"

"Are you fucking serious?"

"I'm afraid it's even worse. She told Terina about the quarters, saying Craig was being extorted to keep her safe."

"That's not what happened at all." He slams his fist on the desk.

"I know, man. But she didn't know that. She went to the cops and saw the crime scene photos."

"*Jesus Christ,*" he breathes.

"She's been blaming herself. I explained the truth. I hope you're okay with that. I know you said you didn't want her to know, but—"

"You did the right thing. I had no idea she thought that. I mean ... she asked one time early on if there was more to it, but that's it. She never said anything else."

"We haven't gone over it too much, so I'm not sure why she didn't say more to you. All I know is what she's told me and what I've looked into. That mother-in-law of hers is a real piece of work. You know she had prostitution charges brought against her?"

"Jesus, you're a font of good fucking news today," he grumbles. "No, I didn't. We did a check on the son, and he was clean. It didn't occur to me his *mother* would be an issue."

"I've cut her off from Terina, but I'd like to do a little more digging in case she makes another appearance. Stains like that have a way of resurfacing."

Renzo nods and grabs a piece of paper. "This is the name of the dealer he was using. I considered taking care of him but decided whoever was responsible for the hit did us a favor, so I let it be." He scribbles the name and gives me the paper. "He's one of Fat Joe's guys. Used to keep shop at the Qwik Wash Laundromat on East 119th, I believe."

"A laundromat?"

"They have a back room with girls."

"Ah, that makes more sense." I tuck the paper in my pocket. "I'll let you know what I find."

Renzo's phone begins to vibrate on the desk.

"It's Enzo Genovese." He answers the call, says a few short words, then scribbles an address on the notepad before hanging up. "We're meeting his underboss, Gabriele Fiore, tomorrow morning."

"What are we going to do with the girls?"

He rubs his face while he thinks. "I'll get with Cosimo. Let's all stay there tonight so we don't have to worry about transporting everyone before the meeting. I'll have our outside detail come with us."

"Sounds like a plan. Guess the girls will get their outing after all."

"Let's hope it gets us closer to ending this thing."

A few minutes later, I'm back in my car. I make the drive to city records, where I confirm the plats I had printed are the correct renderings. The shop is bigger than I expected. That helps explain why he'd choose it as a hideout. Someone with a struggling business, like a taxidermist in the middle of the city, is a prime candidate to pocket some money while letting Pasha run operations out of a back room.

I'm going to put a serious crimp in those plans.

Satisfied, I look up the address for the Qwik Wash Laundromat. It's all the way up in East Harlem and will take a while to get over there, but it'll be worth it if I can find this guy.

Billy Ikes—ready or not, here I come.

CHAPTER 55

DiAngelo

"Hey, you can't just barge in here." A curvy woman in a hot-pink tube top glares at me, hands on her hips.

I ignore her and survey the small room tucked away at the back of the building where I entered from the alley. If they didn't want people coming in this way, they should have locked the door. Now that my eyes are adjusting to the dim light, I can see the walls are painted black. It's an entry room, only big enough for a bistro-sized table and one chair. Each of the four walls contains a door.

"Whatta you deaf?" the woman calls even louder. "This ain't no public restroom or somethin'. You's gotta get out."

"I'm here to see Billy Ikes."

Her eyes narrow as she crosses her arms over her chest. "Never heard of him."

The door behind her swings open, revealing a middle-aged man with a mustache and the beginning of a mullet. And to top it off, he's wearing a blue tracksuit with a thick silver chain.

Honest to God, I didn't know they made assholes like this anymore.

"There a problem out here?" he asks, puffing out his chest. The dude doesn't weigh one fifty soaking wet. His posturing in front of me is laughable, but I let it go.

"I have a couple of questions for Billy Ikes—that you?"

"Who wants to know?"

"Name's DiAngelo. I'm with the Morettis. I understand Billy works for Fat Joe, and we had a couple of questions."

The guy eyes me warily. "Whatdoya wanna know?"

"You Billy Ikes?"

He sniffs, looking briefly at the woman before stepping back. "Let's talk in here."

Excellent.

I follow him into a small office lined with seventies-era wood paneling. The man truly is a relic from the past. Behind his desk is a credenza with two monitors, one showing an empty room with a twin bed in it. If I had to guess, I'd say one of the other doors leads to that room, which is where Miss Pink Tube Top would be working if she had a client.

We both sit. I don't want him getting trigger-happy, so I decide to concede some ground and see where it gets me.

"It's my understanding Billy had a customer named Craig Kirkland about five years ago."

He huffs. "Five years is a long-ass time. You expect a man to remember some rando junkie from that long ago?"

"This rando ended up stabbed five times with a roll of quarters down his throat. That ring a bell?"

Feigned concentration forms an exaggerated frown on his face. "Billy might remember that from the news, but I doubt he knows more than that."

The man across from me is Billy fucking Ikes, and his insistence on playing this little game is grating on my nerves.

"Look, I don't give a fuck about why the guy was killed or who killed him. I want to know what the guy was into—what was his drug of choice and what sort of bets he was making."

"How about this? You let me talk to Billy. Come back another day, and I'll let you know what he has to say."

I sigh with a nod and begin to stand, making sure before I do so that Billy's hands are visible, but instead of turning for the door, I reach across the small desk and slam his face into the wooden surface. I round the desk and fist his hair, only to come away with a toupee in my hand. I curse and grab the man by his throat instead.

"My patience has dried up, Billy," I growl through clenched teeth. "Tell me what the fuck you know about Kirkland."

"Tool," he sputters. "Dude was a tool. One of those finance guys—the kind that toyed with addy and blow—

nothing hard-core." He tugs at my hand with manicured nails. I squeeze harder.

"And the gambling?"

"You know the type—always thought the next bet would be his big break. Ended up down several hundred k. That's all I know."

None of this is unexpected. I was hoping for something that might give me insight into who the guy was or how he went from NYU graduate to deadbeat in such a short time.

"How'd he end up buying from you? Who introduced you?"

"His ma ... she brought him when he was in school."

Jesus, that woman is even more vile than I realized. She got her own son into drugs and then had the gall to blame Terina.

My hand clenches in fury.

"C'mon, man ... told you ... what I know." His breathless rasp reminds me I don't actually want to kill the man.

I let him go and head out the door while he devolves into a coughing fit. He only has himself to blame. Fucking moron. I'll have to call Fat Joe to smooth things over, but it shouldn't be a problem. I can do it on my way to Kristi Kirkland's apartment. It's time she and I had a few words.

I LET myself into Kristi's place when no one answers the door —the building's old enough that cameras aren't a problem. She's got a deadbolt, but that doesn't stop me. I wouldn't be any good at tracking if I hadn't mastered how to get in and out of places undetected.

The apartment would have been stylish back in the late nineties. Ceramic tile countertops with stained oak cabinetry in the kitchen. Floral wallpaper in the living room. Brass fixtures and forest-green carpeting.

Fast-forward twenty-five years, and it's not only dated but dirty.

She's a smoker, so a thin coating of nicotine film mars the windows and mirrors. Every surface is cluttered with crap—magazines and food wrappers and random toiletries strewn about. She even has knickknacks like little troll dolls and stuffed bears wedged between dishes in her china cabinet. None of it looks like it's been cleaned in this century.

I'm going to need to fucking disinfect myself after being here.

I do my best to poke around without touching anything and find several surveillance-type printed pictures of couples having sex, along with a package of manila envelopes. They're piled on her dresser, and judging by the looks of it, I'd say she's running a blackmail operation. The couples are all different, but the room is the same. She's got a camera some-where. Maybe even an accomplice, but I'm not worried about that.

The other noteworthy find is a veritable pharmacy of drugs. Prescription and illicit—she's got them all like some warped collector. Most of the bottles and baggies don't have much in them, but the assortment is vast.

What I don't see anywhere are photos of her son. In fact,

there are no noticeable signs of his existence. No baby pictures. No wedding portrait. Nothing.

People process grief differently. I get that. But after everything I've learned, I think this soulless bitch simply doesn't care.

Every second I spend in this vacuum of humanity makes my skin crawl. I'm actually relieved when I hear the lock click over, announcing her return home.

I wait to make sure she's locked inside before I round the corner. I don't want her trying to run, though I should know better. This sort of evil doesn't know fear.

"Well, if it isn't the Jolly Green Giant," she sneers while dropping a tote bag on the sofa. "Didn't anyone ever tell you steroids shrink your dick?"

"Better than all that Botox eating away at my brain." My jab strikes a nerve. At least, I think it does. It's hard to tell when her face is so immobile from botulism.

"What the fuck are you doing in my house? That bitch send you? She thinks she can ignore my texts, but it's not like I can't find her."

Easy, D. You're not here to kill the woman.

I force my body to relax, which isn't easy. She's got me pissed right the fuck off.

"Terina isn't getting your texts because your number is blocked."

She scoffs. "Little chickenshit can't run from reality."

"And what reality is that? You getting your son hooked on drugs and gambling? Sounds like a you problem," I point out evenly.

"He graduated with honors because of me," she spits angrily. "Besides, it never would have been a problem if it wasn't for you people." She jabs a bony finger in my direction.

My head tilts a fraction. "I know you don't believe that."

"I know he would have run if it wasn't for her. Got his passport and everything. He wouldn't ever get on a plane because of *her*."

So that's it. "You torture her with blame because in the end, he chose her."

The way she glares at me tells me everything I need to know. I shake my head slowly and start for the door.

She lifts her chin haughtily as I walk past. "He was *my* son. He wouldn't have been alive if it wasn't for me. I laid down my life for him, and he was so sickeningly infatuated, he threw it all away for someone who was utterly worthless. I could see it coming, too. Unlike her, I'm smart enough to read between the lines. I even took out a life insurance policy on him because I knew he'd end up dead because of that whore. If she's tortured with guilt, then good. She deserves it."

And there it is.

My breaking point.

Not only has she inflicted horrific pain on innocent lives but she has also profited from it with zero conscience. This sorry excuse for a human does not deserve to take up space in this world.

Fuck the consequences.

My hands shoot out lightning fast and pull her back against my front. With my left arm across her front to hold her in place, I use my right hand to whip her head around and snap the fragile bones in her neck.

Kristi Kirkland is mid-shriek when her body goes slack.

Killing someone has never been so easy or guilt-free. Because *fuck her*.

She's lucky I didn't draw it out. She's not worthy of the time it would take. I don't even do her the dignity of setting her down gently. Her bony body collapses to the floor, hitting the coffee table on her way down. Good.

I get out my phone and dial Grisha.

"You know I hate phones," he says in greeting.

"Yeah, but you answered." I fight back a smirk.

"What do you want?"

Now I'm full-on grinning. "I wanted to know if your boat is going out in the morning."

"It goes out most mornings," he says noncommittally. "You looking to fish?"

"I have a donation if you're looking for chum."

"Aren't you thoughtful." His amusement carries across the phone line.

"I'll have someone bring it by tonight."

"Next time, you should come with me."

My smile flattens. "You know I'm not a fan of boats."

"Eh, one day. I'll keep trying."

"You do that." I hang up. We don't do goodbyes. It's an unusual relationship between us, but it works.

Next, I call my guys.

"I'm going to need you to bring me a suitcase—bigger than a carry-on, but it doesn't have to be huge." I give them the address and instructions to come through the back. They can get cunty Kristi over to Grisha for me so that I can get back to Terina. She's still in danger from Pasha, but at least the Kirklands are out of her life forever.

Hopefully, tomorrow's meeting with the Genoveses will get us that much closer to putting Pasha's head on a spike. He's drawn this out so damn long, there's no way he's getting off easy. I won't allow it. If Renzo disagrees, we're going to have a real problem.

CHAPTER 56
Terina

"I NEED TO TELL YOU SOMETHING BEFORE YOU GO PACK," D says once we're home from Renzo's. It's just a quick stop-in to get a bag together before staying at Isa's dad's place for the night. It sort of reminds me of packing a bag after the snake incident, except this time, everything's different.

Instead of feeling scared and alone, I have DiAngelo. Not just as my bodyguard, but as my partner. I'm still worried for him. I don't think that will ever change. But I'm not battling a constant sense of doom.

"What's that?" I respond warmly.

"While I was out today, I made a couple of unplanned stops. One of them was to see Kristi."

"Oh." That was unexpected. "What for?"

"You already know she was lying to you, but it turns out, she was the one who introduced Craig to her dealer slash bookie. Her shifting any blame to you was pure spite. You know she had a life insurance policy on him?" The disgust drips from his words when he talks about Kristi. I don't blame him.

"No, I ... I had no idea."

"That woman was pure evil. I don't know how you put up with her as long as you did."

His words play in slow-motion through my mind.

"Was? She *was* pure evil?"

D approaches, cupping my face with his hands, his eyes razor sharp. "Evil will not touch you so long as I have breath in my body. That sort of evil had no place in this world."

My chest hollows out on a long exhale as though I've had the breath knocked out of me.

DiAngelo killed Kristi.

He killed her ... for me, and he's telling me because he doesn't want secrets between us. Is it wrong that my first reaction is hope? Hope for us and hope that he doesn't get caught.

"Okay," I say softly, then wrap my arms around his middle and hold him close. His coiled muscles relax beneath my touch. He was worried about my reaction but told me anyway, and that means the world to me. That means he trusts me.

I pull back and raise my lips for a kiss. He doesn't keep me waiting.

An hour later, we're settling into Cosimo's house with Bonny. Renzo and Shae arrive shortly after us with little Liora and all her gear. Isa's staying the night, as well. The chaos is fun in a way, but it amps up my anxiety. I have no control over this situation, and when uncertainty like this hits in the evening, it makes everything worse.

"You're awfully quiet," DiAngelo whispers so the others don't overhear.

We're in the living room chatting with everyone. He and I are sitting smooshed together on the couch—it's the first time we've been close around family. Isa and Shae keep grinning at me like idiots. Ordinarily, it wouldn't bother me, but with all the uncertainty, their scrutiny, even the happy kind, still feels unsettling.

"Yeah, I'm fine." My attempt at a smile must not be all that convincing.

D raises a disbelieving brow. "You sure?"

You can be honest, Rina. Trust him, remember?

"It's just a lot to process—the events, staying at a new place, and lots of people talking and the uncertainty. It's just a lot." That's the best way I know how to describe it.

He presses a kiss to my forehead before rising, bringing me with him. "We're calling it a night," he announces to the room. "Renzo, I'll be ready by seven."

Relief washes over me when he takes my hand and leads me from the room, Bonny close at our heels.

"Thank you, D."

"No skin off my back. I'd rather have time alone with you anyway." He squeezes my hand, bringing a smile to my face that I feel deep in my chest. "I was wondering, though, if you've ever talked to someone about this stuff—a professional."

"Like a therapist?"

"Yeah."

"Not exactly."

"How come? I know I'm probably not one to talk, but if you don't like it when you get overwhelmed, wouldn't it be good to get help with it?" His tone is feathered with worry rather than judgment, which keeps me from feeling defensive at his question. He genuinely wants the best for me.

"I considered it, but it's been drilled into me since I was little that we don't discuss our lives with outsiders. Opening up to a therapist would mean telling them *everything*. I could never forgive myself if the feds went after my family because of me."

"That's honorable of you, babe, but fuck that. Your mental health comes first, and I know your family would agree. Besides, there are some sort of patient confidentiality rules. I say, you should give it a try to see if it helps."

"That's what Isa said."

"You talked to her about it?"

"Yeah."

"Good." He leads us into our room and pauses, a smirk teasing his lips. "If it helps you feel more comfortable, I could always have a word with the therapist first to make sure they understand the importance of discretion."

I purse my lips in thought. "I suppose that would give them valuable insight into what I'm up against."

"Up against?" His brows rise high on his forehead, playfully. "I'll show you up against."

The next thing I know, my back is flush with the wall, and D's mouth is plundering mine. We shower together in the en suite bathroom. It's smaller than we're used to, leading to a lot of touching, which results in a lot of sex.

I'm feeling far more relaxed by the time I crawl into bed. DiAngelo is scrolling on his phone when I join him. He lifts the covers to draw me close to him.

"Come watch with me."

Tucked against his body, I'm wrapped in contentment while watching a video of a horse splashing in a drainage ditch and covering its rider in mud. His chest rumbles with muted laughter beneath me, and I outright giggle. He scrolls to the next video, which is a compilation of dogs twitching and snoring in their sleep.

We spend almost an hour immersed in silly animal videos. It's an incredible distraction, as he intended. I forget my worries entirely, and when the lights go out, I'm too exhausted to dredge them up. Within minutes, I'm fast asleep.

My fears must stay with me, however, because I wake extra early. The sun isn't even up, yet I'm wide awake. I know I'll fidget and disrupt his sleep if I stay, so I ease out of the bed and quietly slip from the room.

We're staying on the second floor, where most of the bedrooms are located. I could go kill time in the living room downstairs, but I'd feel awkward down there alone with Cosimo if he happened to be up. I'd rather find somewhere else to chill for a bit until the others wake up.

Our bedroom is across from Isa's, and Renzo's family is staying down the hall. There's another bedroom by theirs and one next to ours. I decide to check out the one closest to us, hoping I'll hear D when he gets up. Cracking open the door, I turn on the light and realize right away where I am. This was Isa's brother's room.

It doesn't appear as though anything has changed since he passed years ago. There's no dust, so it gets cleaned, but otherwise, the room is a monument to the loss this family suffered.

Their heartbreak bleeds into me.

This room isn't meant to be disturbed. I begin to back out when my eyes catch sight of a framed photo on the dresser. My body locks down tight, refusing to budge.

A boy who I assume is Isa's brother stands between a pair of twin boys—DiAngelo and Elio. They're in their midteens, their bodies in the process of transforming from boys to men. All three wear matching grins of pure joy.

Before I know what I'm doing, I have the picture frame in my hands and am absorbing everything I can about this glimpse into the past. Tragedy struck this group of friends, and poor D is the only one who remains.

I can't imagine how hard that must have been.

While I lost Craig, DiAngelo lost not only his twin but also their good friend, all in a relatively short timeframe. My heart breaks for him, yet I'm so grateful I have the chance to bring a hint of that joy back to his life. I don't fully understand why my neurotic self appeals to him, but it does, and that makes me incredibly lucky.

I wish sweet Isa could know this feeling.

I'd be willing to bet her avoidance of relationships stems from the same fear I was experiencing. A fear of loss. But what I'm now realizing is the loneliness of isolation is still losing, it's just a surrender rather than a defeat.

A guarded heart gives up before the battle even starts.

Instead of suffering an acute injury and subsequent recovery, living in fear is a withering starvation that drains the soul over a lifetime. A pain that never heals.

By setting aside our fears, DiAngelo and I are choosing to fight for a better future.

I set down the photo and say a silent prayer that Isa will meet someone who challenges her to do the same. Not wanting to skulk around anymore, I go back to our room and sneak back under the covers. D pulls me into his arms.

"Everything okay?" he murmurs groggily.

"Yeah, everything's good." Inspired by my revelation, I decide to be big brave and take a leap of faith. "D?"

"Hmm?"

Do it, you've got this.

"I love you, and I'm so grateful you're in my life."

His eyes open and shower me with devotion. "I had forgotten what love was until you reminded me. You have become my everything, firefly."

Tears burn the backs of my eyes as I bring my lips to his in a tender kiss.

CHAPTER 57
DiAngelo

Gabriele Fiore is the underboss of the Lucciano Family, who deals primarily in construction, while the ports are our territory. Business can overlap, but for the most part, we aren't direct rivals. The old Italians set it up that way years ago to stop infighting. The five Italian operations in New York and a couple of Chicago outfits even joined up to form a commission to keep things civil.

All that to say, today's meeting should be amicable. *Should* being the keyword.

I never take anything for granted. We make a show of

leaving weapons at the door, but I'm still armed. I don't care who I'm meeting with, I'm not going in naked.

Fiore has three guys with him. My guess is, they're carrying, too, along with Tommy and Sante, who met up with us before the meeting. Four of us from each family, all eyeing one another warily.

"Renzo, I appreciate your willingness to meet on such short notice," Fiore says after we've all gathered around a rustic wooden table in the basement of an old Italian restaurant in Lucciano territory. Their meeting, their pick of locations.

"We appreciate your cooperation on this and look forward to being able to return the favor."

Fiore nods once, acknowledging the debt. "I'd like to introduce you to Nico Conti. He has an old family connection to Michael Savin. He's done a little digging for us."

All eyes turn to Nico.

"My wife, Sofia, is friends with Michael—the two had a bit of a business arrangement for a number of years. As time passed, we haven't been in contact with him quite as much. He became more involved in Biba's operations, and that was a challenge. Sofia reached out to him this week after you raised concerns. He never responded, which is unlike him. His wife is a therapist. We went by her office and found it locked up with a note to patients taped to the door."

"Sounds like their disappearance was intentional on their part," I note.

Nico nods. "My guess is he's in hiding. I don't know why else they'd vanish voluntarily. But even so, it surprises me he wouldn't reach out to Sofia, especially if he was in trouble. They were close at one time."

Renzo leans back, frowning. "Are you aware that Biba's old garage was fire-bombed recently?"

"We are," says Fiore. "Heard it was Reaper, but I'm wondering if Pasha put that out there to keep the heat off him."

"Attacking his brother would make sense after being cut off from the business."

We're all silent as we consider the implications of Renzo's comment, which makes the basement door opening that much more noticeable. Everyone stills, hands poised to reach for concealed weapons as a young soldier jogs down the wooden stairs.

"Excuse me, sir. I'm sorry to interrupt." The poor kid's eyes dart around the room, and I can practically smell the sweat pouring off him. He leans in and whispers to Fiore, who nods. The kid takes off up the stairs before another booted pair of feet begins to descend.

This new man joining us is no child. His steps are confident and controlled.

Fiore and his men, who had their backs to the stairs, stand and face the newcomer. He's younger than me but not at all wet behind the ears. His jet-black hair is only rivaled in darkness by his calculating stare. The skin of his neck is covered in tattoos, as are the backs of his hands and fingers, which is all that can be seen beneath his black shirt and pants. The man knows how to make a statement.

"If it isn't Michael Savin," Fiore says dryly. "We've been looking for you."

"That's not Michael," Tommy blurts. "That's a fucking assassin working for the Reaper." He draws a throwing knife, which instigates the appearance of an arsenal of weapons and shouts for everyone to calm down.

Nico crosses the room and stands in front of Michael. "Drop your *fucking* guns. This *is* Michael Savin."

The man in all black steps out from behind Nico, looking completely unaffected. "I am Michael, but we don't have time for introductions beyond that. I'm here to let you know Pasha got word of your meeting. He's rigged the place with C-4." He turns his piercing gaze to Tommy. "The Reaper would like you to know, his debt is paid."

We all stand with our thumbs up our asses, stunned as he calmly walks back up the stairs. I have so many questions. So much confusion.

"Shit, we need to get outta here," says one of the Luccianos.

All eight of us bolt for the stairs, shoving our way up as fast as we can.

"Everyone get the fuck out!" Fiore yells inside the small restaurant on our way to the front entrance. "The place is rigged to blow."

We stumble into the street. I note a black SUV turning a corner down the block, which must have been Michael's ride, since the man is nowhere to be seen.

All of us look around, huffing for air and wondering if we've just been pranked when the entire restaurant erupts in flames. The windows explode onto the street while the shock wave sends us tumbling backward. I can feel the goddamn heat on my face from twenty feet away.

"*Fucking Russian scum*," Fiore bellows, wiping dirt and sweat from his face. "They'll fucking pay for this." He turns to Renzo and extends a steady hand. "I believe we now have a common enemy."

The two shake hands, signaling the start of a new alliance.

"I hope you know we didn't mean to drag you into this," Renzo says solemnly.

"Those fuckers had a choice. They knew this was our territory. They chose war. That has nothing to do with you."

Renzo nods. "It might be good for the Russians and this Reaper to have a reminder that the Italians still stick together."

"Agreed." His eyes narrow in thought. "In fact, I propose we go back to old traditions and set a precedent with a wedding uniting our two families. A signal that can't be ignored. I'll need to make sure the boss is on board, but I think he will be if you are."

I watch Renzo carefully, curious how he'll answer. Eventually, he nods. "I'll also discuss it with the family and see if we have anyone willing to fill that role."

The two shake again as sirens grow closer.

"Time for us to go," I prod, relieved when Renzo leads us away from the burning building to our cars. Tommy and Sante abandon their car and pile in with us so we can discuss the situation.

"Does that mean Michael is working with the Reaper?" I ask no one in particular.

"Sounds like it," Renzo says. "Considering he claimed to be The Reaper's messenger. His debt is paid. Only The Reaper would know we killed Biba and left him and his shooter alive."

"Think he could be The Reaper?" That would be something—the man the Russians were at war with for months hiding in plain sight.

"Not unless the rumors were false about his scars," Tommy cuts in.

"True," Renzo responds. "And we've heard word about the scars on his neck from multiple sources."

"Still, how did one of the Russians end up with Reaper?" The revelation floors me. I thought the two groups hated one another.

"I'd like to know how everyone knew our goddamn business—Pasha learning about the meeting and Reaper knowing Pasha knew. We putting up fucking billboards I don't know about?" Renzo is pissed, and he has every right to be. I expect the Luccianos and Morettis are both going to do some major in-house clean-up.

Out of nowhere, Renzo pulls the car into a parking lot and turns around. I meet Sante's eyes in the rearview mirror, both of us wondering what's going on.

"They think they've got us on the run, but they can't know our plans if we move without warning. We're going to go find that fucking Russian piece of shit and rip his fucking heart out. I'm done playing safe."

CHAPTER 58
DiAngelo

PRESENT

Tommy, Sante, Renzo, and I meet with three other guys at one of our safe houses. We arm ourselves with enough gear to wage an all-out battle, including communication earpieces. And last, but not least, we all familiarize ourselves with the layout of the taxidermy shop.

It doubles as a pseudo-museum, meaning it's not just a front desk with a small workshop space in the back. There's over five thousand square feet to hide. Luckily, we should have the element of surprise.

On the way over, we decide that Renzo and I'll take two

soldiers with us through the front, and Sante and Tommy will take the third man with them through the back. I wait for them to get in place before signaling my team to leave the car. We keep our weapons holstered to draw as little attention as possible, then take out our guns as soon as we slip inside.

The door chimes, announcing our arrival.

"We're in," I say softly over the comms device while surveying the entry. Animals and insects of all varieties are frozen mid-motion, posing for eternity. They're everywhere. If I had the time to truly take in the spectacle, it would be creepy as fuck.

"We're in, as well," Sante's voice sounds in my earpiece.

My gaze lands on a man across the room, standing as stock-still as the carcasses surrounding us. He's reed thin with a thick mustache and round magnifiers hinged onto his wire-rimmed glasses. He blinks, then bolts toward the back.

"We've got a man on the run, heading your way," I warn while launching into pursuit. It doesn't last long. After rounding two corners, I come to a halt. The taxidermist stands with his hands raised in the middle of the space. Our two teams have him surrounded.

"Got him," Sante says with a note of wicked amusement.

"Please, I no do anything. Have no money," says the shop owner with a heavy Russian accent.

I charge forward and grab his shirt, hauling him up off his feet. "Where the fuck is Pasha?" I growl the words with unrestrained savagery. He needs to know I'm not fucking around.

"He not here. Please," he whimpers. The acrid smell of urine hits my nostrils.

Jesus Christ, he pissed himself.

I toss him against a nearby wall, then crouch over him, snarling. "Tell me where the fuck he is, or I will skin you alive and stuff you like one of your creations."

His entire body is consumed in violent tremors, but he manages to nod his head toward the opposite wall.

I peer back. "Is there something on the other side of that wall?"

He nods.

"Tommy, circle around."

He takes off, and we all wait for his return, which only takes a few seconds.

"Seems to be a room sectioned off. The door is just around the corner."

I narrow my eyes at the man. "They going to be waiting in there for us?"

"No, they leave. Not here."

"If you're lying, I will kill you. Understand?"

He clenches his eyes shut and nods.

"You two check it out. Be ready," I instruct Tommy and Sante.

They round the corner and disappear.

"All clear." Sante's voice comes through the comms device.

I take two zip ties from a pocket and secure the taxidermist, then join the others in what seems to be the main workshop. There are bright spotlights instead of windows and shelves full of equipment and chemicals. A central table in the middle of the room is covered in peacock parts. There's another table against a wall that hosts a laptop and papers. This looks more promising.

We gather around and see scribbled notes, news articles, and piles of photos. Terina walking into yoga. Terina at a coffee shop with Isa. There's a photo of Azzurra, but the majority are of Terina ... and Isa.

"Why's he got pictures of Isa?" I ask, thinking out loud.

Renzo sifts through the piles. "Those are more recent. It looks like everything beneath is all Terina." He stills, then looks at me. "Do you think he could have given up on his first target and shifted tactics?"

My heart pounds against my rib cage.

"Fucking hell," I hiss.

We both take out our phones, our murderous stares colliding when neither Shae nor Terina answers.

"We've got to get back to Cosimo's," Renzo demands hoarsely.

We all run as though death itself were on our heels.

CHAPTER 59

Terina

PRESENT

"WHERE'S SHAE?" COSIMO DEMANDS AFTER WHIRLING into the room, his eyes manic. Mom, Isa, and I stare back at him, stunned.

"She's putting the baby down to sleep," Isa answers. "What's—"

"There's no time. Come with me." He races toward the stairs with us close behind, including Bonny, whose instincts have her on high alert. Adrenaline surges into my bloodstream as my brain tries to identify what's happened. Or maybe more accurately, what's about to happen.

Cosimo flings open Shae's bedroom door. "Grab the baby. We're going to the safe room."

Shae scoops up Liora and joins us without hesitation, taking an extra second to grab a gun as well. She's a badass like that. Her face is all business, like she's not even fazed. I don't know how she does it. I'm unraveling at the seams.

We follow Cosimo back downstairs to his office, where he angles a book so that it's sticking out of the shelf, revealing a keypad. He enters a series of numbers, and a section of the bookshelf swings open into a secret room. We hurry inside after he turns on the light. The thick metal door clinks shut behind us.

The room is simple with a single overhead light. It's a square—about eight feet on either side—and while it's enough for the five of us to fit comfortably, someone with claustrophobia would be struggling. The only objects in the room are a small chair and a metal desk with a computer monitor.

"What's happened?" Mom asks in a hushed whisper.

"I'm not exactly sure. I just got word from DiAngelo saying we needed to get to the safe room." He sits in the chair and turns on the monitor. There's no computer, just a monitor plugged into the wall.

I have Bonny sit, then join the others around the monitor. When it blinks to life, eight separate camera feeds fill the screen. We can see the guards stationed outside at the front and rear of the house. Several cameras are also inside the home.

I get out my phone with the intent to text D. "I don't have any signal. What about you?" I ask Isa.

She shakes her head. "You can't get a signal in here. It's built so that electronics can't be tracked, but it also means we can't call out."

"There they are," Cosimo says in a grave tone.

My first thought is he means DiAngelo is back, but when I look at the screen, I can tell that's not right. The men approaching the house have guns pointed at our guards. Gunfire rings out a fraction of a second before the delayed feed shows shots fired. The sound is muffled inside this vault of a room, but gunfire is hard to miss.

My hand clamps tight over my mouth to hold back the horror.

We're being attacked.

Is this room bulletproof? What if they try to burn the place down? Are Renzo and DiAngelo on their way? What if they end up in a shoot-out?

Nausea hits me with such intensity that my head spins.

"They've breached the entry," Cosimo reports.

None of us makes a sound as we watch the monitors. The different angles make it hard for me to tell how many men there are. Three or maybe four. It's not a ton, but it wouldn't take many if we hadn't had the panic room to hide in. I pray it holds out until help arrives.

I don't even breathe when I see two of the men enter Cosimo's office. They're only a few feet away from where we hide. And while the door is thick, I have no idea about the walls. I'm wondering how soundproof the room is when sweet, tiny Liora lets loose a wail.

Both men whip around to face the bookshelves.

CHAPTER 60
DiAngelo

I've called all of their phones—Terina, Shae, Isa, Cosimo, and even Azzurra. I've left messages. Renzo has called. We've tried over and over without success. I keep thinking that if I try one more time, maybe I'll get through. Because if they don't get word...

I can't even think about what might happen.

Renzo informed us that Cosimo has a safe room. I can only hope that, if Pasha did go after them, they had enough time and warning to reach safety.

Please, God, let them be safe.

Aside from the phone calls, we're silent on the drive. The concentrated fear filling the car is so dense that the pressure pushes in on me, making it hard to breathe and pounding against my skull.

Renzo breaks at least a dozen traffic laws. He runs lights. Drives on the sidewalk. He even scrapes the entire side of the new SUV along a light post to squeeze around traffic. After what feels like an eternity, we pull up at Cosimo's house, where the guards are now motionless on the ground near the entry.

The car doesn't come to a complete stop before I eject myself, gun in hand. The others are close behind me. I run across the large yard and confirm two of the men down are dead—one is ours, the other is theirs. The third man is unconscious but alive.

"Let's stick to the same plan—Tommy and Sante, your team enters from the rear. D and I will take the others through the front."

Everyone nods to Renzo's command and falls into step with the appropriate team. We're stepping through the front entry when a spray of rapid gunfire bursts through the air in the distance.

"The east wing," I say.

"That's where the safe room is," Renzo adds.

We take a few steps in that direction when two shots ring out behind us.

Tommy's voice comes over the comm. "We got one."

That's one less, but it also means the others are probably aware they're no longer alone. We move down the hallway as one. A head peeks out from a doorway, then disappears. The door slams shut.

Renzo spits out a curse. "It's time to give up, Pasha," he bellows. "We have you outnumbered and surrounded."

"I don't think so, you fucking cocksuckers. You owe me!" He sounds crazed, which is never a good sign.

I tap Renzo's shoulder and motion that I'm heading back outside. He nods, calling out to Pasha again while I hurry back to the front door. Once I'm outside, I hug the perimeter of the house until I get to the office windows. Slowly, I take the tiniest peek into the room, then retreat, careful not to disturb the bushes behind me.

"It's Pasha and two others," I inform our group via the comm. "Very armed. I can take them, but I need a distraction." One of the men is watching the window. The second I show myself, his gun is pointed and ready to fire.

Renzo's voice buzzes in my ear. "Got it. You tell me when."

"Make sure you stay clear of the door." I don't want to accidentally shoot one of my own guys.

I double-check my gun. "Good on your count."

"Three, two, one..."

Gunfire explodes inside the house.

I step in front of the window, gun raised. As I'd hoped, all three men inside are now facing the door to the office in anticipation of being stormed. I pluck them off through the window like apples on a fence post, putting multiple bullets in each of them.

"All clear!" I shout.

Renzo and the rest of our guys, all seven of them, pour into the room. I bolt for the front door to join them back inside, pushing through the crowd until I'm standing with Renzo as the bookcase door swings open.

The first thing I hear is Bonny growling.

"Settle, Bonny," I issue evenly.

She immediately starts to whine with eagerness to see me. Everyone in the safe room emerges in perfect health. I've never been so damn relieved in my life.

Terina's eyes are brimming with tears when she flings herself into my arms. I hold her so damn tight I have to remind myself to let her breathe. Out of the corner of my eye, I see Renzo doing the same with Shae while the others quietly talk among themselves.

Eventually, I pull back, needing to see Rina's face and reassure myself she's okay.

"You're not hurt?"

"No, you?" she asks.

"We're all fine, though the guards here at the house didn't fare so well."

Her face melts with sadness. "It was so awful. We could see it on the monitor but had no way to help them."

I hug her to me again. "I'm so sorry you had to go through that. I was terrified when we realized Pasha was likely going after Isa. We couldn't get here fast enough."

"I don't even want to think about what would have happened if you hadn't warned Cosimo."

"So he did get my message?"

She nods. "He had us so freaked out. I didn't have a

chance to look at my phone until we were in the safe room, and then we didn't have a signal. It was so scary."

"You did incredible. All of you."

Rina's gaze drops to the floor, where three dead men lie at our feet. I'd been so concentrated on seeing her that I forgot to consider how upsetting it might be to see the bloody remains of three men.

"Is one of them Pasha?" she asks.

I force her gaze to mine. "Yes, he's gone now. You're safe."

Her eyes try to stray back to the dead.

"Rina," I say in a low murmur with just a touch of warning.

Her gaze snaps back to mine as though I'd given a tug to an invisible string tethering us together.

"Don't allow him to darken a single ray of your sunshine. Just let him go, okay?"

Her answering smile intoxicates me.

"Okay, D."

I slant my lips over hers and silently thank God she's mine.

CHAPTER 61
Terina

PRESENT

"Your house is shot to shit, Cosimo. I'm sorry about that." Renzo grimaces at his top adviser. We've moved into the living room to talk while the soldiers have gone outside to handle the dead and wounded. I'm tucked into DiAngelo's side, simply relieved to have him close.

"That can be fixed," Cosimo says with a flick of his wrist. "The suffering we endured and the lives lost can never be undone." His solemn words sit like lead on my chest, as I'm sure they do for all of us. Today has been such a tragedy.

"We're not about to move on just because Pasha's dead,"

Renzo confirms. "I haven't had a chance to talk to you since the Lucciano meeting. Pasha had rigged the place with explosives. We all got out, but only because the Reaper sent Michael to warn us."

My breath catches as I peer up at D in shock. I had no idea I'd come so close to losing him twice today. I tighten my grip on his middle, and he places a kiss on my head.

The creases in Cosimo's face deepen with restrained violence. "And Simeon will try to say he wasn't involved. I don't like it. He had to have known more about Pasha's actions than he let on."

Renzo nods. "At the very least, he turned a blind eye, which he may already be regretting since Pasha's attack was staged in Lucciano territory. Gabe Fiore was livid. He tabled a marital alliance between us to show a unified Italian front."

"Interesting."

"Yeah, only problem is, we'd have to find someone willing to make that sacrifice for the family. I'd rather not force anyone." A deep frown carves itself into Renzo's face.

"It would be easy enough to find a willing man. We could put the burden on them to come up with a bride."

My stomach turns, thinking of some poor woman being forced into an arranged marriage. I can't imagine how awful that would be, yet I've seen the depravity of what we're up against. The two families would be exponentially safer united against this common enemy.

Renzo nods. "We can discuss it. I think the alliance needs to happen, if at all possible."

"I'll do it."

The words ring out unexpectedly through the group, our collective stares turning to Isa, who stands a little taller.

"Isa—" Cosimo admonishes her.

My sweet friend shakes her head, her lips drawing into a firm line of determination. "No, Daddy. I'll do it, assuming they can find someone who seems to be a good man. I wasn't going to marry anyway. I'd rather do this and save another woman the heartbreak. My mind is made up."

My jaw hinges wide in disbelief.

Cosimo curses and storms from the room. I snap my mouth shut and go over to hug Isa.

"You take a little time to think about it, okay?" I whisper.

She smiles placatingly, but I see in her eyes that she's truly committed to this decision.

"It's time for us to get going," DiAngelo murmurs to me with a warm hand on my back.

I nod. "I'll text you," I tell Isa before we make our way outside. It's time for this day to be over. Pasha is dead because of the incredibly brave men in our lives. For now, I'll focus on my gratitude for them and their safety. Future worries can wait. Today, life is good.

"You're not going to be able to talk me out of it." Isa crosses her arms over her chest as she speaks in a firm tone.

I gave her two full days to come to her senses. Two days to realize the enormity of what an arranged marriage would entail before trying to talk some sense into her. Yet somehow, it seems as though time hasn't lessened her resolve in the slightest.

"Help me understand, Isa. Why are you doing this to yourself?"

"That's the whole point—I'm not doing anything to myself. I know we haven't talked about relationships, but I truly never planned to marry. I'll be more than happy for my husband to pursue whatever other women he wants. He keeps his freedom. I help my family. No one loses out. But if I don't do this, some poor girl could have her heart broken."

"What about your heart?" I ask softly.

The sorrow in her eyes when she smiles at me sends a brutal ache through my chest.

"You've worked through your losses, and I'm so incredibly happy for you, but mine have changed me permanently. I'm thirty-seven, Rina. If I haven't found any interest in love by this stage, it's not going to happen. I'm okay with that, and I hope you can be, too."

I often forget that Isa is older than me. It's the reason we didn't connect until more recently, even though our fathers worked closely together. She's older than me, but love doesn't have a sell-by date. I want to shake her and insist that thirty-seven isn't remotely old enough to give up.

"What if you agree to this, marry a man you don't love, then run into your soulmate? You'll have trapped yourself with no way out."

"There are as many what-ifs in the world as there are drops of water. If I give them power over me, I'll drown. I can only look at the facts as they are right this minute when making a decision about what I do next, then honor those choices knowing I did the best I could at the time. At this particular moment in time, that means agreeing to be married."

She sounds so steadfast in her resolve that all the fight in me melts away. As much as I hate to admit it, she is the only one who can decide what is best for her.

"Okay, Isa," I offer gently. "I can't say that I totally understand, but I respect your decision."

My best friend squeezes my hand and smiles. "Thank you, honey. I know this isn't easy. Heaven knows my dad is struggling with it more than anyone."

"I imagine so."

"He'll adjust the same way we all do when life tosses us an unexpected curve in the road. A year from now, you and I will be elbow deep in soup, and you'll see that none of the important things have changed."

I smile, hoping that she's right. "Soup, huh?"

"I haven't forgotten. We need to pick the place and get to it." Her grin almost reaches her eyes. Almost. And when I start to think about it, I realize I'm not sure I've ever seen her light at its brightest. That was comforting to me for years. I didn't have to feel any pressure around her to shine brighter than I could manage, but now that I've escaped the darkness, I want to drag her with me.

That's not how it works, though.

A person must walk into the light voluntarily. It's not a destination that can be forced.

"Say no more. I'll get on it as soon as I have a chance." I

can't force her anywhere she's not willing to go, but I can lead the way and hope she'll follow. "Be prepared. I have a feeling D will insist on escorting us."

"Three pairs of hands are better than two."

My body shakes with laughter. "That may send him into grumpy overload. He's not exactly the rubber gloves and hairnet type."

The visual has her giggling along with me.

"No, but he'd do it for you," she says fondly.

I smile and nod. "Yeah, he would." He'd also take payment from me after the fact, but I wouldn't balk at the fee. In fact, the entire arrangement is sounding more and more promising. "I'll have a look at the options next week."

She lifts her coffee mug and clinks it with mine. "It's a deal."

"Hey, Mom and Dad, I hope you don't mind that I brought someone with me. I'd like to introduce you to Terina." DiAngelo holds my hand as we enter the pre-op room where Mr. and Mrs. Farina prepare for her double mastectomy.

I was honored when D asked if I wanted to join him today —to meet his parents and to support him through such an emotional day. Especially when our shoot-out with the Russians was less than a week ago. We're grateful to have all the time we can get together, even if it means a day at the hospital.

The older couple stares at me as though I've sprouted a third eye.

I give a little wave before I'm gobbled into a huge hug from D's dad.

"Mind? Are you kidding? We're absolutely delighted. Call me Rocco." He pulls back and beams at me, then moves to hug his son.

I smile and go to offer a hug to Mrs. Farina, who is in a hospital gown in the bed. "It's so lovely to meet you."

"Yes, you have no idea! Please, call me Nella." Her blue-green eyes shine with warmth.

DiAngelo returns to my side, his arm protectively around my back. I'm not sure if it's a statement to his parents or support in what could be an awkward situation, but I love it all the same.

"Everything good for the surgery today?" he asks.

"We got a big thumbs-up from the doctor," Nella assures us. "They're still filtering in with paperwork and all that crap, but we should be good to get started on time. What about you? Have things finally settled down for you, or are you still hosting that friend of yours?"

Heat singes my cheeks.

D gives me a little squeeze. "That friend is right here, and while she's still staying with me, the danger is over. Everything is much better now."

Nella's mouth rounds as she tips her head back in a now-I-get-it expression. "So that's where you two met."

"She's Renzo's sister," he explains.

Dear God, if my cheeks get any hotter, they'll start smoking, and I'm not even sure why. We're adults. But these are his parents. I can't help but feel awkward.

"You've done an amazing job as parents. D has helped me through a rough time, and I'll always be incredibly grateful."

Nella's chin quivers. "Thank you, sweetie. Oh, D, you did so good."

I peer up at DiAngelo, who looks visibly choked up when he nods. "Thanks, Ma." He crosses and gives her a long hug. "I love you. We're gonna wait with Dad until you're in the clear, then we'll come by again tomorrow to check on you."

Now, all four of us are sniffling back tears.

We exchange another round of hugs before D and I head to the waiting room.

"They seem like wonderful people," I tell him, my fingers still woven with his when we sit.

"They are. I'd say I don't deserve them, but I know you'd only argue."

I give him a playful glower. "You're damn skippy I would."

He lifts our joined hands and places a kiss on my knuckles. "I'm not sure I'd believe it, though, if it weren't for you."

"I can be pretty convincing when I want to be."

"Yes, but that's not what I mean."

My brows furrow in confusion as I wait for an explanation.

"No matter how much I try to blame myself for the past, I know I must have done something right or the universe wouldn't have given me you."

And, there goes the waterworks. Again.

Tears blur my vision. "You didn't have to do anything but be yourself. I never stood a chance."

"And now you're mine forever." A lighthearted smile kisses his lips, drawing the same from me.

"So long as you'll have me."

"Always, firefly."

CHAPTER 62
DiAngelo

IN A MATTER OF WEEKS, MY LIFE HAS BECOME unrecognizable. I went from isolating myself, even from those closest to me, to being a central component of a tightly knit family. The thing that surprises me the most is how oddly familiar it feels.

I think that's because this is the life I had envisioned for myself when I was younger.

Back when Elio was alive.

Family gatherings and gossip, group text threads and inside jokes—elements of a close community that can only exist when connection is a priority. I've spent years denying myself that life, refusing to exist in a world I should have shared with my brother, but it's time to let that go.

It's time to move on from the past.

I've surprised myself at how easily I've shed my old skin. The overhaul has been so dramatic that my two circles have merged into one. Mom's surgery was a huge catalyst. Zuzu and Rina coordinated to make sure my parents didn't have to cook a single meal in three weeks. Mom is doing so well that my parents are joining us for family dinner tonight at Zuzu's house, along with Renzo, Shae, Liora, Tommy, and Danika.

Zuzu is making her famous caponata, and while everyone talks over one another, we have the Sunday evening football game on in the background.

I've been looking forward to it all week.

So has Terina. My firefly has been glowing brighter than ever, and that is the best part of all. She deserves all the happiness in the world. Even if that means Bonny in a bumble bee costume for Halloween. Her nails are even painted yellow.

"We should have gotten them matching costumes," Rina squeals to Shae while holding Liora, who is decked out in a tiger onesie.

Shae's eyes widen. "They could be Daenerys and her dragon."

"Or hear me out," Rina says with a grin. "They could be something adorable like Winnie the Pooh and Piglet."

Shae scrunches her nose. "I'm pretty sure Liora is more dragon queen than little pig."

Rina studies Shae for a second before responding. "Yeah,

you're probably right. Piglet's a bit timid for your warrior princess. Isn't that right?" She coos the last part to Liora, who gives her an adoring smile.

Zuzu comes up behind Rina and also grins down at the baby. "She is a princess, isn't she? I can't wait to see her in a fancy dress for the wedding." She turns her focus to Shae, wiping her hands on her apron. "Have you gone shopping for it yet? It's only two weeks away."

While the two talk, my eyes are fixed on Terina, who visibly deflates. She's been horribly worried about her best friend. Isa has insisted on going through with the arranged marriage. The Luccianos have designated a groom, and all the plans have been made. In two weeks, Isa Costa will marry Mazzi Antonelli.

I'm not thrilled about it, either, but she's a grown woman. If this is what she wants, that's her choice.

"I can go grab it real quick." Rina's words filter through my thoughts as she hands the baby back to Shae.

"What are you grabbing?" I ask, realizing I've missed something.

"Mom didn't get the mail today, so I'm going to run out there and get it."

I'm immediately on my feet. "I'll go with you." As if I'd let her go out alone. We're deep enough into fall that it's been dark for an hour. Her mother's house isn't in a bad area, but that doesn't mean shit can't happen.

She smiles and leads the way.

This same scenario would have played out drastically different had it taken place months ago. I'm reminded of our heated exchange outside this same house on the first night I was assigned to protect her.

Satisfaction thrums in my chest when I think of how she responded to me right from the beginning. The memory elicits another emotion, as well.

Desire.

As soon as we're outside, I bend and fold Terina over my shoulder.

She gasps and giggles. "You're going the wrong way."

"We'll get the mail after."

"After what?"

"After I fuck you against the house." I give her ass a smack and head to the corner directly below the security camera, where I know we can't be seen.

"Oh," she says in a suddenly husky tone.

Yeah. Oh.

Once we've rounded the corner and are tucked away behind some shrubs, I put her down and spin her away from me. "Pants to your ankles, hands against the wall," I growl at her. If anyone overheard me, they'd be certain this was an attack, but Rina knows better. This is a fantasy I know we've shared since that very first night.

As expected, not only does she comply, but she does so in record time. "Someone could come looking for us," she says, but it's not a warning. Her words are laced with excitement.

I wrap my fist in her hair and tilt her head back a fraction to get close to her ear. "Then I suggest you squeeze my cock as hard as you can and try to be quiet."

"Yes, D." The need in her voice makes my knees weak.

Jesus, she's incredible.

I shift her hips out toward me and grip her hips, sinking inside her in three assertive strokes.

We both hiss in pleasure.

"You really did want this, didn't you, firefly? You're so goddamn wet, you're dripping."

"Only for you, D."

I fuck her mercilessly against the wall. The crisp night air and shadowy darkness amplifies the threat of exposure. It's a heady aphrodisiac. The two of us are on the edge of release in no time. I clamp my hand over her mouth. She screams against my skin, pulling the trigger on my orgasm. My balls practically crawl back inside my body I come so damn hard.

Our heavy breaths are visible puffs of steamy air as we recover.

I slide my hands up her hips and find her breasts, giving them a squeeze when I pull her body back against my chest. "You are the best goddamn thing to ever happen to me, you know that?"

"Yeah," she says lazily, making me chuckle.

We collect ourselves, clean up the best we can, then get the mail. Back inside, the chaos has kept anyone from noticing our prolonged absence. Dinner is delicious. Conversation flows easily, and laughter is abundant. We're in the middle of a great evening when Terina announces she and I have somewhere to be.

"I hate to eat and run. We'll be on dishes duty next time, promise."

I stand with her and nod like I know what's happening. I

don't want to call her out if this is her way of taking a breather from the family. We say our goodbyes and let Bonny take a quick potty stop in the yard before heading to the car.

"Everything okay?" I ask once we're outside.

"Yup." She grins smugly. "I have a surprise for you."

Well, well. I'm intrigued.

She tells me where to go, refusing to put the address into the GPS so it doesn't ruin the surprise. I can't imagine where on earth we'd be going at this time of night. Not that it's all that late, but we're not exactly partiers when it comes to nightlife.

My curiosity intensifies when we pull up to a tattoo parlor.

"What kind of trouble are you up to, little firefly?"

Her answering grin is positively wicked.

I love it.

When I open the door for her, she first checks to make sure Bonny is allowed in, then tells the girl at the front desk her name and that she has a piercing appointment.

"Fuck me, Rina. Are you serious?" I ask her quietly.

She nods. "Told you I would. It means they'll be off-limits for a while, but I figured you'd be okay with that."

My lips are on hers so damn fast, our teeth collide.

"God, I love you," I breathe with my forehead resting against hers.

"Love you, too, D."

Finally, we turn back to the girl at the desk, who is now grinning ear-to-ear.

"Ready?"

"I think so!" Terina says with a twinge of nerves.

"What are the chances you guys have time for ink while we're here?" I ask, noticing a guy in the back of the shop scrolling on his phone.

The girl calls over her shoulder, "Jay, you open?"

The guy lifts his gaze. "What are you thinking?" He stands to join us.

I take out my phone and open to an image of a firefly tattoo I'd already saved and show it to him, along with Elio's name already on my chest. "I was thinking the firefly could be standing on the E and shining light across the name. Maybe use white ink for the highlights."

"Oh, man, lighting is my specialty. We can do something seriously sick with this. Let me put a sketch together." He snaps a picture of my current tattoo, then hurries off to his desk, seemingly engrossed in inspiration.

When I look at Rina, her eyes are watering.

"That's really lovely, D. I had no idea," she says softly.

"I thought about surprising you, but now that we're here, I'd just assume we do this together, if you're okay with it. Mine will take quite a bit longer than yours."

"There's nowhere else I'd rather be." The light of love shines in her eyes, and I feel so damn lucky I could burst.

That's my firefly—my very own ray of sunshine—and I will devote every day of my life to ensuring her light never dims because her joy is a gift to everyone around her. She is my priority and my purpose. My reason for being on this earth. And someday, many years from now, when I see Elio again, I know he'll be proud of the life I've led.

EPILOGUE
Terina

PRESENT

It's a week away from Thanksgiving, but I'm struggling to summon feelings of gratitude when my best friend is about to be married off to some stranger. Her wedding day has come, and I'm still in shock that no one has put an end to it.

In less than an hour, I'll do my duty as her maid of honor. I'll make sure her train splays properly and hold her bouquet at the appropriate times, but I'll be fighting back outrage every second of the way.

Everything about this is wrong and so incredibly unfair.

But who is there to stop if not Isa herself?

I know we talked it through to some extent, but my brain still won't get on board. I wish I understood why she would volunteer for a lifetime pledged to a man she doesn't know. I get that she thinks she's saving some other woman the grief, but maybe we could do that by standing up to the system, rather than capitulating.

I don't know why I'm still having these conversations with myself. I've said the same thing to her a dozen times over, and she's dead set in her decision.

"Shouldn't you be with the bride?" D asks when I join him in the church sanctuary.

"She has her cousins with her. I just needed a second."

He offers a grim smile, knowing how much I've struggled with this day. "I'm not sure I have much to cheer you up. I was talking with Cosimo, and I'm concerned he's having memory issues."

"Really? What happened?" I'm shocked because the man is only in his mid-sixties and always seems as sharp as a knife.

"We were talking about the renovations he's making at his house to repair the damages, and he mentioned getting a call from me before Pasha attacked. He was adamant that we speak on the phone, but I never got through to him or any of you. I didn't push the issue because I didn't want to upset him today, but I only ever left him a message. We never spoke directly that day."

"Oh, poor Isa." My heart breaks for her. "I wonder if she's noticed any signs of decline." That could be why she's decided a marriage is in her best interest, though it doesn't make any sense to me at all. There's no telling.

"There's nothing we can do at the moment, so best to let it go."

I nod. "I know I've told you ten times already, but you look divine in that tux." A smile finally creeps across my face. "If I didn't think it would mess up my hair, I'd say we should sneak away for a minute."

He shakes his head. "You're incorrigible." He leans in close, his lips hovering above mine. "Don't ever change." He seals his sweet command with a kiss that curls my toes.

"Okay, I guess I'd better get back before you distract me even further."

His hand snags mine. "She's going to be okay, firefly. Try not to worry too much."

"Thanks, D," I say softly, then head off in search of the bride.

Her three cousins, who make up the bridal party, are standing in the vestibule, chattering among themselves. I continue around the corner to the door leading to the church administrative building, where Isa was getting ready.

When I arrive at the room, it's empty.

Did Cosimo come to get her? It's not quite time for the ceremony, but he could have wanted a word with her.

I check the bathroom first, then head back to the main church. "Have you guys seen Isa?" I ask the group of bridesmaids.

"DiAngelo wanted to talk with her alone," the eldest says, confusing me.

"What do you mean DiAngelo wanted to talk with her?" I was just talking to DiAngelo. He couldn't have been in two places at once.

"Yeah, he said he needed a moment alone with her, so we left." She stares at me like I've lost my marbles.

Hell, maybe I have.

"I went back to her room, and she's not there. The bathroom was empty, too."

They stare back at me blankly.

"Will you guys go look for her in the other building? I'll make sure she isn't over here."

They nod and scurry off in a flurry of whispers. I don't blame them. This feels a little off.

Could Isa have come to her senses and run? Maybe, but it doesn't explain the odd part about DiAngelo.

I continue my search, double-checking the confessional and the transepts. I can't imagine she could have snuck into the main sanctuary without being seen—a bride generally draws a lot of attention—but I want to be thorough.

Once I've walked the church, I head back to the other building. This time, the girls look much more frantic.

"We can't find her anywhere." The eldest wrings her hands together.

"Okay, you guys hang here in case she shows up. I'll go tell the others." I jog back to the church, which has started to fill with guests. I make a beeline straight for D, who is standing with Cosimo.

If she's not with Cosimo...

"Something's wrong," I blurt in a rushed whisper. "Isa's disappeared."

"What do you mean, disappeared?" Cosimo demands.

"The other girls said DiAngelo came by to talk to her—"

"I haven't gone to see her." He interrupts with a thunderous expression.

"I don't know. That's just what they told me. We've looked everywhere for her. She's gone."

"She swore she wanted this," Cosimo says, his brows knitted in worry.

I get out my phone. "Let me try to call her." I only have to wait a second before I hang up. "It went straight to voicemail."

"Something's not right here," DiAngelo says before getting Renzo's attention nearby. Once he joins us, we explain the situation, then go in search of the priest.

"The church has security cameras, right?" Renzo asks.

"Yes, what's happened?"

"We need to see the footage from the last hour, immediately."

The older man with small wire-rimmed glasses nods and leads us to the administrative building, where the bridesmaids are huddled. The priest unlocks the office, and we all pile in.

"It's this building we're interested in," DiAngelo clarifies. "She was over here when she disappeared."

"Someone's gone missing?" the priest asks in a worried tone.

"The bride."

The priest crosses himself, then continues his work at the

computer. "This is the camera at the back entrance. It's motion-activated." He starts the most recent recording.

We all watch in stunned disbelief as Isa rushes from the building, hand in hand with a man.

"Pause it," Renzo demands. "Jesus, look at the knife in his other hand. It's a karambit."

He and DiAngelo exchange a knowing look.

"What does that mean?" I ask.

Renzo's frown deepens. "It's a special type of curved blade." He pauses, as though not wanting to say more. "It's the sort of knife the Reaper is known for using."

"God, no," Cosimo pleads on a heavy exhale.

"Let's watch the rest. Maybe it'll give us a clue as to who he is."

The video resumes. Much to our astonishment, the man stops them and turns, lifting his gaze directly at the camera. The priest pauses the recording.

Our entire group breathes a collective gasp.

DiAngelo staggers backward, his face horror-stricken.

The rest of us look from the computer screen to him in confusion because it's DiAngelo in the video.

"See," the bridesmaid pipes up. "I told you it was DiAngelo."

D's face goes ghostly white, eyes fixed on the screen as he slowly shakes his head. "It's not me. It's Elio. He's alive."

Thank you so much for reading *Hunter's Keep!*

And I KNOW!!!! I'm so sorry to leave you on such a cliffy, but it's going to be totally worth it!
The Reaper is coming for you this fall.
Pre-order now by scanning the QR code below.

Bonus Epilogue

And in the meantime, scan the QR code below and enjoy an encore of DiAngelo and Terina in this *Hunter's Keep Bonus Epilogue!*

SUICIDE & CRISIS HOTLINE

While the characters I write about are not real, the issues of self-harm and suicide are a reality for many. If you need emotional support for whatever reason, there are people willing to help.

Inside the US, call or text the Suicide & Crisis Lifeline at 988.

ABOUT THE AUTHOR

Jill Ramsower is a life-long Texan—born in Houston, raised in Austin, and currently residing in West Texas. She attended Baylor University and subsequently Baylor Law School to obtain her BA and JD degrees. She spent the next fourteen years practicing law and raising her three children until one fateful day, she strayed from the well-trod path she had been walking and sat down to write a book. An addict with a pen, she set to writing like a woman possessed and discovered that telling stories is her passion in life.

www.ingramcontent.com/pod-product-compliance
Lightning Source LLC
Chambersburg PA
CBHW020900060726
47591CB00004B/1010